Pieces of PARIS

G. G. VANDAGRIFF

SHADOW
MOUNTAIN

Library of Congress Cataloging-in-Publication Data
Vandagriff, G. G.
  Pieces of Paris / G. G. Vandagriff.
    p. cm.
  Summary: Annalisse and Dennis seem to be living the American dream until Annalisse's secret past threatens to destroy their family.
  ISBN 978-1-60641-838-3 (paperbound)
  1. Post-traumatic stress disorder—Fiction. 2. Pianists—Fiction. I. Title.
PS3572.A427P54 2010
  813'.54—dc22   2010019438

Printed in the United States of America
Publishers Printing

10 9 8 7 6 5 4 3 2 1

To my persistent, loyal, and brilliant son
Morgan McGill Vandagriff
who would not let this one go

Acknowledgments

To all my dear friends from the Missouri part of my life, who read this countless times—Ginny, Jeanne, Janice, Vicki, and Lavina.

To Dixie, who knows everything.

To my wonderful Storymaker friends who made this their labor of love—Heather Moore, C. S. Bezas, and Rachel Ann Nunes.

To my Storymakers' critique group—may each of them be published!

To the wonderful people at Shadow Mountain, who always give me their support—Jana Erickson, Gail Halladay, and Suzanne Brady.

And mostly to my husband, David, who chased away the past and read the manuscript many, many times.

PIECES OF PARIS

when i feel the incomplete measure

i soothe myself with wood and tusk

at harmonic intervals, playing

my life back into paris

my heart into my hands

my voice more than borrowed

from frederic (who died before his prime)

in each mazurka: a repetition of theme

in each fugue: a counterpoint

nocturnes, preludes and impromptus:

the backs of my hands

the backs of my lover's hands

dolce, dolce

i shan't cry

—ANNETTE BOEHM

Chapter One

I t was the simple things that undid her, Annalisse had discovered. Something as ordinary as the scent of lilacs when the
air was heavy, a brief measure of Tchaikovsky, or a dream. A
dream like the one she'd awakened from last night—so real she
could smell the Paris Metro in it. Any of these things could revive in
a moment the memories she'd spent the last six years burying. They
crept under the leaden shield around her heart and found the small,
secret place where she still had feeling.

Straightening up from picking beans in Dennis's garden, she
drew a hand across her sweaty forehead. She had a family now, she
told herself firmly. Little Jordan and a husband who had rescued her
and chased away the darkness. Thinking of Dennis with his Brad
Pitt good looks and quixotic worldview, she wondered, not for the
first time, whether the tenderness she felt for him would ever be
enough to qualify her as the kind of wife he deserved. She longed to
feel the passion she knew she was capable of, but that woman was a
stranger to her now and thus to Dennis. He had no place in that up

and down and over and under looping past that had made her cry and laugh and perhaps lose her heart forever.

She looked at the wretched green beans in her bucket and stretched to ease the muscles in her back. On the farm growing up she had hated picking vegetables, but now being six months pregnant made it doubly hateful.

Did I make a mistake?

For the four and a half years of her marriage, she had thought she was happy. Of course, that was before they had moved to the Ozarks, of all places. But she must love Dennis. How could she not? His dreams for a better world and his efforts to make it so had seduced her into feeling there was hope after all. Those had been her childhood dreams as well. Marrying Dennis was like coming home.

But he had never met or known the real Annalisse, the one who existed in parentheses between her leaving her childhood farm and marrying him. She had, until now, allowed him to reinvent her, to place her on the pedestal of his dreams. But, lately, flashbacks had been jolting through her daily life, transporting her from their farm back to more exotic times and places. She thought she had expunged those memories from her life six years ago, leaving them behind in the blackness. Why had they begun to resurface, harrowing up her numbed heart with their sights, scents, and sounds?

On the other hand, what was she doing here in the middle of this blasted garden picking beans? It had to be the world's worst irony that she had ended up back on a farm. She had tried to make their life in the country work. With all her might she had tried. But now, not only did her back ache but her heart ached. The bugs were crawling up her ankles and arms, and the dense blanket of humidity caused sweat to trickle down her neck.

"Mom! Bug!" shrieked her three-and-a-half-year-old son.

Annalisse looked at towheaded Jordan, a tiny miniature of

Dennis, and in the midst of her misery, a thrill of fondness lifted her out of the past. "Since when are you afraid of spiders, Anakin? Use your lightsaber!"

She did feel. Maybe not as she ought, but her love for Jordan eclipsed every other love in her life. She would never, ever forget the moment she first held the miracle that she, Dennis, and God had made. For days she had felt as though she were queen of the world.

Jordan assumed a frightening mien, brushed the spider off his leg with the stick, and stamped it with his little green Crocs. "Squash, squash, squash!"

"Good for you! Now, back to the beans." Feelings for her little boy climbed like a vine all around her heart. She hoped that vine would be strong enough to hold together the Annalisse she was trying so hard to become. She hugged and loved Jordan, taught and played with him, joined in his imaginary games.

Why wasn't it enough? Why wouldn't Jules and their tightly woven past leave her alone? Were these sudden violent bouts of memory turning her into a schizophrenic?

But Jordan was not finished complaining. "Mommy, beans are for daddies."

Internally, Annalisse agreed. It was a constant wonder to her how precocious her son was. But she tried to motivate Jordan, just as her mother had always spurred her on in difficult tasks. "I know it's hot, honey. I hate it, too. But Dad's at his office, and he'll be tired when he gets home." She hadn't had the heart to tell Dennis that canned beans from the store on sale were cheaper, considering all the labor that went into growing, picking, and canning. *Why does it have to be done?*

She knew the answer: It was part of the city-born Dennis's dream of becoming the next Thoreau—a dream of light and hope that was a necessary weapon against her past. A dream that was becoming more necessary by the hour, as the haunting grew worse.

Ignoring her, Jordan danced down to the creek and began to splash himself with the glee of a typical child.

"Can you tell me what in the world you're doing here?" Jules was inside her head again. "Green beans? I thought you'd left the farm. What's happened to you, Lisse?"

She felt the tears she hadn't shed years ago sting her eyes, and she turned her back so Jordan wouldn't see. Her nose was running now, and she had nothing but the back of her dusty hand to wipe it. Yanking at the beans, she pulled them up, plant and all, and flung them into her bucket.

"Mom!" Jordan said, standing up to his knees in water, his little freckled face scrunched with worry. "Yo' wecking the gawden!"

Suddenly, she knew she couldn't pick one more green bean. "Let's just forget them, Jordan. Come away from the creek."

As they climbed the hill to the house, her short night caught up with her. She was very tired. Physically tired and more than exhausted by her ongoing mental debate. *Was it wrong for me to have married Dennis? Especially when our marriage was founded on lies of omission?* Guilt struck her so forcibly that she stumbled.

"Go wy down on yo' bed!" said Jordan, the worrywart, when she couldn't keep up with him. "'Membew my sistew in yo' tummy. Daddy said I gotta take cao of you."

Annalisse knew that if she continued to view her surroundings through Jules's eyes, she was going to completely lose it. "Why don't you go play Star Wars, honey," she suggested. "I have a new action figure for you."

Her son jumped up and down. "Who? Who? "

"Yoda. The little guy with the big ears . . ."

"Coool! I been wanting Yoda fo' a wong time."

PIECES OF PARIS

"Go look in my bottom drawer, sweetie."

After Jordan ran upstairs, she walked towards the fridge with the idea of pouring herself a glass of orange juice but stopped in the middle of a kitchen that suddenly appeared strange and unfamiliar. *What in heaven's name is wrong with me?* Grabbing fistfuls of her long blonde hair, she beat her head with her knuckles.

Forgetting the juice, she walked aimlessly into the living room and looked at her baby grand piano, so out of place in the farmhouse. She simply couldn't stay away any longer. They had dragged it halfway across the country, and as far as Dennis knew, it was her father's gift for the children. But now, as though she were sleepwalking, she went over to it and caressed the keys. Then she did something she hadn't allowed herself to do in six years. She sat on the bench and put her feet on the pedals. She was swept away by a memory so intense that she had no strength to fight it off.

⌒⤳

The door was open, but Jules was so lost in his practicing that he didn't see or hear her. Leaning against the door frame, Annalisse listened to him master the Tchaikovsky violin concerto.

Light filtered in from a high window, making the small practice room with its bare green walls look like a monk's cell. On the floor was a ragged denim jacket, a pack of Marlboros spilling from one pocket. Across a folding chair lay his violin case, open, so that the ruby velvet lining caught the light and gleamed like wine.

Overlaying the sparseness of these few details was music so vivid and rich that Annalisse was compelled to close her eyes against it, reducing the meager visual surroundings to a color negative on the back of her eyelid.

Such music! Minor chords striving heroically toward a dissonant

5

climax, and then, abruptly, a hauntingly melodic interlude where the bowing slowed. Slavic melancholy, Jules called it. Climbing, reaching desperately up the scale, the wistfulness grew into feverish, teeth-gritting longing, made more poignant still by Jules's obvious identification with the work.

When she could stand it no longer, she opened her eyes. Perspiration had plastered a fringe of dark curls to his forehead, and a grimace distorted his expressive mouth. He looked the picture of a suffering El Greco Christ. Annalisse's prosaic Lutheran upbringing had done nothing to prepare her for the pain of her heart stretching to contain this new world of feeling.

"Oh, God, help me!" she pleaded silently. Usually very self-possessed, she felt the logical, practical organ she knew to be her heart fly out of her breast and lose itself in the dramatic foreign terrain where Jules dwelt.

Piano Performance was only her minor, but when she had first heard Jules play, she started coming every day to the practice rooms. Their acquaintance was only weeks old, but it was clear that she could never expect more than friendship from the violinist. Her native universe—anatomy cadavers, soybeans, and solid Swedish parents—was far too ordinary. Before coming to Stanford, she had gone only once a week to study with a former great concert pianist in Madison, Wisconsin.

Then, Jules was looking at her, and she felt the color flooding her face. For a moment the spell of the music held, and then they were just Jules and Annalisse again. He scowled.

"Sorry," she said. "The door was open, you know."

Without speaking, he stowed his violin reverently in its case. It was the only possession he treated properly.

"What's happening?" he asked finally, with the vague air of one returning from a long journey.

"Nothing much."

"You finished?"

She nodded. She had been lost for hours at the piano next door, struggling with her Rachmaninoff. Jules had set her the task, claiming that she needed to stretch herself with a Russian composer. The music was beyond difficult, but a rare, unknown flower of feeling had begun to unfurl just below her breastbone. She had never known it was there. It possessed the mystery and sweetness of a secret. A secret Annalisse.

Together they walked out into the wet afternoon. A mass of students milled around the plaza between the union and the post office, dressed in a variety of garb—sombreros, berets, army surplus fatigues, frayed work shirts, sandals, cowboy boots—pervading the area with the smell of wet wool and leather. Above the long-haired throng, Stanford's fountain, Memorial Claw, displayed its barbs like some malevolent goddess.

"Want to go to the beach?" she asked suddenly.

Jules looked at her for a second as though she were deranged. "In the rain?"

"It's only a mist."

For just an instant, his eyes softened, and then there, right in front of the post office, he gave her his first kiss—long, lingering, and hot. Cupping the back of her head with his hand, he said, "You're adorable."

"Me?" She felt giddy as her heart did flips. Jules never used words like "adorable." And he certainly never kissed her.

"But crazy as a loon."

Annalisse studied her dirty hands with their chipped, begrimed fingernails. Once, they had played a concert grand for hours each day. Since then she had thrust music, along with Jules, to the most distant place in her personal universe. The flower inside her was dormant now. Bare and barbed with thorns she shouldn't go near.

Her hands had found other occupations—wiping baby bottoms, planting gardens, canning beans. But there, somewhere amid the tendons she could see beneath her skin, was a magical chemistry, a memory of muscle, linked to a banished part of her brain-life. Would the connection still work? Did she even want it to? Would she dare to open Pandora's box?

Hesitantly, she put her work-soiled hands on the smooth ivory keys and began awkwardly to play one of the pieces of Paris.

Chapter Two

Dennis woke slowly to the sound of a violin somewhere in the house. For a moment he lay and listened, watching a shadow of a birch branch blow against the bedroom wall in the moonlight. High, mourning notes gathered in the stillness of the room, pulling him out of a deep, luxurious sleep, carrying him into the heart of some Slavic drama. A dark girl, part princess, part gypsy, was running through a twisted, blackening forest, her red dress tattered by thorns. Dennis groaned, rolling over.

The space next to him was empty. Squinting at the alarm clock, he sat up. *Geesh!* Two A.M.

He followed the music downstairs, where it rose to an unholy keening, robbing the cozy living room of its familiarity. Even the big farmhouse kitchen seemed strange. Dutch blue cupboards, white lace curtains, and geraniums were not at home in an atmosphere of high tragedy. But there it was, singing through the house, his house, setting everything atremble with frustrated longing. In the middle of the night, in the bare gray light of the moon, it didn't seem nearly as ridiculous as it should have.

And of all places, it was coming from the laundry room. Dennis took hold of himself. Even if he were overly imaginative, Annalisse wasn't. She was probably ironing. But why this heavy, emotional music? She had always chosen Bach and Vivaldi concerts when they went to the LA Philharmonic. Shaking off webs of sleep, he started toward the half-open door, when, barred by some strangeness, he halted in the passage until the final coda died away. Then, resolutely, he entered the room.

Framed by shelves of detergent, bleach, and fabric softener, Annalisse stood in her bare feet, ironing his shirts. Her CD player was balanced precariously on an oversized package of toilet paper. At first, she didn't see him. Then she looked up, and he saw that tears were falling unchecked onto his shirt where they sizzled one by one under the iron. For a moment he stood, disoriented, wondering if this was part of his crazy dream world.

"Swedie?" His alarm returned. "What's wrong?"

She looked as though she were trying to place him. Slowly the spell broke, and she turned off the iron and tried a grin. "I should have known better," she said with a shaky laugh. "Too much Tchaikovsky in the middle of the night. Sorry I woke you."

Nobody could look more innocent than Annalisse, but he wasn't buying it. In more than four years of marriage he had never once seen her cry. He was the emotional one. She didn't even cry at funerals.

Moving the ironing board aside, he took her face in his hands and wiped her tears with his thumbs. "C'mon, Annalisse. Tell me. Something's wrong. Why are you unhappy?"

She hid her face in his neck, sniffing, clinging to him with a ferocity that alarmed him. "I'm not unhappy," she insisted. "I just got carried away. I came down here because I couldn't sleep. I always get restless when a storm is coming."

That at least was true. But Annalisse just wasn't the type to weep over storms or concerti. Anyone with a less Slavic temperament, it would be hard to imagine. Built along the lines of Juno with the heavy blonde hair and the pink-and-white complexion associated with milkmaids, his wife possessed a disposition of stoic calm. Traits of her Swedish pioneer ancestry stood as a bulwark against any inclination to hysteria.

This behavior was a mystery. One she apparently didn't want to share with him. At least, not yet. At a loss, he asked, "How about some cocoa?"

She lifted her head, and he saw that her face had relaxed into its customary calm. "Sounds good."

And so they sat up until three, drinking cocoa on the swing of their screened-in porch, talking about other things.

"I didn't tell you," Annalisse said with a laugh. "When I took Jordan to get his hair cut today, he produced his Anakin Skywalker action figure and insisted that B. J. cut his hair exactly like Anakin's. He even instructed him in the right way to comb it over his forehead."

Dennis laughed with relief. This was the Annalisse he knew. "What are we going to name our little girl?" he asked, placing his hand on her abdomen with the reverence he felt for his unborn child. "She's going to be here soon, Swedie. How have you been feeling?"

Annalisse laid her hand on top of his and looked into his eyes. He could barely see in the dark, but he could read the normal tolerance and amusement with which she regarded him. The knot in his stomach finished untying itself. She was still his Annalisse.

"I don't like any of the names on our list," she said. "How about Bronwyn?"

"Bronwyn? For heaven's sake, what have you been reading now? That sounds medieval!"

"It's Welsh. Your mother's Welsh. I'm sure there's a Bronwyn in your family history somewhere."

He could feel his face stiffen. "She won't thank you, you know."

"I know," Annalisse said softly. "But I wasn't thinking of her. I was thinking of you. I think names should connect with the past. Have I ever told you about mitochondria?"

He laughed. Yes, this was definitely his Annalisse. Only she would bring up some abstruse biological reference during a tender moment. "No, but let's save it for another time, shall we?"

She grinned. Bringing his palm to her lips, she kissed it. "Now, tell me how the campaign is going. Do I need to cart Jordan around in a wagon and go door to door?"

He kissed her behind the ear. "You know, that wouldn't be a bad idea. Sounds like a Norman Rockwell painting. Perfect for Blue Creek's image of itself: the last bastion of Americana."

They kissed then with the tenderness and sweetness that marked all their intimate encounters. Annalisse was his Madonna. One didn't go around passionately ravishing Madonnas. He stroked her hair tenderly, outlining her cheekbones with his hands, feeling the softness of her skin. The sky grew darker as clouds blew in to blot out the moon and stars. When at last, they climbed the stairs to bed, the house was very dark, all trace of the eerie gray light gone.

Curled against him, Annalisse sighed and fell asleep almost instantly, but he lay awake, drawing calm from her closeness and her warm skin, listening as the wind blew a summer storm nearer.

The scene in the laundry room—why had it troubled him? She was in the sixth month of her pregnancy. Tired. Uncomfortable. And pregnancy hormones did strange things to women. His unease was absurd. But the idea of anything being wrong with Annalisse . . .

He chided himself. It was just because it was the middle of the night. How could there be anything really wrong, just out of the blue like that? Annalisse wasn't the type to harbor secret sorrows. But she had been crying over Tchaikovsky, of all things. Or was it something else?

Burying his face in the downy nape of her neck, he smelled the lemony-vanilla of her soap and, reassured by this familiarity, drifted off to sleep.

"Oatmeao. Oatmeao with bananas and bwebewies." Dennis was awakened by his son whispering into his ear.

Grumbling, Dennis threw back the covers and gazed sleepily at Jordan. "Why do you always wake at dawn?"

His son grinned and pulled at his arm, trying to yank him out of bed. "Mommy's in the showoe. I heaw thundew outside."

Dennis put his feet over the edge of the bed. So Annalisse was already up and showering. The incident of the night before receded further into unreality.

Struggling into his gardening Levi's, he rallied his offspring. "Your cereal can wait, shaver. C'mon. We'd better get the chickens into the barn before I go to work."

Outside it was tremendously windy, and Dennis heard Jordan's thunder, though it was still in the distance. It looked like this was going to be more than an ordinary storm. His son ran ahead down the steep slope that bottomed into the creek. Dennis walked more slowly. The sight of his land revived him as it had every morning of the three months he'd owned it.

He had dreamed of finding a place like this ever since he discovered Thoreau his junior year at Northwestern. In those days, he and his friends had philosophized over *Walden*, their "Green Dream." One night, Sam had summed it all up: "The trouble with this country is that there's too much technology. We've forgotten the simple beauty of the cow." Today Sam Cohen was a hedge fund guru on Wall Street. But Dennis had been luckier. After graduation from law school, he'd scoured the country until he'd found this Eden in the Missouri Ozarks, where he'd hung out his shingle.

The long-saved inheritance from his father had been enough to put a down payment on this little farm that had just seemed to be waiting for him. All around him the land undulated in gentle hills of silver-green fescue grass. His own Walden Pond, complete with geese and a willow tree, lay in a hollow next to a gray barn Wyeth could have painted. The barn housed Henrietta, his Brown Swiss cow. Across the creek, a thick oak wood sheltered deer sometimes. And right now the wind carried the sweet smell of peaches ripening in his orchard. Of course, only a fool would try to make it farming on eighty acres, but with the income from his law practice they were comfortable enough. And if he was elected county prosecutor, the extra salary would top things off nicely. Most important, Jordan had clean air to breathe, pure water to drink, and acres and acres of safety extending in every direction.

"Jordan!" he called. "Henny Penny's over there by the pond. I don't know where the other chickens are, but shoo her into the barn."

Grabbing a bushel basket from inside the barn door, he went down to his garden by the creek bed. If the bottom land flooded, he might lose the last three rows of green beans, which were ripe for picking.

Gathering beans as fast as he could, Dennis felt the sky darken around him. After half an hour, he realized he'd never accomplish the task alone before work. Spying his son starting up the hill, he yelled, "Tell Mom to come! We've got to get the rest of the beans in!"

Thunder boomed as he harvested, and by the time Annalisse joined him, the wind was bowing unwieldy sunflowers and blowing July dust into their eyes. The forest across the creek rustled violently.

Putting hands on her hips, his wife laughed. "Go to the office, Dennis. Jordan and I will save your precious beans." With her tow-colored hair whipping around her face and her nose peeling from a recent sunburn, Annalisse looked reassuringly normal.

He grinned. "Sure you don't need my expert supervision?"

Shaking her head, she bent over the beans. "We'll manage. At least the wind is cool. Oh, and I've got that luncheon, don't forget, so I won't be home at noon. Jordan's going to Grandma Betsy, but there's leftover chicken in the fridge for your lunch."

He pulled her upright into his arms and kissed her cheek. "You're really okay?"

"I'm fine," she insisted, lightly returning his kiss. "Stop worrying about me."

"Okay, then." He saluted obediently. "Over to you."

"Ham and corn muffins for breakfast," she said.

Climbing up the hill to the house, Dennis let the wind strip the hair off his forehead, cool his sweaty brow, and fill his nostrils with the fertile scent of summer rain. Exhilaration burst upon him suddenly.

As he looked back down the hill at his wife and child, they seemed oddly bright against the dull green of the approaching storm. Waving at his son, who was fighting the bean plants with a stick (no doubt his light saber), Dennis finished climbing the hill and went in to his ham and corn muffins, amazingly content with his life.

Chapter Three

Annalisse dreaded the Cherokee County Republican Women's luncheon. Nothing but Dennis's bid for election as county prosecutor could have forced her away from her piano.

For an hour today, she had revisited her past. She had made contact with it, albeit clumsily. Her hands still worked. The thorny stem might yet bear at least a bud. Unless it was dead. It was excruciating trying to recover at twenty-six what had been so easy in her teens and early twenties. *Why does my soul suddenly crave my music?* It made her feel disloyal to Dennis. It gave Jules a place in her present life.

On the other hand, if she didn't strive to regain her gift soon, she would lose it altogether. Did she want that? Did it even matter what she wanted? Then an idea hit her with a boldness she wasn't prepared for. Perhaps the piano was the only way to fill the void in herself in this land of green beans, peaches, and yes, Cherokee County Republican Women. Dennis had his dreams, his life, his career. Her children would eventually grow and leave her. Why had God given her this talent if he didn't expect her to use it?

After dropping her son off at their stout neighbor's (who adored Jordan and insisted on being referred to as Grandma Betsy), Annalisse forced her way through the storm that had finally struck the town. She tried to put Jules out of her mind, but the ugliness of the town dug at her in the sore place where he dwelt. This was not where Annalisse had expected she would be living at this time of her life.

Blue Creek was not one of those graceful Southern towns possessed of old mansions draped with wisteria. Having begun life around the railroad turntable, it was a working class town of six thousand souls. The houses were ugly and squat, built by poor men out of the rock they found in the ground. The concrete sidewalks were cracked, corrupted by huge untidy trees that had taken over the streets. Latino immigrants had moved into the most squalid housing on Buchanan Hill, sold to them at extortionate prices over the last few years.

In the square, the only presentable building was the bank—red brick and white columned—made slightly ridiculous by its neighbors, the green corrugated aluminum Sears catalog store and Calhoun's Video World and Appliance Repair. Calhoun's had originally been a four-story opera hall at the turn of the last century but was now missing much of its roof. White stucco with a yellow marquee that proclaimed Bingo on Tuesdays, it was now a dingy hangout for the good ol' boys.

Annalisse was headed for the Turntable Club, a white-painted cinder block building which, despite all efforts by the Cherokee County Republican Women to refine it, remained what it was—a greasy-spoon truck stop on State Route 60.

Pulling her Prius into a parking place against the eroding curb, she opened the door, spread her umbrella, and stepped into the swirling stream of water. She had worn her L. L. Bean waders. She wasn't about to ruin her best shoes.

"Lisse, this is absurd. You look ridiculous in that getup! What are you doing at this thing? You hate politics!"

"Oh, go away, Jules," she said to her ghost. "There are a lot of things you never understood about married life and responsibility." And now *she* was talking to *him*. Aloud, of all things.

Once she was inside, the steamy heat hit her like a wave. The smell of the inevitable chicken à la king mingled with burnt grease immediately made her nauseated.

Caught in the act of removing her waders, she was greeted by the state senator's wife, Mae Cavanaugh, a smooth-skinned, white-haired lady who resembled Dame Judi Dench with bouffant hair. Annalisse shook herself mentally and commanded herself to be cordial.

"Why, Mrs. Childs, it's so nice to see you! Isn't this weather awful? Bad for the turnout, I'm afraid. But the senator will be so glad to know you were able to make it. We wives can make such a contribution, you know, and I want everyone to meet you. When you have your shoes on, you just might want to make your way over to the candidates' wives' table. It's the one with the maroon iris." Mae poured this avalanche of words over Annalisse as she struggled with her waders.

"Good afternoon, Mrs. Cavanaugh," she said with a forced smile before moving on to the table with the name tags. Annalisse noted that some optimistic florist had attempted to alter the seediness of their surroundings by placing silk irises in green Styrofoam blocks on each of the unsteady Formica tables that were now shrouded in white cloths.

Pulling the back off her gummed tag and slapping it on herself just below her collarbone, Annalisse felt as though she had entered an alternate reality. Drawing a deep breath, she reminded herself that she actually was a Republican. The trouble was, these women managed to make her ashamed of the fact.

Annalisse wore a yellow maternity jumper with a large-collared white blouse and a navy blue ribbon tie. A matching ribbon tied back her long hair at the nape of her neck. Of course, she stood out. Like a pregnant Alice in Wonderland. Her credentials as a human being included nothing these women would comprehend. To them she was and always would be a foreigner—the Northerner who lived at Peach Tree Farm and took the *New York Times*.

"Can you believe it? Silk irises in the Turntable Club?"

Annalisse turned around in surprise to see who had voiced her own thoughts. It was the diminutive Whitney, Sheriff Tom Webster's wife. A country singer wannabe, she was one of the few politicians' wives Annalisse knew. They had been canoeing together one memorable day when their husbands had succeeded in capsizing them in Blue Creek.

"Whitney!"

"I was gambling with myself about whether you'd come or not. Dennis make you?"

Annalisse felt a moment of discomfort. "Not exactly. But he's so enthusiastic about his campaign and everything. I guess it's the least I can do."

"Well, just don't let Mae run you. She takes everything for granted, you know. She and the senator figure Cherokee County is a dictatorship."

Annalisse laughed. "Then the senator will have his hands full with Dennis."

Raising an eyebrow, Whitney said, "Why do you think Mike Green's quitting the prosecutor's job?"

"Because he's going to Jeff City . . ."

"Guess who got him the job?" Whitney grinned wickedly and then looked past Annalisse. "There's Tom's mother. I promised I'd sit with her. She's totally confused at these things. Talk to you later."

Disturbed, Annalisse made her way through the milling, chattering women with their shrill voices. What was that about Mike Green? Obviously, Whitney thought it had some significance. She must remember to ask Dennis. If the senator thought he had Dennis Childs in his pocket, he had better think again. The idea gave her renewed resolution, and with a deep breath, she faced the CCRW.

"And you? Where do you fit in this screwy little world?" Jules inquired. "Are you going to grow old here and wear flowered jersey, doing good works? I can't see it, you know."

Jules's presence was making this almost unbearable. Mentally, she kicked him and put on another smile for Mae Cavanaugh, who was welcoming her to the "Wives' Table."

"I've told you all about Dennis Childs, who's going to be our new prosecutor, if the senator and I have anything to say about it," she was telling the other wives. "He's a very smart young man."

The women looked at Annalisse politely and smiled but seemed slightly shy. After a moment, they resumed conversation among themselves.

Mae pronounced imperiously, "The senator tells me you're from Los Angeles."

"Actually, from a little town in Wisconsin. But Dennis went to law school at USC. That's where we lived before moving here."

"Oh! She's from the country, girls," Mae announced, her smile softening as she looked Annalisse over, a calculating gleam in her eye. "We were all a little in awe, you know. We thought you were a big-city girl."

Annalisse eased back in her chair. No point in telling them she preferred the bright lights. Let them think of her as Dennis did—the wholesome farm girl.

"My mother raises hogs, as a matter of fact," she said. "My father is a judge."

It was at least a part of who she was, anyway. And if it put them at ease, so much the better.

"Well, you must have had your fill of Latinos, living in California," Emily Canliss said, her nostrils flaring. *Dame Maggie Smith?* "Do you know they want to take over the state?"

Startled, Annalisse felt her stomach tighten. For Dennis's sake, she must keep her cool. But an imp prompted her to reply as kindly as she could, "You know, I really think they're more concerned with feeding their children."

Mae looked at her sharply. "How many Latinos did you actually know?"

Clearly, they thought she was naïve. "I knew some very well, in fact. They were my neighbors." She paused and smiled almost apologetically. "I tutored Latino children through an outreach program when I lived in San Diego. Some of them were very bright. If I could find anyone who was interested, I'd start something of the sort here."

The senator's wife drew back and viewed her with a shrewdness that made Annalisse uncomfortable. "Well, dear, I must tell you that it won't do your husband's career any good to make friends with the Latinos in Blue Creek. They're taking over the town with their slovenly ways. The chicken factory hires them because they'll work for almost nothing. One of the things your husband will be expected to do as prosecutor is to cooperate with the government to rid this town of the illegals."

Annalisse looked at the calm, superior Mae in her pearls and pink linen suit, and she felt herself losing it. Maybe it was her resemblance to Dame Judi, but it seemed to her that the woman spoke as though she were playing the role of "M" in a James Bond movie, giving Dennis his assignment: exterminate the vermin. She felt her jaw harden.

She said, "Dennis will do what he thinks is right, Mrs. Cavanaugh."

The woman narrowed her eyes. "Who do you think you are, missy? One of those misguided bleeding hearts? We will *not* have gangs and drugs springing up in our town!"

"Have they?" Annalisse asked mildly.

"Not yet. But it's only a matter of time."

"As long as you treat them as outcasts, that is exactly what will happen. With a name like Cavanaugh, your husband's ancestors must have been Irish. Surely you can understand. There was a time when this country saw the Irish as a plague, too. It left them in the streets to starve."

Mae looked as though she'd been slapped. But Annalisse continued, "Fortunately, things changed as they were assimilated. I believe that the ability to assimilate minorities is part of the strength of our country."

Mae drew herself up and her eyes sparked danger. "I suppose you think we're just poor and ignorant and need to be enlightened. Well, Blue Creek has kept itself free from your type. That's why we like it here. It's not like the big city. We could never assimilate those people!"

Closing her eyes, Annalisse took a long breath, telling herself to be calm. She had long suspected that Blue Creek was a bastion of bigotry, but Dennis had refused to see it. Yet these women must have some good qualities. Perhaps she could find some common ground. "They need education so they can become useful, with a future . . ."

Emily Canliss broke in, her nose high as though smelling something unpleasant. "Before you know it, it's going to be another Tijuana if we don't drive them out somehow. This is exactly the type of situation the KKK used to handle."

"There's always Sonny's Boys," a tiny lady Annalisse didn't know said in a cracked voice.

"Sonny's Boys?" she echoed.

Though the small woman said nothing else, her eyes gleamed behind their folds with the hard, excited light of the fanatic. Annalisse had no doubt that she was referring to some sub-rosa group that had taken on the Klan's mission. Horror crept over her as she imagined a group of tattooed skinheads attacking small Latino children with clubs. Looking from the self-righteous Mae to the vinegary countenance of Emily, she could no longer stop her outrage from surfacing.

"If Sonny's Boys are who and what I think they are, I can tell you that my husband would never tolerate such people. Believe me, Dennis Childs knows no fear."

"You've got it all wrong, Annalisse," Mae said in a silky voice. "We're true Americans here in Cherokee County. So we don't believe in your political correctness. What's wrong with speaking our minds?" Then changing in an instant, she slapped the table with her palm. "At least the Irish were white. Those Latinos are filthy, girl! Filthy and disgusting!"

The cafe had gone dead silent. Annalisse could no longer remain at the table. "From my experience, their manners are considerably better than yours," she said simply. Standing, she made her way out. Not even pausing to put on her waders, she grabbed them and barged out into the downpour. The water gushing down the street between her and her car was her Rubicon, and she knew it. The look on Mae Cavanaugh's face had been positively malignant. Annalisse had never seen such a transformation. Dame Judi could take lessons from Mae Cavanaugh.

She had no idea where she was going. Not home. Driving over the bridge, she noticed vaguely that Blue Creek was skimming its belly. She headed instinctively for the high ground of the city park, beating the steering wheel with her fists. If she'd had to insist on seeing the scene as a film, she should at least have played it like Emma Thompson—straightforward, honest, and unflappable.

As it was, she had probably ruined Dennis's career. But was she supposed to just sit there and listen to such flaming fascism?

For heaven's sake, calm down, Drama Queen. As her heart slowed, she told herself that if it hadn't been for the ever-present Jules, she would have been able to swallow hard and keep quiet. Maybe.

But snatches of that other life kept seeping up through those cracks she'd tried so hard to patch over with her marriage and children. She was totally unreliable emotionally, and she hated it.

Nothing like this had ever happened before. She'd never lost it so completely, so totally beyond saving.

In her head she recreated the scene she had just left. The KKK! How could she be expected to keep her cool in the face of *that?* What would Dennis have done?

Annalisse began to feel a little better. The KKK or Sonny's Boys would surely be a deal-breaker for him. He wouldn't want any part of the government in a county like this. Maybe he'd even want to move.

Then she sighed and shook her head. Dennis was a fighter, it was true. But he was sold on Cherokee County and so happy to be here, she almost wanted to shield him from disillusionment. That was, she realized, an instinctive reaction she practiced all too often.

With this thought, her mind returned to its rut. *Was* her marriage a cop-out? She certainly didn't seem to belong in the life she had chosen. Dennis and Jordan thought she was someone she wasn't, but they loved her. Together they had built a cozy little world, much like the one she had been raised in. And, of course, there was Bronwyn. Up until now, she had tried with everything in her to make her new life succeed. Especially since there was no going back. She couldn't, even if she wanted to.

Annalisse headed up the hill to the barbecue pavilion, parked within the dense screen of evergreens that surrounded it, turned off her lights, and slumped back, glad the windows were beginning to fog.

When she had been listening to his music last night, Jules had been so vivid, so alive, standing on the beach that wintry day, eyes as gloomy as the sky, salt spray tangling his hair. It was the world around her that seemed dead.

She felt like some kind of volcano. She never knew when the lava would spill over her, smoldering with memories of a life long dormant. *What has caused the volcano to become active, suddenly, without warning?*

And Dennis. Poor Dennis. On the day she'd found him, she'd found hope to begin anew. And so, she'd put Jules behind her and never spoken of him. Tried never even to think of him. But apparently the wounds were too deep. Four years of marriage to Dennis hadn't stitched them shut, and now Jules and everything he represented were yanking out the sutures. The pain was beyond description.

❧

The ocean was always foreign to Annalisse. A mesmerizing disorientation settled on her as she stood at the base of the cliff on San Gregorio beach, watching the waves of the Pacific crash into a white boil at her feet. She was no longer an unimaginative biology major but the wispy denizen of a mysterious world fraught with dangerous potential. Salt spray tangled her hair. Jules put his arm around her shoulders.

Punching him playfully, Annalisse turned and ran back to their picnic blanket. "I used to dream of making castles in the sand when I lived in Wisconsin."

He threw himself down beside her, breathing hard. "Sand castles? Seriously? Sometimes you're too good to be true, Lisse."

"Well, wasn't this picnic a good idea?" She sprinkled a pinch of sand over his curls. He grinned a rare grin but made no effort to rid himself of her offering. "Or would you rather be back in your dorm studying for midterms?"

"When I first met you, I thought you must be either naïve or stupid," he remarked. He began idly to dig a trench with one hand. "But you're just honestly happy, aren't you?"

"What are you doing?"

"A castle has to have a moat, doesn't it?"

She laughed. "Yes, and pie crust turrets. Where's that plastic knife we used on the cheese? It's just what we need. And our paper cups."

"How do you do it?" He stopped his activity and studied her.

"It shouldn't be too hard, but the sand's got to be real damp."

"I didn't mean that, you crazy kid," he said. "I'm asking you how you manage to stay so optimistic all the time."

"I know it would be more politically correct for me to be fraught with angst over my weight or the environment or the future in the Middle East, but I love life here in California. It's like a dream come true for me." She didn't add, *and I'm with you.*

They worked in silence for a few minutes, and the castle took shape. With the help of the plastic cheese knife, Annalisse fashioned a turret fit for Rapunzel.

"Just how far into the future do you look, Lisse?"

Surprised by the question, she looked at him. His moody, dark eyes punctured her mood.

She returned to her castle-making, trying to rescue the afternoon. "Oh, I don't know. I picture getting my degree. Going to work for a lab somewhere."

"And your music? What about your piano?"

"I'm not in your class, Jules."

He put his sandy hands up to her face and turned it so she was looking into his intense black eyes. "Listen to me, Lisse. I've heard you play. Deep inside you, you have not only the passion but the core of genius. I don't know where it came from, but it's there. And that kind of genius comes along so rarely, it's your duty to develop it. Why do you think I put you on to Rachmaninoff? You don't choose music. Music chooses you." He paused and kissed her forehead lightly.

Annalisse bit her lip. Jules had never talked to her about her talent before. She had no idea he felt this way about it. Genius? Her? Annalisse Lundgren?

"But you've got this complex," he continued. "You think your being just off the farm instead of out of some fashionable conservatory makes you inferior." Brushing his thumbs over the sensitive skin under her eyes, he continued. "But I'm telling you that you've got a huge advantage over most people. You just need to work at it harder. Stop treating it as a hobby and start treating it as your life."

"You're right. I can't really see me making it as a concert pianist." She tried to laugh it off. In spite of Jules's words, she knew deep inside that something about the picture was wrong. She belonged in a lab, probably bent over a cadaver.

"I'm going to need an accompanist," he said softly, still looking directly into her eyes. "I'd like for it to be you."

"Me?" Annalisse was suddenly breathless. "But I'm not nearly good enough! Why would you want me?"

"Because of that passion. Underneath that Scandinavian calm of yours, there's a lot of excitement brewing."

"How do you know?" she demanded, feeling herself go scalding hot.

Taking her by the shoulders, he tumbled her back onto the sand. Then, slowly and delicately he began to kiss her, running his fingers through her long hair, tasting her cheeks, her forehead, her ear, and finally her lips. She couldn't believe this was happening, couldn't believe he was kissing her, couldn't believe he thought she had a genius within. Her world was turning upside down. As he stroked the planes of her face, she kissed him back with a fierce tumble of emotions. The world twirled around her in lover's vertigo. Jules laughed, a joyful carefree laugh, as they played like children on the beach until they were both thoroughly covered with sand and their castle lay in ruins.

Jules whispered, "I wouldn't be surprised if the talent buried in you is greater than mine. You understand me, Annalisse. You understand my music. You want to be part of it, don't you?"

She looked into his face and saw the earnestness he had always reserved for his violin. "Yes," she stumbled, out of breath. *I want to be part of you.* "Yes, of course I do. But there are so many things against it. I mean . . . I don't know if I'm really cut out for that kind of life. I'm so ordinary, Jules."

"You're deluding yourself. You're not ordinary at all. Don't you want to travel the world? Play in the great concert halls? What could be more fantastic?" His eyes shone.

She looked away. There was no way she could picture herself in such a role. But why would he lie to her about her talent? What motive could he possibly have? "I . . . I'll have to think about it, Jules. That's a huge change. It's hard for me to wrap my mind around."

"There are things you don't know about me, Lisse. I need your buoyancy, your happy view of life." He cast his eyes down, and he drew a heart in the sand. "This last month, seeing you every day—things have changed for me. I've been waiting to see how deep your strength goes, whether it's real or not. I'm convinced it is. And I know I'd be crippled without it."

Stunned, she struggled up onto her elbows. What did he mean by that? Crippled? She watched as he deserted the ruins of their castle and walked to the edge of the water once again. Jules was incredibly moody at the best of times. For a reason she couldn't define, she feared those moods, and so she was unable to ask him to elaborate. Instead she concentrated on the sheer unexpectedness of his praise.

He thinks I can do it. He wants me. These thoughts drummed in her head. She still didn't know what to make of them.

At length, she stood and joined him. "It's starting to rain again," she said, putting a hand out to catch the mist.

"I know," he said, taking her in his arms. "It's making little crystal beads in your hair."

Chapter Four

Hillbilly Law could not be called a cerebral experience by any stretch of the imagination, but here in Blue Creek, unlike Los Angeles, Dennis felt the law was still considered an honorable profession.

This morning he was attempting to write a title opinion on a piece of real estate located down on the creek—a largish farm that originally had been granted by the United States government to the St. Louis and San Francisco Railway Company. When the right mood was upon him, he could really get into an abstract of title, fleshing out with his imagination the tale told on the yellowing pages.

But today ominous rumblings rattled the windows, breaking his concentration, and he found himself resenting the trivial nature of the task. A pervading dampness seeped through the thin walls, accentuating the mustiness of the old chiropractor's office he rented, and he felt the nagging annoyance of being unable to afford something better. Of course, this office was about as good as it got in Blue

Creek. A rare longing assailed him for a client in pinstripes with a Gucci briefcase and a complex corporate tax problem.

Following a brisk knock, Dennis's secretary, Leila, entered the small office. This week her bobbed hair was a sort of fuschia. He and Annalisse laid bets on how long each color would last. Leila ruled him with an iron fist and was probably the only reason his law practice made a dime. "Ada Lou Horneby's out there. Appears she's got another poor lost soul along with her. If you take her on this time, Dennis, I'm not doing anything, not even one letter, unless you promise to bill her."

"How can I bill Ada Lou? The only thing she's got is the gold in her teeth."

"Well, she can't expect you to handle every charity case she comes across. How do you know she hasn't got a secret stash? She must know lawyers don't come cheap, but every time she leaves here she gives me a lecture because I haven't sent her a bill."

"She's very proud, Ada is."

"Dennis, you don't understand these people! If you don't let them pay, they don't respect you. She must owe you at least three thousand dollars."

He told her to show Ada Lou in.

Entering heavily, an enormous woman turned out in an iron gray wig and a "town dress" of lavender-flowered jersey gripped her lawyer powerfully by the hand. "Mr. Chiles, this here's my nephew, Lonnie Warner. He's havin' an awful time over some money's owed him."

Dennis had trouble restraining his instinctive reaction to the poor specimen of humanity who mutely trod in her wake. He was probably not as tall as he looked. It was just that he was all angles and legs. It appeared that he hadn't had a square meal in years.

Missing his front teeth, he looked almost comic under his perplexity and three days' growth of beard. He also smelled.

Dennis invited them to be seated.

"I'll pay all the expenses, o' course. I just wanna see this boy get what's owed him, Mr. Chiles."

"Suppose one of you tells me about it, Ada Lou."

Lonnie sprawled limply in the brown Naugahyde chair and left the talking to his benefactress.

It was a standard case. Dennis wondered only why they had waited four years to see a lawyer. Warner had apparently injured his foot while doing odd jobs for a local hauling company. The small number of employees in the enterprise precluded any provision for workers' compensation benefits.

"We'll see what we can do, Mr. Warner," Dennis assured him, looking up from the brief notes he was making on his yellow pad. "I'll need to talk to your doctor. Who is it?"

"Lonnie. Call me Lonnie." The man spoke finally in a soft, flat voice.

"Lonnie." Dennis corrected himself.

"His doctor's young Gregg Gregory," Ada Lou interjected. "Does Lonnie need t' sign somethin'?"

"Leila has a form out front. Now, Lonnie, perhaps you'd wait for us just a minute outside. I need to talk to Ada Lou here about another matter."

Incurious, the fellow unfolded himself, stood, and wandered out into the hallway, his face still wearing its mask of puzzlement.

Dennis got up and closed the door. Seating himself on the arm of the chair Lonnie had vacated, he addressed the formidable old woman. "Now, Ada Lou, we've talked about this before. This boy needs Legal Aid, that's what he needs. Just take him into Springfield.

It's free, and that's what it's there for. We can't have you taking on every hard luck case in Cherokee County."

Ada Lou narrowed her eyes. "Mr. Chiles, I thought you was a religious man. That's why I come to you. You oughta know it ain't no business of the gumment t' take care o' these kinda problems. The good Lord expects *us* t' help out our brothers when they're in need. I ain't got no one else t' care for, an' I got my Social Security and that bit ol' Horneby left when he passed on. The Lord's been real good t' me, Mr. Chiles. I gotta show my gratitude by helpin' these poor unfortchnates . . . Y' know Lonnie ain't got no folks except me. An' probably ya didn't notice, but he's a bit simple." She touched her forehead. "He needs special handlin'."

Dennis sighed and looked at his elderly client's stubborn face. Then he grinned and said, "All right, Ada Lou. You win." Patting her shoulder gently, he showed her out into the hall.

"That'll be fifty dollars for the consultation, Mrs. Horneby," his secretary announced, defiance evident in her cool voice.

Ada Lou said nothing for a moment. Then, "Why sure, Leila. Just a minute."

Dennis cringed and shut his door quietly. While Leila waged her war against charity, he sprayed lemon air freshener around his office. Then he tried to resume work on the abstract but found he'd lost what little interest he'd had in the first place.

His mood of the morning had faded. This was turning into one of those days when it was hard to romanticize the Ozarks. There was too much poverty here, too much ignorance. Maybe it was the ominous green light of the storm making everything dark and strange at eleven o'clock in the morning, but something summoned up the scene in the laundry room. There was the same air of heavy foreboding, the same sense of ordinary things being out of place. Not for the first time, he reflected on how much he counted on Annalisse, counted on her strong sense of family and her stoic disposition to anchor him in his swings of mood while fighting the battle of good versus evil. It made him uneasy to realize how much he relied on her steadiness.

Sighing, he pushed his forebodings aside and picked up the telephone to call Gregg Gregory.

"We still goin' fishin' tomorrow morning?" their family doctor greeted him.

"Maybe this storm will bring the fish to us," Dennis answered as a sudden percussion of rain hit against his windows.

"Well, if it floods, you can just about count on it that half my OB patients'll go into labor."

"One of your other patients came in this morning with a potential lawsuit. Lonnie Warner."

"Right." Dennis heard the doctor draw a deep breath. "I told Lonnie to find himself a lawyer. I specifically mentioned you, as a matter of fact. Didn't think anyone else in town would touch it, to tell you the truth. Are you still up for a good crusade these days, Dennis, or have you sold your soul to politics?"

"Don't be cute. What've you got?"

"Well, what I've got, or rather what Lonnie's got, is gonna raise one heck of a stink. Can you meet me over here around five-thirty? I want you to see for yourself."

Intrigued, Dennis agreed, hung up the phone and resumed his scrutiny of the chain of title on the Watson farm.

"Milkey Mae Montgomery," he mused. "Now, there's a name. Bet she packed a shotgun and was known all over Cherokee County for her corn liquor. No children, apparently, as she passed the farm on to a nephew. Probably widowed in the Civil War . . ."

It was no good; he couldn't jolly himself into it. Gregg's talk of crusades had gotten his blood running. An abstract was much too tame to hold his interest. Taking his old London Fog raincoat off the peg, he went home for an early lunch.

~

"It's a good thing we've got this thing," Gregg commented later, referring to his SUV he was shifting into four-wheel drive. The street outside the Cherokee County Hospital was swirling with knee-high muddy water. "Wooee!" he crowed as they pulled out into the stream. "You ever seen rain like this in July?"

"It's a monsoon, for crying out loud," Dennis replied. "Probably drown my chickens. Where're you taking me, anyway?"

"To the scene of the crime," Gregg answered, suddenly grim. He pushed up his horn-rims with a forefinger. He'd graduated first in his med school class at the University of Missouri and managed to look like the quintessential Ivy Leaguer, but Dr. Gregory was another big city dropout. His wife was a Blue Creek girl, and once he had realized the dearth of doctors in the area, he determined to settle where he could do the most good.

"You mean where Lonnie had his accident?" Dennis asked. "Who was his trucking outfit hauling for?"

"Amalgamated."

While his friend maneuvered the Bronco out onto the highway, Dennis considered Amalgamated Chemical, the single biggest employer in Cherokee County—in this part of the state, for that matter. The company had moved to Blue Creek from St. Louis during the sixties to take advantage of the open shop, unions being a rarity in southwest Missouri. People were glad of a near minimum-wage factory job close to home to supplement their shrinking farm income. With a spirit of independence dating back to Civil War days, the people of Cherokee County were an island of tough, self-sufficient

35

Republicans in a sea of Southern Democrats, shunning all manifestations of liberal thinking. "We Take Care of Our Own," was their motto, and that suited Amalgamated Chemical just fine.

Gregg turned off the highway onto a rocky dirt lane that tunneled its way through a dense canopy of oak trees. Thick red mud spattered up on the windshield.

"You sure we're not going to get stuck?" Dennis queried. He could feel the mud churning under the wheels. "This goes down to the creek, doesn't it? It's probably flooded."

"We're not going that far. This is the back way into the Amalgamated property. My boys come down here frog huntin' on their bikes. No more, though, I can tell you that."

"They get caught?"

"No. You know what Amalgamated's been dumping back here on this vacant lot?" Gregg asked as he pulled off the road into a clearing. "Dioxin."

"What?" Dennis stared at his friend and then at the wasteland around him. The only things he could see were a rusted-out old truck chassis, spare tires, and empty beer cans.

"Dioxin. It's a by-product of that wonderful Agent Orange the army used in Vietnam. It's also a by-product of hexachlorophene, which they probably still produce. It's one of the most toxic substances known to man. Provides you with a great shot at a variety of different cancers, among other things."

Dennis looked out over the muddy lot, afraid of what he was going to hear. "How does Lonnie fit in?"

"That's what he was digging up and hauling. That's what he got on his foot. First it turned into an acne-like rash, and he didn't think much of it. But Ada Lou brought him into see me about four years ago. At the time, I didn't put two and two together. I gave him some cortisone cream or something. It didn't touch it, as it turned out, but

Lonnie never came back until recently, when he started going off his feed and Ada Lou finally got him to come in and see me again. He's got leukemia, Dennis. Stage four."

For a moment, Dennis said nothing, letting the seriousness of this charge sink in. Was that poor wreck of a human being who was in his office that morning going to die because of criminal negligence on the part of the company that most of Cherokee County considered to be its savior?

"He said he didn't know what was in those drums," Dennis maintained stubbornly. "What makes you think it was dioxin? Have you ever seen it before?"

"Unfortunately, yes. The army paid my way through med school, remember? I did an internship at Walter Reed. That rash appeared right after the dumping incident. When I was an intern, I actually specialized in patients who had been contaminated by toxic waste. It's partly my fault that I didn't follow up on his story four years ago. I might have saved him."

"Geez! Amalgamated would have to be crazy to mess with that stuff! I mean, what in the world are they doing with dioxin buried in the back forty?"

"It's not really as unlikely as you'd imagine. What are they going to do with the waste? They didn't want it around, so they buried it."

"Above a creek that floods every spring?"

"Nothin' to stop 'em." Gregg shrugged. "You know how lax they are about the environment around here. They hate government regulation of any kind. After I saw Lonnie again recently and determined his condition, I had him bring me back here and show me where it was he was digging. I marked it with that stack of three tires. Maybe they finally realized the danger and that's why they hired Lonnie to haul the drums off somewhere else, but that's where

37

they were. The one that leaked on Lonnie probably did some leaking into the ground, too. He said it had rusted through."

"You realize what this means?" Dennis demanded, his anger finally unleashed.

"Sure," Gregg replied. "The contaminated soil could reach the creek any time. Dead frogs, dead fish, and poor dead Lonnie. And that's just the start."

Dennis stared through the rain, trying to take in the magnitude of it all. "Why haven't you sounded the alarm on this thing? That creek waters dairy cattle all the way down to Arkansas, for crying out loud."

"Humans, too. Some people build spring houses on it. But they've moved the drums, Dennis. Lonnie delivered 'em out behind that old Quonset hut that sits in back of Amalgamated, but they're not there anymore. We checked." Shifting the SUV into reverse, he continued. "The problem is to find out what they've done with them. And what they're going to do for Lonnie. That's your job. No one listens to doctors, but lawyers can hit 'em where it hurts." Gregg pushed his glasses up onto the bridge of his nose. "I haven't told Lonnie about the dioxin and what's going to happen to him yet. You care to do it?"

Dennis shook his head. "That's your job, thank heavens."

Taking it easy because of the mud, Gregg nursed the SUV slowly backward, steering clear of the truck chassis, and made his way back to the lane.

⌒‿

Annalisse must have managed to chase the chickens into the barn. They were there, cluck-clucking at the rain through the barn door from the safety of their perch on the hay. Dennis was relieved.

There was some new intelligence that chickens were smart, but he'd never noticed it. Still, he wouldn't like to see them drown.

Henrietta was also safe and dry. Pulling up the milking stool, Dennis settled himself to milk. For him, the barn functioned as a decompression chamber. This was where, most of the time, he put off the lawyer and took up the farmer. But today as he pumped Henrietta's teats, his head next to her placid bulk, the worldly concerns remained. First there was an overwhelming pity for poor, simple Lonnie Warner. On top of that was pure rage. For such a matter to land in his law office was some sort of cosmic joke. After searching high and low for his Eden, he wasn't about to see it poisoned. There were steps he could take.

To the sound of milk streaming rhythmically into the pail, Dennis mapped out his strategy. First, he'd get the State Department of Natural Resources to test the soil where the barrels had been. That area was under water every spring, making it likely that more than one barrel had rusted through.

When they had the evidence, they'd tackle Amalgamated. He'd send out press releases to the *St. Louis Post Dispatch*, the *Kansas City Star*, and the *Springfield Daily News*. He and Lonnie would probably be swamped by reporters from the local TV stations, and maybe one of the networks would even feature the story on the national news. He could see it: Lonnie, a symbol of Dickensian proportions—the innocent, ignorant boy used up and destroyed by careless corporate greed.

The milk streamed faster and faster into the pail. Finally, Henrietta stirred mildly in protest, stepping away from him and switching her tail. Dennis straightened up and smoothed her hide apologetically. "Sorry, old lady. Guess I got carried away."

Commencing again at a more sedate pace, Dennis reflected wryly upon his preoccupation. *Here we go again. Dennis Childs, ace muckraker, crusader extraordinaire. And yet, all I really want out of life is peace. Peace to raise my children, grow my garden, milk my cow. But how can there ever be peace without justice?* That was where he always came up against it. And how did you maintain justice without a fight?

These days all his fighting was done in the courtroom, but even there it could be plenty brutal. At least you never *saw* the other guy bleed. With real blood, it was different. How far did you go? Some nights he still dreamed about that cop. Still saw his little pig eyes as he raised his nightstick and went after Jill.

Annalisse maintained he'd be bored with true peace, that he was never happy unless he had a cause. Maybe she was right. There was nothing that got your adrenaline pumping like a worthy cause. He relished a challenging duel—going up against the other guy, who was doing his best to pulverize you. You were alive then, colors were brighter, sounds sharper, smells more pungent. And when you won, when you downed your Goliath, well, there was no high quite like it.

The irony of all this didn't escape him. He'd lived with the contradiction in himself for too long. And the fact that he had moved here to pursue his Green lifestyle mocked him.

But there could be no possibility of ambivalence in this situation. No one could dispute the pure evil represented by dioxin in the water table.

❧

Jill's hair was a long cascade of platinum silk as she bent over him, screening their kisses from Sam as they stretched out on the floor of his apartment, fugitives from their first demonstration. Even in her army fatigues, she smelled like gardenias, and her perfect Nefertiti face was the most beautiful thing he had ever known. The short round creature they called Sam because he was precisely like the Hobbit, Frodo's devoted friend, was carrying on about the event that Dennis was trying to forget with Jill's kisses.

"You were awesome, man! How could that cop go after Jill, of all people? What if he'd hit her?"

"I'd have been a martyr to the cause," Jill said in her surprisingly husky voice. "But Dennis was my white knight, as always." Sitting up, she looked at her watch. "Time for the news. I think we actually made history today, guys. Turn it on, Sam."

Sure enough. There it was on Sam's plasma TV. Evidence in spades of police brutality. The camera had actually homed in on their pig of a cop, just one among many called in by Lakeland Steel to break up their demonstration. He was about to crush Jill's skull with his nightstick.

Dennis could still smell the man's garlicky sweat as he wrestled the weapon out of the cop's chubby grip and then brought it down squarely on the guy's head. For a moment, Dennis's heart stopped. *Was he a murderer?*

This fear distanced him from the scenes that flashed in front of him as he was jostled by the mob of cops and students protesting Lakeland's pollution of Lake Michigan. He stood, hands hanging at his sides, blinded by the memory. He glimpsed his father, the gentlest man on earth. Dennis imagined his eyes—sad and uncomprehending. Finally, he hoisted the tiny Jill over his shoulder and wrestled his way out of the crowd, down the street to where Sam's Lexus was parked.

Now, watching the cop on TV as he recovered from being hit, standing up and looking around him for his assailant, Dennis was extremely relieved that the man was all right. And that his own back had been to the camera.

"Aw, man!" Jill said in disappointment. "You didn't kill the guy, after all, Dennis."

"You wanted him dead?" he asked.

"At least. He was repulsive. And totally without a sense of proportion, which is worse. But it made a good news story. Only if you hadn't hauled me off, I would have been interviewed, Dennis. How could you?" She punched his arm playfully.

"Hemingway tradition, Jill. Don't gush over your hero. Just make his favorite dinner," Sam said with a laugh.

"Chinese takeout, Sam. And, as usual, you're buying."

As his friend shrugged and put on the giant fleece that made him resemble a grizzly, Dennis knew he was secretly pleased to be of use.

He looked at Jill as the door closed behind his friend. "That stuff really turns you on, doesn't it?"

"Wasn't it great? And we made the news! Maybe even the national news!"

"Jill, I thought I killed that cop. I was almost a murderer."

She pushed him back down on the floor, and as the curtain of her hair fell about him, he forgot everything but the sensation of her kisses as she rained them all over his face.

Chapter Five

H ey, Daddy, Mommy got a pizza!" Jordan greeted his father as he emerged from the shower after milking.

Annalisse presented her cheek for a kiss. "Sorry," she said. "I hope you don't mind. It's not a frozen one. It's from Pizza Hut."

"One hundred percent natural, then, I'm sure," Dennis answered, putting the milk bucket onto the tile counter.

"I want pizza evewy day!" Jordan said, carefully arranging the forks on the table. "Mommy's in the papew!"

Sitting down, Dennis opened the *Blue Creek Sentinel*. It always struck him as quaint that a town this size should have a daily evening paper. Jordan pointed out his mother's picture on the front page. The caption read: "Mrs. Dennis Childs and Mrs. Jesse Cavanaugh discuss plans for the busy months ahead at today's Cherokee County Republican Women's luncheon." Whoever had written that caption was imaginative, at least. Annalisse looked self-conscious; Mae, thunderous.

"You see this?" he asked his wife, laughing.

Annalisse nodded but said nothing.

Normally, his wife was welcoming and greeted him sunnily with a kiss. What was wrong?

"Thanks for chasing the chickens into the barn," he said. "That couldn't have been easy in your condition."

"It was fine," she said, her voice flat.

Over dinner, Annalisse continued to be uncommunicative. While Jordan noisily consumed his pizza, smacking his lips, Dennis watched his wife. She looked unusually drawn—her skin was as translucent as an onion's, revealing the purple veins at her temples and under her eyes. She wasn't well, he told himself. No matter what she said, she wasn't well. Tonight he would get to the bottom of it.

"You don't look good, Annalisse," he told her later, helping her pull the spread off the bed. Jordan was asleep in his own room. "I'm an idiot. I shouldn't have left you with all those beans."

"I'm just tired," she sighed, her expression dull as she sat on the bed. "It wasn't the beans."

Remembering the picture in the paper, he asked, "Was it the luncheon? Mae looked like she was out for someone's blood."

Annalisse didn't answer for a moment. Then, turning her face away, she said in a low voice, "I didn't handle things very well, Dennis."

Such dejection alarmed him. Was she going to cry again? "Annalisse, look at me," he said as gently as he could. "Look at me."

She faced him, her jaw clenched. "I didn't," she insisted.

"What happened?"

"Don't you ever get sick of this place?" she burst out, clenching her fists. "Sick of the reactionaries and the prejudice and all the little old ladies in flowered dresses?"

He forbore mentioning that such little old ladies were his bread

44

and butter. But reactionaries? Prejudice? "What happened at the luncheon?"

"Oh, to heck with the luncheon!" she exploded, hands flying. "What's important, Dennis, is that somewhere in the world someone is playing Chopin tonight. Maybe in Vienna they're sitting up still, drinking *schokolade mit schlag* and talking about the opera . . ."

Her sudden vehemence and abruptly foreign train of thought astonished him. "Geesh, Annalisse. What are you getting at?"

Instead of replying, she got up and began to undress. He went on, "You sound like a transplanted New Yorker or something. I mean, you can't tell me it was all that different in rural Wisconsin. And since when do you speak German?"

She didn't answer.

"Well?"

Finally, she said with a sigh, "I wasn't all that crazy about rural Wisconsin, Dennis. But at least it was in the North."

This was a surprise. "What do you mean?"

Pulling her nightgown over her head, she shrugged and went into the bathroom. "There's a lot more to life than soybeans and hogs."

Stunned, he listened to the water running as she brushed her teeth. What she said was true, of course. There was more to life. But he'd been under the impression he'd married a country girl. Leaning against the door frame, he groped for the real issue. The Tchaikovsky episode probably figured in here somewhere . . .

"Something must have brought this on, Annalisse. I mean why, today, do you suddenly decide to tell me all this? If you felt that strongly, why didn't you say something back in LA, before we moved here?"

She began to wash her face. When she had finished, she looked as scrubbed and pink as her old cotton nightgown. But she was using a new talc or lotion or something. It wasn't the lemony vanilla he was used to. He wrinkled his nose. She smelled like lilacs, he decided.

"I'm sorry," she said, getting into bed. For a moment she closed her eyes and leaned against the headboard. "It's been a bad day, Dennis. I'm taking it out on you and Blue Creek. The truth is, I'm not who you think I am."

Now he was shocked. "Annalisse. Look at me." She opened her eyes but kept them focused straight ahead. He had never seen them so full of misery. "You're my touchstone. You mean everything to me. More than the farm, certainly. More than Blue Creek. Tell me what's wrong! Something's happened."

Rolling away from him onto her side, she drew her knees up as though protecting her baby. "I've ruined everything, Dennis. I insulted Mae. I walked out on the luncheon, and everyone watched me go. You could have heard a pin drop."

Then she was crying, her face averted from him. Completely bewildered, he could only look on, trying to make himself understand that this was his wife, this was Annalisse. She had been nothing but nurturing, calm, and pragmatic all their married life. What was happening to her? He felt helpless, desperate, as though the sun were going out. He had always thought that his various causes and pursuit of Eden had made him the one with the chaotic inner life.

Placing a tentative hand on her shoulder he whispered, "Swedie, it doesn't matter. Whatever it is, it doesn't matter. I just want you to be happy. I don't care about anything else. We'll go back to LA if you want to. Just please, please stop crying."

After a while her sobs lessened, but she still lay tense under his hand. When he removed it, she relaxed. He felt suddenly cold, lost. Whatever had happened was closed inside of her, closed against him. For some reason, he was the enemy.

Standing up, he began to undress. Much as he wanted to, he couldn't cross-examine her. It went counter to everything in their relationship. Picking up his shoes, he threw them one by one into the closet and then, wearing only his shorts, trotted noisily down the stairs, hitting the wall with his fists as he went. His wife obviously wanted him gone.

From the living room he could see the rain slashing at the windows. It was so deafening, so relentless. And it made his charming farmhouse smell moldy. Wandering aimlessly, he picked up stray Star Wars creatures from the oatmeal-colored carpet. He had been right to be uneasy last night. Maybe part of it was this weird storm. He was all on edge. He'd never seen rain go on and on like this. It still pounded the roof like an artillery barrage. Was she really unhappy here? No. People didn't cry as if their hearts were breaking because they didn't like living in the country. Did they?

Incredible as it seemed, he must be the problem. Annalisse had snapped, somehow. She was unhappy with him. Perhaps she no longer loved him. He would have thought it impossible that Annalisse might simply switch off her feelings, but such a thing had happened to him before. *Something is going on.* His chest tightened, haunted by days past. The disillusionment he had suffered was still painful in retrospect. He cringed, remembering it.

～

The sun was shining. His psych paper was finished and turned in. Jill was due back today from the anti-nuclear-energy demonstration in Washington.

As he made his way down Ridge Road to her apartment, he felt the exultant freedom that virtue brings—it was a good, possibly brilliant, psych paper—and he allowed his thoughts to dwell on Jill.

Not that she was often out of his thoughts, but he'd had to force his mind into academic channels over the Thanksgiving vacation. He'd wanted to go with her to D.C., but he hadn't any money and he was failing psych.

Now he anticipated her with a poignancy made sharper by deprivation. She would smell like gardenias.

Last night he'd rested from his studies by writing some poetry. There in his crummy dorm room by the light of his clip-on lamp, he'd penciled a small gem. It came to him now:

> *when we are in love*
> *we love gas pumps and daffodils*
> *diamonds and old denim*
> *small-town stoplights*
> *blinking all night long*
> *under star-strewn skies*

He threw his gloves in the air, caught them, and then, feeling like a kid at the beginning of summer vacation, ran the rest of the way.

Bob Dylan's rasp came through the door at the top of the stairs. Jill's patron saint. The landing smelled like Chinese takeout.

Unlocking the door, he called out, "Jill?"

He was in the middle of the neat-as-a-pin living room before she emerged from the bedroom, silky blonde hair disheveled, wearing a man's shirt, and as far as he could tell, nothing else. The shirt wasn't his.

The velvety pupils of her eyes seemed big as pansies, oddly unfocused. She gave a belated grin of recognition and started toward him.

Before she reached him, however, the bedroom doorway was filled with a bare-chested man the size of a fullback. Rodney

Coleman, the campus rooster with the brain to match. "Hey, what's happening?" Rodney yawned.

Dennis's withdrawal from the scene was pure reflex. It wasn't until he was back down on the street, halfway to the dorm, that he could think.

His whole being constricted, recoiling from the vision, but he kept seeing it, over and over, until he shook with it. Jill, his brilliant Jill, stoned and in bed with the stupidest man at Northwestern. By the time he reached his own dorm, the shock had worn off, and the rage began. Instead of opening his door, he put his fist through it.

Late that night, after consuming enough alcohol to obliterate him, he lay in his bed sober as ever, staring at the cracked ceiling. His naïve poem mocked him from the nightstand, and the pain started.

~e

When she was sure Dennis had dozed off, Annalisse put down the book she'd been pretending to read and turned off her reading lamp. She lay quietly, listening to her husband breathe. She'd consciously shut him out for the first time in their marriage. On top of ruining him by her behavior at the luncheon. It was all the fault of these unremitting flashbacks. Dennis would be better off without her.

No! She couldn't start thinking that way. Forcing her thoughts out of the widening abyss, she reminded herself that Dennis didn't know the whole story. Even if she'd messed up today, Dennis would forgive her. Tomorrow everything would be all right. Or at least as all right as it could be, given the choices she'd made.

Fitfully, she turned on her side. Had Jules ruined her for leading a predictable life? It was important for children to know what to expect, for her to see ahead to safe tomorrows.

Jules hadn't been safe. But he'd been alive—exciting, brilliant. He'd pulled things out of her she'd never known were there, made her stretch and steel herself.

She tensed. It was a false picture she was drawing. It was only sweet in the looking back. In real time, she knew the ending—a time as black as any cave, where events had wrestled her to the bottom of the world. Remembering the good times stirred up this storm that pulled her life out of shape with its whirling force, exposing all her faulty foundations.

Face it. I married Dennis on a pendulum swing away from Jules. It was wrong of me. For more than four years, she had fostered her husband's hope and idealism, thinking it was enough for the two of them. But now, her internal tsunami had ripped away the self that was Dennis's wife. Who was she? What did she want?

Annalisse threw off the covers and went downstairs to the screened-in porch. The smell of wet earth drew her out of herself, stimulating her senses. Jerking open the screen door, she ran outside, barefoot, feeling the pouring rain cold and sharp on her skin, the saturated grass oozing between her toes. She wanted to be alive—all alive. She wanted to shed this sensible shell she lived in and be someone different—maybe the person she used to be, someone who did outrageous things, who loved and was loved to excess. Someone who would sit up all night in a Paris cafe, or eat garlicky deep-fried *Langos* from a street vendor in Vienna, or play Rachmaninoff's *Third* until the sweat poured down her body like rain.

Chapter Six

Annalisse awoke the next morning with a throbbing head. For several minutes she lay feeling heavy and overripe. When finally she got out of bed, she groped her way to the bathroom and brushed her teeth. It took her a few bewildered seconds to understand why her feet were dirty.

Memories of yesterday and the dull prospect of today muffled her mind. Laundry, grocery shopping, putting up green beans.

Stepping into the shower, she scrubbed herself briskly and began an accompanying lecture. *Who do I think I am? Madame Bovary? It's time to get back into my skin and quit behaving like such a fool.*

Annalisse slammed the faucet off and emerged from the shower. She would put yesterday's fiasco behind her. Perhaps a note to Mae, apologizing and repenting, would salvage the situation. And, of course, she would explain the whole thing to Dennis. It was way past time that she did. Perhaps he could even help her through this, if he wasn't too wounded by her revelations.

First, however, she had to send Jules into exile. There was plenty

51

to be glad of in her life with Dennis. Pulling the muddy sheets off the bed, she sent them down the laundry chute. Then she shunned her jeans in favor of a white sundress, tying a sky blue scarf around her neck with a rosebud knot she'd seen in a catalog. On impulse, she changed the part in her hair from the center to the left side and used a bobby pin to fasten it back from her face, exposing her ear and cheekbone. One foot was out of the rut, anyway.

Now, breakfast. She would make waffles and serve them with wild blackberries, fresh whipped cream, and brown sugar.

"Mommy, you look diffwent," Jordan commented. "Did you get wet? Is it still waining?"

"Why don't you go see? It looks pretty clear. Dad must be in the barn."

The waffles looked beautiful, but Annalisse couldn't eat them. She had absolutely no appetite.

"The rain's stopped, finally," Dennis commented as he and Jordan walked in through the kitchen door. He looked at her guardedly, taking in the changes in her appearance but making no comment. "Springfield paper says we got eight inches before they went to press at midnight. Probably another four or so since then."

"Cool!" Jordan declared. "How much is that?"

"Why don't you come into town with me and see, Jordan?" his father offered. "I won't be going fishing this morning, that's for sure. I'll bet downtown's a mess. We can help clean it up before I get ready for court."

Annalisse was grateful for whatever had put this idea in Dennis's head. Jordan was not only precocious, but relentless, and this morning she needed to concentrate on getting her bearings.

There had been flooding. When Annalisse drove over the bridge into town to shop for groceries an hour and a half later, she could see water, deep as the hubcaps, standing everywhere. It had begun to recede, but tree limbs, garbage of every description, and thick red mud covered sidewalks where it had been washed up against the storefronts. There was a rotten, decaying smell in the air.

Instead of driving straight through town on the highway, Annalisse turned into the square to see how the business district looked. She was surprised to see a hive of activity. Now the band shell (missing a chunk of its roof since the storm) housed white-haired ladies dispensing coffee and sweet rolls to the volunteers clad in overalls who were busy digging Blue Creek out from under the mud. She recognized Mae Cavanaugh and Emily Canliss.

Wearing his straw boater, Old Joe, the retired mayor, was shaking his head over the ruined flower bed that surrounded the band shell. Here and there Annalisse could see him poke his cane at a bedraggled zinnia or snapdragon peeking through the mud. All the doors on the square stood wide open, and shovelfuls of mud came flying out at frequent intervals.

Annalisse saw Dennis and Jordan as she drove past Calhoun's. Jake's Feed and Garden Supply, down at the south end, looked especially hard hit. When the river flooded the square from the north, the only things in its way were the band shell and Jake's store. His front window was broken.

It would be heartless to drive on, Annalisse decided. Jake was Jordan's friend, having won the child's heart with mousetraps and sunflower seeds when the family first came to Blue Creek and friends were scarce.

She parked the car on an island of mud. Taking off her sandals, she waded across to the store. *Well, I wanted some action, didn't I? This wasn't particularly what I had in mind, but it will have to do.*

"Need some help?" Annalisse called as they entered. All around her, men and boys shoveled mud into wheelbarrows. Annalisse understood for the first time why Jake kept the original unfinished oak floor in his shop. A new one would have been ruined by the ankle-deep mud.

"Miz Chiles? That you?" Jake answered from the back. "I didn't reco'nize you at first." The friendly giant walked through the dim light and ancient seed bins to greet her. His orange mane and beard were wild as ever, and his massive shoulders were shiny with sweat under the straps of his overalls.

"Can I help?" she asked. "Looks like you really got hit."

"Oh, this ain't nothin.' Look over there." He pointed to a patch of plaster exposed between two metal shelves. "See that brown water mark 'bout three foot off the floor? Flood in '58 did that. My granddaddy had one back in '32, like to tore the place down. Least I know 'nuf now t' keep m' seed stored up off the floor. Didn't lose much this time 'cept some lawn seed I hadn't put in bins yet."

"Is Trixie okay?" she asked, referring to Jordan's favorite hamster.

"She's fine, Miz Chiles. That boy of yours already been an' asked."

Annalisse crinkled her nose and laughed.

Picking her way carefully through the mud and between the wheelbarrows, Annalisse moved farther into the store.

"There's got to be something for me to do, Jake," she said.

"Naw, you look too purdy in that white dress. That husband o' yours already been an hour in here shovelin'. He's one of the first ones here. Rolled up them fancy pant legs of his, put my coveralls on, and got right t' work. I sent 'im on down to Crabtree's a minute ago. Seems they got trouble with a wire shortin' out or somethin'."

"I hope Jordan stays out of the way," she said. The mud was oozing through her bare toes. "He thrives on disasters for some reason."

"Oh, that's just bein' a kid, Miz Chiles. No, you can be real proud of that boy. He's gonna go places with a vocab'lary like he's got. You can be proud of that husband o' yours, come t' that."

"You gonna stan' there all day talkin' to that purdy lady an' let us do all the work, Jake?" Little Dan Perkins asked. He was even bigger than Jake and was also working without a shirt.

"Aw, Little Dan, you wuzn't doing nothin' afore this flood but sittin' in front o' yore TV. Thiz the most excitement you had all year, so you keep quiet."

Turning his back on Perkins and crew, Jake began vigorously to clean out his left ear with his little finger. "Guess Louise an' I need to get on in to see Mr. Chiles 'bout our wills. Mah Aunt Ada Lou, she's been on at me. Says it don't do no good t' pr'crastinate. You know we think a lot o' that husband o' yours in this town. He's gonna make a fine prosecutor. Which puts me in mind of somethin' I been meanin' to talk to you about."

Annalisse inclined her head.

"The senator, he don't make a habit of hirin' anybody that ain't a yes-man, if you see what I'm drivin' at."

"Dennis isn't a yes-man, Jake."

"Now, I know that, and you know that, but it'd be best if you kinda kept it to yourselves until after the election. Might spoil his chances. An' we need him here. Yes, ma'am. We could sure use someone who wasn't a yes-man."

"Any reason in particular?"

"Let's just say, I might not be real educated, but I b'lieve in democracy."

Annalisse reflected on the similarity of this to Whitney's warning. "Well, don't worry, Jake," she said with a sudden smile. "Dennis is a lot tougher than he looks." When the giant still looked doubtful, Annalisse was inspired to confide, "He escaped from jail in Africa once. The police chased him all the way to the border."

Her friend looked mildly shocked, and Annalisse hastened to explain. "He was helping the freedom fighters."

"Mr. Chiles fought with them nigras?" Jake threw back his head and hooted. "I'd like to be a fly on the wall when ol' Jess hears about that! If there's two things in this worl' he can't stomach, it's nigras and Mexicans."

"Then maybe we'd better keep it a secret till after the election," Annalisse said.

The man picked up an old Coca Cola bottle that had been dislodged from some hidden refuge. He presented it to Annalisse as a souvenir of the flood. "I have me a little somethin' from ev'ry time this place been under water," he told her. "Maybe someday I'll start me a museum." Then, wading with her out to the car, he cautioned, "You take care now. Yore brakes might not grab just like you want 'em to."

Waving at Jake, Annalisse backed carefully out into the square. As she drove past Crabtree's Variety, she waved at Dennis, aloft in Empire Electric's cherry picker. He appeared to be having the time of his life.

Annalisse smiled to herself. In today's sunlight, she could tell herself that if Madame Bovary had been married to Dennis and lived in Blue Creek, she would never have taken herself so seriously.

❧

Annalisse's waffles had been a peace offering, Dennis surmised. Whatever was wrong with her, she was clearly trying to compensate for it. He still had no idea what the problem was, but this morning's adventures had restored his optimism. Maybe it was just her pregnancy. He was now convinced that he had overreacted. Annalisse wasn't Jill. How could he ever have thought she was?

At any rate, as he showered, he was finding the prospect of an afternoon in court rather tame. The physical activity had exorcised

56

his demons. As he watched the red mud swirl down the drain of his shower, he reflected that working beside his fellowman to bring order out of tangible chaos was infinitely more satisfying than this afternoon's scheduled divorce hearing.

While he drove to the courthouse, his mind refused to concentrate on the details of Sprague v. Sprague. Instead, a jubilant fragment of Lewis Carroll echoed in his head:

> *"And hast thou slain the Jabberwock?*
> *"Come to my arms, my beamish boy!*
> *"O frabjous day! Callooh, Callay!"*
> *He chortled in his joy.*

Pulling into a parking space by the square limestone courthouse, Dennis forced himself to inhale slowly. To counteract the Carroll, he recited severely, "Carolyn Sprague, abused wife of Joe D. Sprague, mother of Matt and Sarah . . ."

The hearing went the way he had expected it would. Carolyn got custody of the kids but not enough child support to raise them. Cavanaugh was the opposing attorney. Too bad being state senator didn't occupy all his time. He was the toughest courtroom opponent Dennis had ever met.

He was almost across the marble lobby when he heard the senator hail him. "Wait a minute there, son!"

Turning, he saw the big man approach, his shiny silver-gray suit flapping open, the black tie loose at his neck now that the hearing was over. "Got a minute?" Cavanaugh asked, herding him to the door. "Let's go over an' get some o' Naomi's pie. It oughta be comin' outta the oven right about now."

Naomi Nielson ran a diner across the street from the courthouse. The farthest green plastic booth was unofficially kept for the "Gang of Four" as Dennis called them—county clerk Norm Canliss,

Judge Thompson, Cavanaugh, and Lou Fisk, county chairman of the Republican Party.

Now the senator led Dennis to this privileged seat and called to Naomi, "You save me some o' your blackberry pie?"

"You just keep yourself patient now, Sen'tor. It's gonna be just another minute 'r two. Yore early t' day."

Cavanaugh pulled his coat off expertly with one arm. He'd never used a prosthesis. According to legend, he maintained that lawyers didn't need two hands, just guts.

Recalling now that he'd missed his lunch, Dennis also ordered a chili dog and a glass of milk. "Hope you didn't get flooded out at your place, senator," he remarked. "I heard Norm Canliss's soybeans are under two feet of water."

"I always did tell Norm he hadn't oughta plant soybeans. This ain't Iowa. God meant this t' be cattle country. Only crop you can count on here is fescue. But, no, Norm's gotta plant soybeans. Gotta show the rest of us how t' make money outta these ol' red rocks." The senator laughed, and then he leaned forward confidentially. "Dennis, I got a little matter t' discuss with you, but before that I need t' tell you, I heard from Bill Blanchard this morning."

"The attorney general?"

"Yes, well, it seemed to me that with all those worker's comp cases Ada Lou keeps sending your way, you're gettin' to be somethin' of an expert. I thought I might put a word in young Bill's ear. He's got those appointments t' make, namin' attorneys to represent the state in Second Injury Fund cases."

Dennis nodded. It had been all over the Springfield paper recently that Blanchard was awarding the appointments, which could result in substantial fees paid out of the state treasury to people who were contributing to his gubernatorial campaign.

"Well, now, I was good friends with Bill's daddy, Senator Richard

Blanchard, God rest him, and I've known the boy since he was a tot. When I told him all the things you been doin' for Ada Lou's poor lost souls, he thought as how you probably earned the right to the Cherokee County appointment. Could give a boost to your practice, you know, and I don't foresee any conflict of interest when you get elected to the prosecutor's job. What d'you think? Like to try it?"

Dennis felt immensely flattered. Other people had been wary of the new young lawyer from California, but Cavanaugh had gone out of his way from the very first to make him feel at home, to help him succeed. It hadn't been easy being the only attorney in town who wasn't homegrown. The funds from his father's inheritance were running low, which was one reason he was running for the prosecutor's job.

"Yes, I would. Thanks, senator. I appreciate it."

"Now, for this other matter . . ."

"Shoot."

"Well, now. Mah wife tells me she met Mrs. Childs yesterday, over t' the Republican Women."

Dennis nodded, trying to appear only casually interested, and put a napkin in his lap. Naomi placed his chili dog in front of him. "There was a luncheon or something, wasn't there?"

"Did your wife tell you what they talked about, b' chance?"

Shrugging slightly, Dennis answered, "Just that they had a little difference of opinion. She didn't say what about. Is it important?"

The senator sat back in his seat and fixed Dennis with a probing eye. "'Twas more than a difference of opinion. 'Twas a real conflagration. 'Bout illegal immigrants, as a matter o' fact."

"Oh, yes?" He took a bite of chili dog, trying for nonchalance. *Illegal immigrants? What in the world?*

"Your wife feels powerful about Latinos, don't she?"

59

"Annalisse?" He looked up from his plate in disbelief. "I'm afraid I don't follow you."

Cavanaugh continued, studying his protégé carefully. "Y'mean t' tell me, son, you didn't know your own wife called Mrs. Cavanaugh un-American and ignorant because she wants to deport the illegals in this town? Your own wife wants to go against the law?"

"Now hold on, senator." Dennis held up a palm. "Something's been lost in the translation. There's no one alive more law-abiding than Annalisse."

"Suppose you just hear me out, son. Seems she tol' Mae that she didn't see nothin' wrong with Latinos comin' here illegally and takin' all our jobs."

Dennis sat immovable in disbelief.

"Didn't even eat her lunch. Just got up and left. Now, what do you think about that?"

Genuinely stunned, Dennis's mind could not stretch far enough to imagine Annalisse having such a conversation with anyone, let alone Mae Cavanaugh. He knew she was upset about something. But Latinos? "I still think there must have been a misunderstanding, senator."

"No. You gotta face up to it, son. That's what she said. An' Em'ly Canliss, she heard it, too. Upset both of 'em, I can tell you. Matter of fact, I think the whole cafe heard 'er."

So that's what Annalisse had said. She hadn't been exaggerating, then. But what was this about?

"I'm sorry if what she said offended Mrs. Cavanaugh, senator," Dennis told him. "But it's evidently something she feels strongly about. And, you know, when all's said and done, it's no one's concern but hers."

"That's where you're wrong, son." The big man began rummaging for his tobacco. "That kinda talk might be okay in California, but around here it could be real damagin'. D'you have any idea how many Latinos work at the chicken factory below minimum wage? D'you know how many of our law-abidin' citizens have lost their jobs? At the shoe factory, too. Our people are leavin' Blue Creek, and the town's soon gonna be full of nothin' but Latinos. People who got no right to be here in the first place."

Dennis tried to ignore the welter of feelings inside him. He saw his own stepfather, a self-made man who had once been an illegal, and the familiar hatred swarmed up inside him. He knew he had issues, and he could certainly see the senator's point. All he could do was stare at his chili dog. No matter what his personal feelings were, he owed Annalisse his loyalty.

Two slices of pie were placed in front of them. The senator began to eat his in silence. Taking a deep breath, Dennis looked his erstwhile mentor in the eye. "I'm deeply sorry, senator, and so is Annalisse. I didn't know what had happened, but she spent last evening in tears. I have no idea what prompted her remarks, but believe me, she didn't mean to upset anyone. Annalisse is the kindest, least belligerent person in the world. I'm certain she was only explaining her point of view, with no idea of how upsetting it would be to anyone."

"But you aim t' be a politician, son, and in politics there's only one way t' look at things," the senator told him, taking another bite of pie. "You gotta look at everything outta the eyes of your constituency. Those Latinos can't vote, so they don't count. You aim to represent Cherokee Countians—you gotta see the world how they see it, you gotta love who they love, hate who they hate. The less ya say about your own opinions, the better."

But it was not Dennis's own opinions that troubled him on the way back to the office. It was Annalisse's. What had gotten into her? Never in the entire span of their relationship had she expressed any feelings about illegal immigrants. Was it possible that she had just been being contrary?

Sighing, he drove into the square. What with one thing and another, life had certainly departed from expectations. First, he didn't seem to know his wife of more than four years. Remembering her withdrawal from him, he was still more troubled. Then the dioxin. Poisoning his Eden. Right now, he could only see it as symbolic. Was there poison buried somewhere in his marriage as well as in the limestone of the Ozarks plateau?

Chapter Seven

J ake had been good medicine. After shopping for all of Dennis's favorite foods, Annalisse had returned home to write and post a note to Mae:

Dear Mrs. Cavanaugh,

I sincerely regret my behavior yesterday at the luncheon. I hope that you will not allow my unwise remarks to stand in the way of our friendship and Dennis's career. I did not speak for him. You certainly have every right to your opinions. Please forgive my rudeness.

Sincerely,
Annalisse Childs

With that off her conscience, she had baked oatmeal cookies (Dennis's favorite) and resolutely shunned her piano and the road not taken.

She felt she had things fairly well in hand by dinnertime. So why was Dennis measuring her with his professional eye?

"Did you see me, Mommy?" Jordan was asking about his ride in the cherry picker.

"I saw Dad. Were you there, too?"

"Yeah. I was up theo. It was weally weally cool."

"Finished, everyone?" Dennis broke in. "You want to watch *Star Wars*, Jordan? I'll set it up for you."

Clearly delighted at this unexpected treat, Jordan followed his father upstairs to the DVD player.

"You're looking at me as if I just held up the 7-Eleven," Annalisse told her husband after he returned. They had settled into their familiar dishwashing routine. It struck her as a parody in that moment. Husband and wife working side by side in apparent harmony with no idea of what was going on in each other's minds. Dennis was fidgety and nervous. He had never been that way around her.

Her husband surveyed her. "You seem to be feeling better."

Annalisse attempted to turn his thoughts away from her. "How did your case go today?"

Dennis grimaced. "Par for the course, I suppose. Went up against the senator." His face lightened. "He made me an interesting proposition."

Annalisse's heart plummeted. He'd talked to the senator. He must know about yesterday. No wonder he was looking at her so speculatively. "Which was?"

"He got the attorney general to appoint me to represent the state in workman's comp Second Injury cases. Give me some recognition in Jefferson City. Might even help the bank balance a little."

Annalisse felt herself grow wary. For a reason she couldn't explain, even to herself, the senator's partiality towards Dennis had always made her uneasy. After Jake's warning, she felt doubly so.

"Are you entirely sold on Cavanaugh?"

"What do you have against him?" Dennis stood, propping

himself in the dining room doorway, arms folded across his chest. The dishes were in the dishwasher, and she was wiping the counters.

Shrugging, she said, "Maybe I just don't trust that wagonload of country charm. You know he can talk perfectly normally when he wants to. I've heard him talking to Mae. He puts on that drawl."

"You sure you're not down on him 'cause he chews tobacco?" he asked, grinning.

It annoyed her when Dennis was patronizing. "For heaven's sake, Dennis, Jess Cavanaugh's a good ol' boy through and through. It just doesn't make sense that he'd do all these things for you out of the goodness of his heart. Why isn't Mike Green running again?"

"Cavanaugh got him a job in Jeff City."

"Have you ever wondered why?"

"What are you suggesting? That Jeff City is the Gulag Archipelago or something? He's going to be part of the new drug task force. He's pleased as heck about it."

"How competent was he?"

"Outstanding. Had the reputation of being incorruptible, as a matter of fact. That's something rare these days."

Annalisse got up from the table. "It's never occurred to you, I suppose, that incorruptibility can be inconvenient for some people?"

Dennis laughed. "You've got a suspicious mind, haven't you? Maybe the senator just likes me. Have you ever thought of that? Maybe he liked Mike Green and wanted to help him out." He took her hand. "C'mon. Let's go outside." Before heading out the door, Dennis called up the stairs to Jordan that they were going to sit on the porch.

She allowed herself to be led to the screened porch, where they settled on the swing bench. The air was balmy and the sky still overcast with a pall of clouds. The grass meadows were matted down as though they had been trampled. The air smelled different tonight, as if the storm had brought new scents in its journey through Texas and Oklahoma. Sweet grass, fresh-cut lumber, and pine sap.

"What's turned you into a saber-rattling radical all of a sudden?" her husband asked cheerfully.

"Maybe it's a role reversal," she offered, trying to match his humor. "For someone who's always been such a cynic about politics, it seems to me you've gotten awfully gullible."

"Because I won't believe Cavanaugh's a rascal?"

Annalisse felt the irritation swirling inside of her—a tiny whirlwind of impatience. "I'm sorry, Dennis, but I don't trust Jess Cavanaugh. And I think you're being more than a little naïve." She delivered Jake's warning, knowing as she did so that Dennis would only laugh it off.

"If ever there was a good ol' boy, it's Jake McClellan," he teased.

They sat a few moments in silence.

Finally, Dennis spoke. "Are you sure you're not feeling a little paranoid because of what happened yesterday at the luncheon?"

"Paranoid!"

"Well . . . sensitive."

Annalisse stared at her husband. It had never occurred to her that he might side with Cavanaugh against her. That he would be surprised, yes. That he might be a little irritated, yes. But not this!

"Are you going to tell me about it?" he asked gently. "What was all that stuff about Latinos?"

Annalisse felt herself flush hotly. Rising, she started back into the house, stumbling slightly over the doorstep. Her husband followed. "He told you?" she asked.

"Hey, I'm not condemning you or anything. I just want to hear your side of it."

"Before you hand down your decision?" she snapped. Rage, red, implacable rage, was skyrocketing inside her, rattling her all over, shooting up into her head, making her dizzy . . .

"Is that fair? Listen, Annalisse, the account he gave me didn't even sound like you. I told the senator that. Something must have gotten lost in translation."

"Thanks for sticking up for me," she retorted. "How do you know I didn't mean exactly what I said? I think your hatred of your stepfather has warped your objectivity about the subject."

"That was a low blow, Annalisse," her husband said. She could hear the suppressed fury in his voice.

"Do you realize Emily Canliss actually regrets the downfall of the KKK in Cherokee County? She said they would have taken care of the dirty Latinos. I'm sorry I rocked the boat, and I wrote Mae today to tell her so, but it doesn't mean I feel any differently about the subject."

"How can I possibly know your opinion, or know anything for that matter, if you don't tell me what it was you said?" he asked, his voice rising in exasperation.

"And what're your orders? To muzzle the little woman?" She walked into the kitchen.

"Geez, Annalisse, be reasonable. The senator was just explaining to me how your remarks might be misconstrued . . ."

"Misconstrued!" she shouted, shaking. "I can't believe this is you talking, Dennis. Since when do you worry about being misconstrued? I always thought your idea was that you said what you thought and to heck with the rest of the human race . . ."

"Okay. I deserved that. But for the hundredth time, won't you please tell me what you said? Forget Cavanaugh. It has nothing to do with him. I was just surprised, that's all. I mean, I've never even heard you mention Latinos. How did the subject come up?"

"I don't remember." She couldn't control her anger, even with the memory of her shame. "She was going on and on about how the Latinos were filthy and disgusting. People like her always say that."

"And?"

"Your stepfather, whatever his faults, is certainly not filthy and disgusting."

He shrugged. "All these people probably know about Latinos is what they see on the TV about the gangs in East LA. I'm sure none of them knows one Latino personally."

"Exactly my point. And yet they are ready to persecute them. Like a bunch of fascists."

"More likely just ignorant." He tried to take her hand again, but she jerked away. "Annalisse, I don't understand you. I've never seen you yell or get so steamed up . . ."

"When it might put a cramp in your political ambitions? Or is it just that you honestly don't care? Do you realize that it's going to fall to you to deport them? Do you even know what life is like for those people? A lot of them come from towns where the only choice they have is to deal drugs or risk their lives stealing across the border. They work two or three jobs just so they can feed their families. Sometimes three or four families to a house." Savagely, she kicked across the kitchen a fork Jordan had dropped. "Can you imagine living with the threat of deportation hanging over you? It makes people desperate in a way you and I can't possibly understand. Have you forgotten what it says on the Statue of Liberty?" Angry tears spilled down her cheeks, but she continued, her voice raised precariously. "But we're happy, white, and well fed, so let's not talk about it!"

Ignoring the contractions of her womb, Annalisse stormed back to the mudroom and, not even stopping to turn on the light, clattered down the basement stairs into the bowels of her house like an animal in flight. She took refuge on an old mattress in the corner farthest from the stairs, leaving Dennis to manage Jordan. She had to have this time alone.

She cried for a long time in the underside of the home where she had thought she could be happy. Now she had torn it apart.

Exhausted, Annalisse looked up from the piano music to Jules's face. She felt she had just come through a war. Never before had she understood the concerto as a duel between the soloist and the orchestra or, in this case, the accompanist.

"That was pretty good, Lisse." Jules moved over to the piano and pointed out a measure with his bow. "Now here, you want to slow down just a little—you were rushing. And here . . ."

He proceeded with his instructions, and she noted them mechanically with her pencil. She must have done passably. He wasn't out of temper or anything.

"So, was it generally okay?" she asked, hoping she didn't sound as timid as she felt.

"It was more than okay." His smile, brief and occasional, was what she lived for. "It was meant to be."

Suddenly shy, she studied her fingers. He hadn't kissed her since that day on the beach, but now, cupping her chin in his hands, he tilted her head up and kissed her with a new passion—an extension of the Tchaikovsky. Her entire body responded as his lips explored hers. In that moment, her inexperienced mind and body whisked away to a foreign dimension that included only a piano, a violin, two rapturous bodies, and Peter Illyich Tchaikovksy.

I'm really in over my head here.

Too soon he broke away and grinned, a thing he rarely did. "Time for a break," he told her. "Coffeehouse?"

She nodded, shutting the piano as he stowed his violin. It had been a month since that day on the beach, and since that time she had struggled here at every available hour with this music. She had done her bio labs at midnight, rushing them to eke out more time for the piano. Today was the first day they had completed the concerto together. And jointly entered this new plateau. Perhaps there *was* more ahead for her than labs and cadavers.

The yeasty smell of exotic pastries and espresso enveloped them as they entered the smoky coffeehouse. Jules ordered their espressos. Annalisse felt a new love for this place with its womblike booths, live folk music, and ringing debates. It and the music rooms were now branded on her as the essence of Stanford, replacing labs, lecture rooms, and cadavers.

Jules sat across from her at the rough-hewn wooden table. "You need to know something."

His voice was so heavy with meaning that her heart dropped. It could only be bad news.

"I'm leaving the country. My violin master has arranged for me to study in Vienna with Erwin Horst."

He paused while this announcement sank in. Annalisse sat stunned, staring at his chiseled face that gave nothing away. The present faded in and out, showing snapshots of the last two months—the day at the beach, their many discussions of music theory and the puzzle of Tchaikovsky's life as they lay under the stars by Lake Lagunita, and their two kisses—both hot, desperate, and Annalisse-shattering. She was dumbfounded. Of course, studying with Erwin Horst was a major opportunity. It would undoubtedly make his career. But why was he only telling her now?

"You make it sound like it's an immediate thing. Why haven't you said anything this past month?" After all this talk about her being his accompanist and all her hard work, he was going to leave her?

But he wasn't finished. "The problem is, you're such a part of my life that I don't think I can get on without you, Annalisse. I haven't tried to sleep with you, because I didn't think it was fair to start something and then leave. You probably imagine I think of you as a sister."

Until that kiss after their practice, she had. Since that day on the beach he had never tried to kiss her again. She hadn't been able to understand it, because the magnetism between them was so strong she was surprised it wasn't visible. It had nearly driven her crazy to be so close to him. She had taken her frustration out on the Tchaikovsky—hurling herself at the concerto as though it were a beast to be tamed.

But what was he telling her?

"How soon are you leaving?"

"As soon as I can. It's a long story, and I'm no good at explaining things. Just take my word for it that the sooner I get to Vienna, the better things will be."

She drew herself up, looked down at her short fingernails, and forced herself to ask, "Why in the world do you need me? Vienna is full of pianists."

"I have never in my life been as happy or as at peace as I have been the last two months," he said slowly, the lines between his brows furrowed in earnest. "You are the only bright thing in my life, Annalisse. I need you more than you can imagine."

She could only stare. Why on earth did he need *her?* But then the kaleidoscope shifted, and she realized what he was asking. He expected her to go to Vienna with him? Now? To sacrifice her own education? To leave her family? And with no explanation about this dire need to leave instantly? She came to earth with a harsh thump.

"Jules, despite what you say, I can't believe I'm a musical genius. You expect me to step out of my life and follow you to Vienna, like some sort of happy pill? With no explanation?"

He knit his heavy brows together in irritation. "I have explained. I can't do this without you, Annalisse. I tell you, without you, everything is dark. I've used my music to stay afloat, but that isn't enough most of the time."

It was impossible for her to believe she had that much power in his life. Annalisse had hoped she was important to him, but she didn't see how anyone like her could be. She was plain old vanilla. He was rich, dark, mysterious chocolate. It didn't surprise her that he had dark times. But being Annalisse, she had a very practical turn of mind.

"Jules, what in the world would we live on? And I can't speak German."

"I have been offered a position with the Vienna Philharmonic on the basis of a CD audition. My music master has a lot of influence. It will pay enough for us to live on, if we're frugal."

She rose from the table, her head too full of objections that her heart was trying to discount. "I have to think, Jules. I have to talk to my parents."

Jules grasped her hand and squeezed it until it hurt. "What I have been trying to tell you is that I love you. I literally cannot live without you. You've become part of my soul, my music, everything that matters."

Tears sprang to her eyes as she stood looking into the face that suddenly seemed fearful and tragic. "Why?"

"Because you've gotten inside me and made peace there. Because every time I'm with you, there's this huge crescendo of joy building in me. I need to be part of you. Physically, emotionally, in every way. I want us to be together, Lisse. And what's more, I know you feel the same."

Annalisse couldn't deny it. But she knew somehow that much as she loved him, Jules was unstable. There would never be a white picket fence or scriptures in the parlor in the evenings and on Sundays. Instead, life would be a whirlwind that would catch her up and deposit her somewhere foreign to everything she knew. Unless she refused. Unless this was the end.

Why hadn't she thought more about the future of her possession by this man? Was she willing to take such a chance? She felt as though he were pulling her off-kilter, leading her away from everything that made her Annalisse. Or the person she had always thought was Annalisse.

Chapter Eight

Dennis didn't know what to do. Standing at the top of the stairs, he looked down into the dark well of the basement and debated with himself. After a moment, he went back to the kitchen, seized a pot he had left soaking since yesterday, dumped some cleanser into it, and began to scour. If only elbow grease and a little cleanser could solve all his problems.

Annalisse's rebuke had stung. Was he really as self-satisfied and smug as all that? Remembering the interview with Cavanaugh now, he wasn't at all comfortable. Hadn't he been just a bit intimidated? A little too acquiescent? Annalisse was right. In earlier years he would have told the man where to get off. Graphically.

But all that was really beside the point. The actual words she'd hurled at him weren't important. She would have said anything to keep him away just then. As shocking as her bitterness and vehemence had been, even more appalling was the way she'd looked. Like an animal at bay. With the instinct of the trapped, she had grabbed at the first weapon that came to hand. He had come too

74

close. It was the same sense as last night. In this matter, whatever it was, he had ceased to be her friend, lover, husband and had become, instead, the enemy.

It hurt, but it made things plain. Annalisse had been more distressed and passionate than he had ever seen her. Why? Annalisse cared about people, not ideas. She was very practical. There must be a specific injustice she had witnessed sometime in her life before him.

Absently straightening the kitchen and starting a load of towels in the washer, Dennis searched his memory for every fact he had acquired, no matter how slight, about Annalisse's life before they had met. There were plenty of impressions, vignettes grown into legend, about her life in Wisconsin—Papa's Socratic Sundays, Mother Lundgren's improbable meals during the farrowing season, her sister Marta's determination to become a lawyer so she could just once beat Papa in an argument, Annalisse's rescue of little Louisa from death in the stock pond. He knew nothing of her Stanford years or even the years after that except that she was one heck of a biologist. When he thought of Annalisse before their marriage, he saw her sunburned and freckled, on horseback among the soybeans of the Lundgren farm.

"I wasn't all that crazy about rural Wisconsin, Dennis." Hadn't she said that? A reproach, and he hadn't heard it, hadn't taken it seriously. To do so would have been to destroy his precious image of her.

Now it seemed he would have to do just that. But how to begin?

Sitting alone on the porch, he heard the melancholy whistle of a freight train pulling through town. Everything was still and languorous in the aftermath of the storm. He sighed heavily. Once again familiar things had taken on a foreign look, but this time he knew they would never be entirely familiar again. What was real and what wasn't?

Why had he never wondered about Annalisse's college years? Had he just assumed she had leapt from the farm into his arms, untouched? That day he'd met her on Sam's boat—he remembered how she'd looked in those crisp white shorts, her long blonde hair pulled back with a wide cornflower ribbon that matched her serious eyes. She had seemed to know all about him at a glance. But what had she been feeling then? She'd been in Chicago, visiting her cousin Karin, Sam's girl. There was something, a glimmer of a memory . . . yes. He'd been annoyed because Sam had said he should try to make her laugh. Karin's cousin had had a bad time.

It seemed strange to be back on the boat again, almost as if Dennis had never been away—Sam's Sousa marches thundering in the background as he bustled around polishing the brass fittings like a fussy housemaid, the wind, seldom gentle on Lake Michigan, promising a good, exciting sail. But it wasn't like the old days. There were things inside his head that hadn't been there then . . . memories, sights and smells that intruded themselves upon moments like this when he wanted to forget.

"Ahoy there!" Karin was approaching the slip, her long black hair flying behind her. The tall girl with her would be Annalisse.

"Well done, Karin!" Sam leapt from the boat to the pier, surprisingly agile for such a short, round person. "Welcome aboard, Annalisse. You ever been sailing before?"

Dennis extended a hand and helped the girl onto the boat. She smiled at him, and his surliness fell away. Some quality about her warmed him instantly. He'd been expecting another brittle creature like Karin, who smoked incessantly and craved excitement. This girl was calm. Her smile suited the May morning.

"No, I haven't." She was answering Sam. "I hear you've turned Karin into quite a sailor."

Sam laughed. "Is that what she told you?"

"Don't mind Sam," Dennis advised her, grinning. "He thinks he's the only one who truly comprehends the soul of *Waldo*."

"Waldo?"

"My boat," Sam explained. "The good ship *Ralph Waldo Emerson*. I mean, you can't name a ship *Ralph*. This is Dennis, by the way. Late of the Ivory Coast. Dennis, meet Annalisse from San Diego."

This time her smile was a little shy, and he recognized a fellow victim of Sam's plotting. He'd try to make it as painless as possible for her. After all, it was only for an afternoon.

They spent the next half hour getting the boat underway. Then Sam and Karin assumed command, and Annalisse and Dennis had only to move their respective bodies from port to starboard as directed.

"The Ivory Coast?" Annalisse quizzed him. "What were you doing in Africa?"

"Looking for the Garden of Eden," Dennis answered, studying her face. Why were her eyes so sad? They didn't go with the rest of her.

"Did you find it?"

He laughed. "No. But I sure eliminated a lot of possibilities. How come you've never sailed before if you live in San Diego?"

"La Jolla, actually. I don't know anyone who has a boat, to tell you the truth. I haven't lived there long."

"What do you do?"

"I'm a biologist. At Scripps."

He'd heard of it. "You must be some biologist!"

She grinned and looked self-conscious again. "What are you going to write?" she asked him.

Now it was his turn to be uncomfortable. "Sam?" he queried ruefully.

"You're not a writer?"

"Let's just say that Africa didn't have the same effect on me that it did on Hemingway."

She said nothing, just looked at him steadily and waited for him to go on. He did. "Oh, it's beautiful, all right. But it's poor. Have you ever been to an underdeveloped country?"

"No, not even Mexico. What was it like in Africa?"

"I had crazy hopes about getting back to some sort of essential, untouched civilization. But I'll have nightmares about those little kids scratching in the dirt till I die. All sores and flies and swollen bellies. And there's not a thing you can do. The governments are completely corrupt."

"No," she answered quietly. "I suppose not." He was grateful to her—no denial, no pseudo cheer.

"I know I'm not the first one to discover poverty. It sounds sophomoric, but I thought I could help somehow . . . Albert Schweitzer stuff . . . but it's so hopeless. I stayed just long enough to get in a fracas alongside some people who were doing their best to overthrow a dictatorship."

"You're a Romantic," she said. It was a statement of fact, not an accusation. "What are you going to do now that you're back?"

Orders were bellowed for the ballast to move itself to starboard.

"How well do you know Sam?" he asked after the shift.

"I don't. I met him for the first time only last Saturday."

Nodding, he acknowledged, "He's shrewd. A lot shrewder than I gave him credit for."

She didn't pretend to misunderstand him and looked away shyly. "What did you do before Africa?"

"Construction, just to make enough money to go to Africa."

"And before that?"

"Northwestern. Speech major." He gave a mock bow where he stood. "And there, ma'am, is my resume. What do *you* think I should do with myself?" This was the real issue, of course. How quickly she had gotten to it, and how much her opinion mattered!

He was surprised to see a flicker of pain cross her face. Her gaze shifted away again, this time to rest on the gray-blue water of Lake Michigan. The wind was stinging color into her fair skin.

"Don't give up," she said.

"What?"

"Whatever it was that took you to Africa, don't give up on it."

Her words and the quiet gravity with which they were spoken had an extraordinary effect. Here was understanding—a great well of it. The bleakness that had blanketed him for months began to lift, and he felt the sun hot on his back. He took a deep breath. His chest expanded fully, freed from the awful constriction that had kept all his movements, all his thoughts shallow for a long time.

"Annalisse, what's your last name?"

"Lundgren," she answered, turning to him again.

"Annalisse Lundgren." He said her name slowly and then grinned. "D'you know what? I just remembered something. I need to go see my mother."

For the first time, she laughed. "Your mother?"

"Definitely."

"How nice. Does she live around here?"

Chuckling, he pushed a blowing strand of hair out of her face and held it against her head with his hand. "No, she lives a long way away."

"Where?" she persisted, sitting very still.

"La Habra. About two hours from La Jolla by motorcycle. You ever ride on a motorcycle?"

"No."

"You'll love it."

⌒ℯ

Long after Jordan had been put into bed, Dennis prowled around the darkened house. Everything looked so normal—Annalisse's red, white, and blue afghan, a gift from her mother, over the back of the couch, a half-finished jigsaw puzzle on the coffee table, books to be returned to the library stacked on the chest freezer, mud-caked rain boots littering the mud room floor.

He stood still suddenly, transfixed by a terrible thought. *Could I be a narcissist? Have I seen Annalisse only as an extension of myself? Does my Annalisse exist only in my mind?* He was as bad as his stepfather, sweeping his mother away from him into the Latino culture and the Catholic church, ignoring who she really was.

What would his real father do in this situation? Closing his eyes, he leaned against the chest freezer, summoning the vision of the man who had helped so many people. Tonight, he envisioned him in his clerical robes supervising the soup kitchen in Watts. Though his father had died when he was only ten, Dennis had realized in his adult life that his father never judged people. He saw them as individuals. He learned their names, their hopes, their dreams. *He would have loved Annalisse, and if he saw that she was troubled, my father would have gone to the ends of the earth to find out why. He wouldn't have counted the cost to himself.*

Dennis stood by the open basement door, peering down into the gloom, hesitating. From below the smell of damp and decay wafted up to him. Was she still crying? Descending the stairs, he began a wary search among stacks of boxes and shelves of bottled strawberry jam from earlier in the summer. When he found her curled in a ball on Jordan's old mattress, she was asleep. Even in the dim light, he could tell she'd cried a long time.

Moving cautiously, he knelt down on the cold concrete floor, studying that face, so strange with its angry blotches, trying to reconcile it with the calm, brave one of his recent memories. *What had happened to her?*

He wanted to take her into his arms, to hold her as he always had and make everything all right. But something lay between them, as real yet as elusive as noxious gas. Perhaps there were such things as ghosts.

Annalisse stirred, and he whispered, "Swedie, you'd be more comfortable in bed. C'mon, honey."

Helping her awkwardly to her feet, he steered her up the basement stairs, through the house, and up to their bedroom.

They undressed in silence. In bed, he pulled her into his arms. This was their bed, after all. She moved to him willingly, sleepily, nestling her head into his shoulder but still silent. He wanted very much to make love to her, to prove that she was still his, but he recognized the urge as that of a Neanderthal and resisted the temptation.

Instead, he asked, "Annalisse? Tell me what is really wrong."

She moved her head off his shoulder. "Not now, Dennis."

"Why not?" Her evasion was even more disquieting.

Rolling on her back, his wife stared at the ceiling. After a moment, he could see moonlight glinting off the fresh tears on her cheeks. "Dennis, I'm sorry, but I really can't go there, okay? Maybe some other time, but not now."

He knew then that she was grieving. There was shattering familiarity in her anguish.

Dennis closed his eyes against the moonlight. He was ten years old again, sitting in his father's closet, burying his face in a brown tweed jacket, smelling that evocative hint of his father—Old Spice and something else—trying vainly to summon the dead man's essence. It had seemed impossible that someone so vital, so important, could simply be gone. Even now, the memory was not an easy one.

For hours he had remembered, reliving in digital clarity his trips with his father, riding on his shoulders as they hiked the national parks—Yosemite with its perpendicular cliffs, the "dinosaur" trees of the Sequoias, the red arches and magical cliffs and mesas of Bryce and Zion's canyons. His father had somehow taught a ten-year-old about the order of the world.

It was Dad who taught me that living was an adventure to make the world a better place. And then, Dad was gone in a blink from an aneurysm while planting flowers in the garden of the widow next door. And the hollow had never been filled. Until Annalisse.

I've been asking too much of her. I had no right to sweep her into my idea of life. What are her ideas? What hopes and dreams did she grow up with? They certainly didn't include a farm, an orchard, and a cow.

Opening his eyes now, he studied the shadow of the birch branch outside the window. It was perfectly still tonight. "I love you, Annalisse," he whispered. "I'm sorry you're not happy. I'll do anything I can to make it up to you. Just please tell me what that is."

She reached her hand into his and squeezed tightly. They didn't say anything else.

Dennis remembered that his mother had left him in that closet until he was ready to come out.

Chapter Nine

Dennis awoke the next morning, feeling less mellow. Dread sat on his chest. It was the first time in his marriage that he hadn't felt in perfect sync with his wife. He couldn't allow this state of things to become permanent. Where should he start trying to understand Annalisse?

Letting her sleep, he informed Jordan it was time he learned to fry eggs. The boy hadn't done too badly, but there was still quite a mess. By putting his instructions into silly lyrics, Dennis kept Jordan's enthusiasm high until everything was cleaned up. No matter what anyone said, children were a comfort.

He showered, shaved, and dressed, and still Annalisse slept. This was so unlike her that alarm replaced his frustration. Getting Jordan's train set down, he instructed him to play quietly in the living room after he left for work.

At the office a message was waiting from the Department of Natural Resources.

"Sid? This is Dennis Childs returning your call."

"Yeah, Dennis. Your e-mail about that mess down there was forwarded to me. Have you got anything else?"

"No. We're trying to get a lead on what they've done with the drums, but we've got to go pretty carefully. We don't want to scare Amalgamated into moving them off somewhere we'll never find them."

"Oh, we'll find 'em," the man said firmly. "Sooner or later."

"Right. How do you want to handle it?"

"How's this sound? We'll send a team down some time next week to look at that soil. Once we get that and your client's affidavit telling how it got there . . . how's he doing by the way?"

"He went into the hospital yesterday," Dennis said.

"We'd better move fast, then. We'll want to get his statement before he gets any worse. Once we have that and the soil samples, the attorney general can slap a suit on them. We'll get depositions on the whereabouts of those barrels before they have a chance to sneeze."

"Right. When can we expect you?" Dennis scanned his calendar, pencil poised.

"I've got to go through the formalities first, so I'll let you know. But I'm sure they'll want to move on this thing. Probably not later than Wednesday or so, next week."

Today was Friday. "That'll be great, Sid. Looking forward to working with you on this."

"Same here. Next week, then."

The conversation did a little to restore Dennis's sense of well-being. He called Gregg with a report.

"Great news, Dennis. Not that it's going to do Lonnie much good."

When Annalisse awoke, she could scarcely open her swollen eyes. Memories of the night before made her cringe in the reality of morning. When would her mind and body realize that Jules was no longer part of her life? She didn't have to fight those demons any-more. She had Dennis and Jordan and Bronwyn. At least she hoped she still had them. Any more of this behavior and Dennis might check her into a psych hospital somewhere. That's probably where she belonged.

Chilled by this thought, she was glad when the ringing phone jerked her away from it.

"Mrs. Childs?"

"Yes?" Annalisse couldn't identify the voice on the other end of the line. It sounded strangely muffled.

"You don't know me, but I've called to give you some advice." The voice continued menacingly, "Tell your husband to give up his Amalgamated investigation. If he doesn't, he might not like what happens."

It had to be a joke. People didn't really make telephone calls like this.

"Who is this? Gregg?"

"This isn't anyone you know. And I'm serious. He's messin' with things he hadn't oughta be messin' with. Could be real bad for his health."

The caller hung up. Immediately dialing Dennis's office, she told Leila it was an emergency. In a moment, she was speaking to her husband.

"I just had a really weird phone call," she said, giving him the gist of it.

"Hmm. That is weird." Dennis sounded intrigued rather than alarmed.

"Should I call the sheriff?" Annalisse asked.

"No. He doesn't know anything about this issue. I'd rather we kept it to ourselves. I wonder how this caller found out about my investigation?"

"What are you doing anyway?"

"I'll tell you when I get home tonight. It's my latest crusade, and it's not a pretty picture."

"Skullduggery in Cherokee County?" she joked, feeling that maybe they were back in normal territory.

"Looks like it," Dennis answered. His voice sounded grim. Maybe the territory wasn't so normal. Maybe he was still upset over last night.

The phone call had the effect of pulling her midway out of her funk by reminding her why she'd married Dennis in the first place. He was a fighter. He loved a cause. With a sigh, she turned determinedly away from her piano and descended into the basement to collect canning jars. It was time to put up his green beans.

"Leila," Dennis inquired, "have you talked to anyone about the Lonnie Warner case and the call to the DNR?"

Today, his secretary's hair was blue-black, and at his words she looked mortally offended.

"I know better than that, Dennis. You know I wouldn't break lawyer-client confidentiality."

"Can you get me Gregg on the phone? Someone's let word of this leak out."

Leila buzzed him a moment later.

"Hey, Gregg," Dennis said. "Sorry to bother you, but someone's leaked the information about Lonnie's barrels. Annalisse got a threatening phone call telling me to leave it alone."

"Dennis, I'm a doctor, for heaven's sake. I know how to keep secrets!" Gregg replied. "Maybe you'd better call the sheriff and get a deputy out at your place."

"I'm not bringing the sheriff in at this stage. He's in too deep with the establishment."

"Well, if you're being that careful, something must have leaked at the Jeff City end."

Dennis thought about this. "That means someone at the DNR has connections down here, probably with Amalgamated."

"Well, stranger things have happened. Amalgamated carries a lot of clout in this state, Dennis. You're not going up against a ma-and-pa organization, you know. They're going to put up a fight."

"I just wish someone hadn't tipped them off. Now they're going to get those barrels moved, and we'll never find them. How's Lonnie?"

"He's not going to last long. He wasn't strong to begin with and doesn't have a lot of will to live. Seems the only one in the world who cares about him is Ada Lou. His wife left him a few years back."

"Poor guy." Dennis felt pity mixed with futility. He could never be a doctor.

"Say, Dennis, I've been meaning to ask you—I mean, it's really none of my business, but is Annalisse okay?"

"Why?" he asked.

"Cindy said there was some big blowup at that luncheon. She said she wanted to call Annalisse but didn't know what she should do."

Dennis felt an unusual desire to confide in someone. Who better than a doctor? "There's something going on with Annalisse, Gregg. I'm worried about her."

"You mean physically? Has it to do with her pregnancy?"

"Possibly." Dennis hadn't seriously considered that Annalisse's hormones might be involved.

"Maybe I should see her."

Dennis knew that suggesting this would not be a good idea. "What did Cindy say, anyway? All I got was Jesse Cavanaugh's version."

"Don't let him intimidate you or Annalisse, Dennis. She wasn't out of line—just pointed out their prejudices. It was the sort of thing I might have expected from you. Mae was outraged, of course. Then Annalisse left. I guess she'd had enough, and I don't really blame her. I just wondered because she's always seemed like the last person on earth to rock the boat."

Dennis squirmed in his chair. *It was the sort of thing I might have expected from you." No wonder Annalisse had been so outraged at his pointing out the senator's concerns.*

"Yeah. She always has been before. But I don't know what's going on. She won't talk about it."

"Anything I can do to help?"

"I wish there were. But I really think it's my fault. Possibly exacerbated by her hormones. We need to work it out between us. I hate to admit it, but I've just now realized that life isn't all about me."

Gregg chuckled. "An amazing admission for a lawyer."

"Yeah. I'm not naturally benevolent like you."

"Seriously, it must be difficult for Annalisse here in Blue Creek," the doctor said. "Cindy tried to get Annalisse into her book club, but it's completely closed to 'outsiders.' Same with the garden club and the mothers' club."

"It's that bad? Annalisse never told me."

"She has good reason to be miserable, if you ask me. Does she have one friend in town other than Cindy?"

Dennis thought this over. "No. Now that you mention it. Well, there's our neighbor, Betsy. They're tight. But she's about two generations older than Annalisse."

"I'll have Cindy give her a call. Maybe Annalisse just needs to let off some steam."

Though he knew it was more than that, Dennis thanked Gregg and hung up with new food for thought. Why hadn't he seen how isolated his wife was? Why had he thought she'd be contented being a farm wife in this day and age? She had had a good career going when she married him.

All these self-revelations were deeply unsettling. And now this threat against his family. He had no idea what quarter it had come from nor how seriously to take it.

Thinking that Sid might know something, he placed a call to the DNR. Sid was in a meeting and his assistant had no idea when he'd be out but promised to give him a message. Frustrated, Dennis composed an e-mail to the man.

He arrived home later to find twelve quarts of green beans displayed on the counter and his favorite summer salad on the table. His wife was dressed in the baby blue sundress he liked, with Bronwyn jutting out ahead of her. She even smiled a greeting, kissing him on the cheek.

Instead of being grateful, he wondered if Annalisse was trying to make up for her behavior of the day before. Or perhaps something else had happened. What was really going on in his wife's head? "I didn't expect you to put up all the green beans at one time!" he said.

"I needed the brownie points," she said, hoisting the milk can onto the counter.

"Why? What have you done now?"

Annalisse stared at him. "Now?"

"I'm sorry. I shouldn't have said that." Dennis felt panic rise in his chest. Why in the world couldn't he control his tongue anymore?

"I suppose you're referring to my conversation with Mae again?"

Dennis was silent. "Uh, how are you feeling after putting up all those beans?"

"You can finish straining your stupid milk," she told him. And walked out the kitchen door into the sultry evening.

Suddenly it was just too much. For nearly five years he and Annalisse had lived in almost perfect accord. Now it seemed everything was wrong. Annalisse, dioxin, threats against his family. The ground beneath him was no longer solid. Everything was shifting.

What would Dad do?

He was reluctant to follow Annalisse again. She had every reason to be angry. Maybe when she had calmed down a bit, she would accept an apology and they could make some headway against all this confusion that had come down on them like a horrific ice storm. His confusion was really irrelevant compared to her evident unhappiness. He knew part of his reluctance sprang from cowardice. And disappointment. Something vital had changed in his marriage, and it was never going to be the same. But Dad would stick with it, endeavoring to understand. Dad hadn't been a coward. A minister must surely have known about imperfection, but it didn't keep him from trying to make things better.

As he strained the milk, he realized he had fallen down on the job in more ways than one. His father would certainly show some compassion towards poor Lonnie. He wouldn't see him as simply a symbol the way Dennis had. He needed to visit his client.

After checking on Jordan and ascertaining that he was sitting in front of the computer, tongue between his teeth, fascinated with a PBS kids' game, Dennis changed from his milking clothes. "Mom's out back taking a walk, shaver. I have to go visit someone who's sick. Do you want to come with me, or would you rather go out back with Mommy and feed some bread to the geese?"

Jordan looked up. "I wanna play my game."

"Okay," Dennis said with a sigh, unplugging the laptop, closing it, and tucking it under his arm. "Come with me. I won't be long."

Dennis entered the hospital, aware of the nervousness that always accompanied him on such visits. He parked Jordan with the computer in the front lobby under the eye of the receptionist, one of his divorce clients, Christy Wellington, who promised she wouldn't let the child move or be bothered.

Room 117. Here it was. Peering around the doorway, he saw his client lying in bed, staring at the television.

"Lonnie? It's Dennis Childs."

The man turned his head, and Dennis was sickened to see how pale he was. He sat by the bed in the room's only chair and plucked Lonnie's nearly transparent hand from the top of his sheet, holding it in his own, as he had seen his father do. "I just thought I'd pay you a visit. Dr. Gregory says you don't get many visitors."

"I'm gonna die," Lonnie said simply. He turned his eyes back to the television. He was watching cartoons.

Desperation and rage overcame Dennis, pushing aside his own problems. How could this happen? What kind of life had this man had? What had he done in his forty years to deserve such a death?

Leukemia. The word had scared the liver out of him ever since he was a kid. What could he possibly say to the man?

"I'm sorry," he whispered, squeezing the cold flesh. "Is there anything you want?"

Lonnie sighed. "I jes' wanna go home."

Dennis felt even more ashamed of his previous anger with his own circumstances. Home. *What kind of home does this poor man have compared to mine?* And yet, he still wanted it. Still wanted the comfortable familiarity of his own things, his own place. Even without a wife. Was there really any reason for a terminal patient to be in the hospital if he wasn't hooked up to anything? That was what hospice was for, wasn't it? And he and Ada Lou could look in on him, couldn't they?

"I'll see what I can do, Lonnie. I'll talk to Dr. Gregory about getting you back home, but I can't promise you anything, much as I want to."

"That'd be nice," Lonnie said taking his eyes from the television screen. They looked as lifeless as pale stones.

Then Dennis remembered the reason for Lonnie's suffering and became more determined than ever to nail the people responsible. "I need to ask you something," he forced himself to say.

"Ask me anythin' you want."

"Have you told anyone that we're trying to find those drums you lifted?"

"No, sir. Doc Gregory told me to hold my tongue. He said you were filin' a lawsuit and that I had to keep quiet or I could ruin everythin'."

"What about before Dr. Gregory warned you?"

"I only jes' talked to Ada Lou. But she don't know nothin' 'cept that I had an accident."

So. The source of the leak had to be the DNR. Looking at the poor, skinny body in the bed, Dennis vowed to fight a good fight. He hoped and prayed there wouldn't be any more Lonnies before he nailed the perpetrators.

Chapter Ten

As soon as she heard Dennis's car drive off, Annalisse returned to the house and sat defiantly at the piano. Picking something that matched her mood, she decided to bang out one of her Paris Chopin Études. Once she had played it with ease. Now it seemed light years beyond her skill level, a fact that only made her more angry. Why had she thought putting up the beans would make any difference?

~

"Look, Annalisse," Jules was saying through her dorm door. "We've got to talk. It's been a whole week. Why have you been avoiding me? Please open up."

Sitting on her bed, her hair freshly washed and wrapped in a turban, she knew that she desperately wanted to see him. But should she? Was it safe? Was their attraction so strong that he could make her act against her good sense? How could he expect her to just abandon her life? She had discussed it with her parents, and they were of the opinion that Jules was a manipulator and that she needed to go forward with her career as a biologist.

Because she had trouble believing in her own talent, their common sense had brought her down to earth. For that reason, she was reluctant to expose herself to the mind-melting attraction she felt for him, not to mention his beseeching eyes.

"At least let me explain myself," he pleaded.

It was the note of desperation in his voice that did it.

"Meet me in the lounge in ten minutes," she said. "I've got to dry my hair."

"Lisse, what I have to say is private. I don't care what your hair looks like. Just open the door."

Taking a deep breath, she said, "It's the lounge or nothing." She wouldn't put it past him to try seduction to gain his ends, and she wasn't at all sure she would be able to resist.

She heard his footsteps as he walked back down the hall.

The first sight of him was a shock. His eyes were sunken. Hair uncombed, it stood out from his head, making him look more than ever like an El Greco figure. An ashtray beside him showed he had been chain-smoking in just the short time he'd been sitting there. He raised to her a face tortured by some black emotion.

Annalisse backed away a step from the easy chair he had chosen at the rear of the lounge. This was not the Jules she knew.

"I know what you're thinking," he said. "I look like roadkill."

"I talked to my parents," she said, still standing at a distance. "They want me to stay here and study biology. They know I'm not a talented enough pianist to accompany you."

"I thought you were over eighteen," he said dully.

"I love and respect my parents. They are rock solid and certainly responsible for any common sense you see in me. My father is a judge. My mother is as down to earth as they come. And, besides that, I agree with them. They left the decision up to me."

It took everything in her to make this statement. What would her mother say if she could see the dreadful condition Jules was in?

Jules plunged into speech. "I'm not sure I can go to Vienna without you, Lisse."

Looking into his hopeless eyes and knowing what she knew about the incredibly talented human being before her, she felt her resolutions falter. "Why not? You'll do brilliantly!"

"What you see at this moment is Jules Kramar at his lowest ebb. The place I live most of the time. It's like being in a hole with no light and no way out. I told you, Lisse. You're my only bright thing."

Annalisse shivered. What was she supposed to do now? He needed rescuing from this darkness. He didn't think he could make it without her, and looking at him, she wondered if he was right. Perhaps he hadn't been exaggerating after all. Loving him as she did, she wanted to embrace him, to feed his body and his spirit, take care of him, and shelter his genius for the rest of their lives. Knowing what she did about brilliant musicians, Annalisse realized in that moment that most of them had made a mess of their personal lives. She sat in the chair by his side.

He reached over and took her hand. "I've never really wanted to believe in love till now. The world has always been such a hellish place for me, I was determined not to see any good in it. I worked it out in my music." He looked into her eyes, appealing, "I think a lot of composers felt the same way I do about things. It gives me a link with them."

Annalisse looked at their joined hands, unable to respond to his confidences.

"What do you really think about us?" he asked finally.

There was such a note of despair in his voice that she had to fight down her urge to rescue him. "I'd like to make this easier for you, Jules, but I can't. As long as you expect me to drop everything and follow you this moment, I'm going to feel manipulated."

"You're right. I really messed it up." He sighed deeply. "I still can't tell you everything, because I don't want you to get dragged into the situation. It's potentially very dangerous. But I guess I can tell you part of it."

Another couple walked into the lounge, hesitated when they saw the intimate conversation, and walked out again.

"I'm an illegal, Lisse. From Mexico. My father brought me across the border when I was six. He died when I was ten, and there's every possibility that I will be deported to Mexico or worse if I don't get out of the country fast."

He lit a cigarette and focused steadily on the ashtray, waiting for her answer. Annalisse was shocked. She said the first thing that came into her head. "But, Jules . . . you don't look Latino. And your name. I always thought it was Czech or something."

"My family line goes straight back to Spain. I have no native Indian blood, though most Latinos do. As for my name, it's actually Julio del Gallego. My violin master thought it politically and artistically important to change it."

"Who is your violin master?"

"The concertmaster of the LA Philharmonic. My father had a lot of money. My teacher in Mexico City suspected I had talent, so Father hired the master right after we arrived here. You see, my mother was a concert violinist. She died at my birth."

"What happened to your father?"

"That's part of the story that can't be told, Annalisse."

She was silent, digesting it all: Jules was exhibiting the classic signs of a manic-depressive. He was also a genius who was in danger for some reason too frightening to tell her. How in the world did she get involved in this dilemma? Her natural ebullience failed her completely.

But she was ready to ignore all these signs of danger because she loved Jules. Body and soul, as Jane Eyre loved the flawed Mr. Rochester. She certainly didn't want him deported to Mexico, out of the sphere of his protective and generous teacher. Now that she knew his reason for leaving really was urgent, she no longer felt emotionally coerced. But her father was a big stickler for the law.

"But your passport and visa, Jules. How can you go live in Vienna with no passport?"

"My mentor got them somehow. He's risking prison for me. The passport is forged, of course."

"Couldn't you possibly wait until the end of the quarter? It's only weeks away."

"This thing is breathing down my neck, Annalisse. I have airline reservations for tomorrow."

"I can't just pick up and go with you tomorrow!"

He bowed his head. "I'd hoped you loved me enough."

She searched frantically for some solution to this mad situation.

"Jules, do you think you can go to Vienna on your own and wait for me until after Christmas? Try to find a piano instructor for me. If I spend Christmas with my family, I can tell them that I want to explore my talent. That I want to take a quarter off school. That I'm doing this for myself, not because you have forced me into it."

"Is it so important what your family thinks?"

"My family made me who I am, Jules."

Sighing gustily, Jules looked into her eyes, his own red-rimmed and sad. "Do you promise you will come?"

"I want to, Jules. I want to very much. Vienna with you would be wonderful."

When Dennis came in, she went up to bed, feeling limp with memory and the effort of playing the piano.

"I'm sorry, Swedie," he said with extraordinary plaintiveness. "You've got to forgive me."

Looking up, she was jolted by the pain on his face. It was the same pain she had just been remembering on Jules's face. "What is it, Dennis?"

He sat down beside her on the bed. "That phone call today. It was about a case I have. I've just been to the hospital and seen my client. He's dying, and it's really shaken me up."

"What's he dying of?"

"Leukemia. He was poisoned with dioxin. Amalgamated's got it buried somewhere around here. He was moving it, and it spilled on him."

"Oh, Dennis!"

"I've really got a fight on my hands this time. And someone in the Department of Natural Resources must have leaked it to Amalgamated that we're on to them, which makes things that much tougher."

"The phone call?" Annalisse was finding it a little hard to emotionally invest in this crisis, but at least it explained Dennis's mood. It must have been a blow to find yet another Eden corrupted. And she had been so horrid. Climbing out of her alternate reality was growing daily more difficult. Still, this was now. This was Dennis. This was important.

"Yeah. I've checked and no one else has let out a peep. The guy from the DNR e-mailed me back this afternoon. Nothing there either."

Dennis stood and paced the room. "If only I didn't feel so helpless! I mean, the guy is dying!"

"Even you can't keep someone from dying," Annalisse said softly, getting out of bed and enfolding him in her arms, trying to ignore the irony of her words.

Startled, he looked into her eyes.

"You've always had a Messiah complex, honey," she said. Then swamped with sudden remorse for her earlier behavior, she kissed him and led him gently back to bed.

Chapter Eleven

The next morning Annalisse had a prenatal exam with Gregg. She felt more of a kinship with him and his wife, Cindy, than with anyone else in Blue Creek. This morning, Dennis wouldn't be coming with her because he had a court appearance. When he left, it was with the old affectionate look in his eyes. She must keep making an effort, or she was going to lose her present-day life to the past.

Grandma Betsy, however, looked at her with concern when she dropped Jordan off. The very tall, plump woman was dressed in a Mother Hubbard apron and was set for canning her own green beans. Her heavily seamed face was puckered as she clucked over Annalisse.

"You been taking that raspberry leaf tea I gave you?"

"Yes, ma'am," Annalisse said to her surrogate grandmother.

"You're looking peaked, dear. Could be you're anemic. Get that young doctor to test you for it. I've got some liver in the freezer from a calf we killed in the spring. It'll fix you right up. If you make it with lemon juice, it takes the curse off it."

Calves' liver reminded Annalisse of her childhood. And Betsy's 1950's vintage kitchen was nearly a replica of her Grandma Swenson's. She had spent many a steamy Saturday afternoon helping her mother and grandmother put up the garden vegetables, and she had vowed, even at the age of ten, that when she grew up, she was going to have air conditioning in her house. Dennis hadn't failed her. They had a good unit pumping cool air through the house, and she was grateful for that blessing. Missouri was even more humid than Wisconsin, and she would have found her canning chores completely unsupportable without it. Yet Grandma Betsy still operated without it, doing her canning in the early hours of the morning. She was now finished for the day and ready to entertain Jordan by having him assist her in making cinnamon rolls. She also possessed an old rocking horse and a play set in the backyard.

"You go on off now and make sure that doctor checks your blood count," Grandma Betsy said as she shooed Annalisse out the door.

Driving into town, she thought of how hard it had been the night before to bring herself into the present. Would Gregg have any idea of what was wrong with her? Did she dare confide in him?

She was still wondering when she arrived at his state-of-the-art office that his wife's family's money had built next to the Cherokee County hospital.

His nurse, Angela, another big-haired friend of Whitney Webster, greeted her warmly.

"Annalisse! It's so good to see you! The doctor is at the hospital, doing rounds, but he just called and said he'd be right over. Shall we get your weight?"

As usual, Annalisse took off her shoes before she stepped on the scale. With her large Scandanavian build, she carried her babies well but tended to put on too much weight.

"A hundred and seventy," Angela pronounced.

Annalisse groaned. Then she remembered Dennis's words last night after they had made love. "You're always beautiful, honey, especially when you're pregnant."

However, now Jules added his two cents. "Does he intend to keep you barefoot, pregnant, and in the kitchen bottling green beans for the rest of your life? Look at your ankles!"

I want this baby, Jules! She almost screamed the words out loud instead of saying them in her head.

Shaking off Jules's intrusion in her head, she followed Angela into the examination cubicle, where she prepared for the exam. The clinical smell grounded her. It reminded her of her lab at Scripps. As she sat up on the paper-covered exam table, she decided she would approach her problems like the scientist she was.

Then she felt a little dart of anticipation. She was due for another ultrasound today. Annalisse realized she hadn't even been thinking of her baby since the haunting began. Now she would see her on the ultrasound and hear her heartbeat. She wished mightily that Dennis were here. The experience had been such a bonding one last time.

Gregg strode into the office briskly a few moments later. "Annalisse! So good to see you! So, where are we now?" He consulted his chart. "Ah, yes, six months! You've passed the critical period. Congratulations. The baby is fully developed and just growing and putting on weight from now on."

Taking the stethoscope from around his neck, he put its cold metal disk against her belly, moving it around. "Ah, good strong heartbeat. We'll do the ultrasound in a minute."

Annalisse smiled with relief. Her sister, Marta, had given birth to a stillborn at seven months. It had been horribly traumatic, but

Annalisse had actually forgotten that concern since she had descended into this twilight existence between the past and present.

As Gregg put on his gloves for her pelvic exam, he said, "So. Tell me. How have you been feeling, Annalisse? You look a bit tired."

Should she tell him? Did he really care? The clinical surroundings reminded her that he was a doctor, not just a friend. He was looking straight into her eyes, his own somber. "Did Dennis say something to you?" she asked, suddenly suspicious.

"He's worried about you. Thinks he hasn't been treating you well."

Tears filled her eyes, and she turned her head to the side so she couldn't see the doctor's eyes on her. How like Dennis to take the blame for her moods! "I think I'm going crazy or something, Gregg. What is it like when someone goes schizophrenic?"

"There are lots of symptoms, none of which I have ever observed in you. The most common, of course, is that schizophrenics hear voices or see people that aren't there."

Annalisse's heart pounded. Had she been hearing actual voices? Was Jules going to appear to her one of these days? Were they going to have to institutionalize her in some place where she would have to live with other weird people, away from Dennis and her children, with only the taunting ghost of Jules for company?

Tears streamed down her face.

Gregg sat down on his stool. "Let's talk this out, Annalisse, before I call Angela in for the pelvic. This is serious. Why do you think you're schizophrenic?"

She struggled to speak through her sobs. "I experience these periods where . . . where I'm completely carried away into the past. I remember everything—sounds, smells, and worst of all, the emotions."

"Flashbacks," Gregg pronounced. "Have you considered talking to Dennis about them?"

"No," she said instantly. "I couldn't. It would totally freak him out. He thinks I'm a different person. I used to be that person. I thought I could go back. I wanted to go back, to put these other things out of my life, but . . ." Annalisse covered her eyes with her hands and said in a small voice, "Some of them were good. Some of them are just part of who I am, and Dennis doesn't know that person. I don't know if this makes any sense, but it's getting harder and harder to live in the present."

Gregg's eyes were soft and full of understanding. "Was there some trauma associated with that other life that you are trying to forget?"

Annalisse nodded, unable to go on.

"Something so terrible that it's caused you to try to forget everything associated with it?"

"Yes," she said. "And I thought I had, until recently. I have no idea what triggered this."

"It was bound to happen, Annalisse," Gregg said gently. "There's a clinical name for it—post-traumatic stress disorder. PTSD. It's not a character weakness. It's a real disorder of the brain."

PTSD? "What do I do?" she pleaded, her heart accelerating in panic.

"There is no way out but through. It sounds like you cut those memories out of your life before you could feel the emotions associated with them. I know you well enough to know that your natural temperament is serene and stoic. You, of all people, would be uncomfortable with strong emotions. You're no drama queen."

"You would be surprised," she differed. "You don't know me as well as you think. Dennis is completely bewildered."

"Well, the emotional facts are that you are going to have to face that pain and deal with it. It's the only way you'll move through it. It would be better if you could confide in Dennis. I'm sure he'd help."

"He could never live with it," she said. "He's quixotic, but I've known him long enough to know that he runs away from things that aren't perfect. He's on this desperate search for Eden. He has been for years." Annalisse picked at the seam of the hospital gown. "His idealism was like a tonic; my world had become so barren. But he thinks I'm Eve, for heaven's sake."

"You might be surprised, Annalisse. Dennis really loves you."

"If he ever finds out who I really am, I won't fit into his life, Gregg. He'll leave me."

"Dennis isn't made that way, Annalisse. He's the most caring man I know. I would give him a chance to help you through this. It's undoubtedly being exacerbated by hormones."

Annalisse wiped her tears as a little wave of relief washed over her. At least her problem had a name. She'd have to research it on the Internet. "Can we do the ultrasound now?"

Sobered and depressed by her conversation with the doctor, after her exam Annalisse could not face going back to the stage set that was her home. She had voiced her worst fear. Would Dennis stay with her while she worked her way through this PTSD and tried to become the person she used to be? Or would he get totally fed up, as he had with the environmentalist movement, Africa, and California? Pulling into the park, she again drove to the spot where the evergreens screened her from view.

⌒◞

Vienna was a fairy tale to the girl from rural Wisconsin. Its magic was spun from the ancient buildings—Gothic, baroque, rococo, and neoclassical rising out of the snow. She was, for the first time in her life, seeing evidence of a civilization that had spread over central and eastern Europe for half a millennium. Strolling through the Hofburg Platz alone while Jules practiced, she felt very small and overpowered, as she imagined troops marching in splendid red tunics before the emperor's palace.

Of course, the Spanish Riding School was her favorite spot. With her love of horses, sitting inside the elegant ballroom with its painted panels and crystal chandeliers, watching the white Lipizzaners was the ultimate in equestrian beauty. She smelled the unmistakable horsey scent, so at odds with the surroundings, and tried to comprehend that the pedigree of these horses went back to the sixteenth century. The riders were gallant and handsome, making the complicated moves seem effortless.

The *Schatzkammer*, with its plethora of royal jewels, was, to her surprise, a disappointment. It was just too hard to comprehend the value and history of so many crowns, pendants, and rings. More to her taste were the art museums where she viewed the paintings of early twentieth-century master Gustav Klimt. His gold leaf painting *The Kiss* was chaste but far more erotic than his nudes. The tenderness of the couple depicted gave her the same ache in her breast as when Jules kissed her. She stood looking at it for a long time, thinking. The painting showed a once-in-a-lifetime love, she was certain. The kind that used to exist before everyone started bed-hopping. Jules was her once-in-a-lifetime love. She was so enmeshed with him spiritually and emotionally that she would love him until the day she died.

She remembered her first argument with Jules at the airport.

"You're going to love our little flat," Jules had said when he met her outside Customs.

"But, Jules, I told you to find a separate one for me! I'm not going to live with you. Isn't it enough that I've come?"

He had stopped in the middle of the airport, his black eyes probing hers. "Why won't you sleep with me, Annalisse? The magnetism between us is part of our work, part of our joy."

"I've thought this out, Jules, since we've been apart. If I had an affair with you, I'd be burned alive. There would be no Annalisse left. It wouldn't be casual, Jules. For me, it would be forever."

Jules had shrugged. "How Victorian you are. How do you know it wouldn't be forever with us? I can't imagine life without you, but this isn't the time for either of us to consider marriage."

"I don't want marriage. I want to know if this is the kind of life I want. If I am talented enough."

He had smiled a little then and caressed the hair that fell over her shoulders. "Okay, we'll find you a place. But I don't think you'll live there long, so it might be wise to get a month-to-month lease. We're yin and yang, Annalisse. We complete each other. Nothing, not even your caution, is going to keep us apart."

Staring at the embracing figures in the Klimt painting, she knew she had an overwhelming drive to physically complete her relationship with Jules. But no matter what he said, she really couldn't be certain that their relationship wouldn't come to an end once his career was established. He would go on—miles ahead, leaving behind his farm girl from Wisconsin. And so she sublimated her physical desires by discovering all she could about her new environs. If fate was fickle, this might be her only chance.

Music was everywhere—the symphony, the opera, chamber music, impromptu concerts, even in the lobbies of the hotels. It served to loosen the anxiety she felt. While lost in Chopin, she couldn't take her own warning that this time-out-of-time was only temporary.

Though she hadn't expected it, the food was fabulous. Especially the *Sachertorte*—a "death by chocolate" bittersweet torte spread with raspberry jam and served with whipped cream in the restaurant of Vienna's most elegant hotel, the Sacher. In fact, the whole city reminded her of chocolate with whipped cream. It was a feast for the senses.

But she was giving the experiment only three months. After she had discussed the matter with her parents, they had agreed to advance her the amount of the tuition and room and board that they would have paid (minus her scholarship) for the quarter. That was to cover the cost of her independence.

The flat she occupied was small and cramped, but it had once been part of a grand townhouse, situated on a street of similar accommodations—biscuit-colored and adorned with white trim that resembled cream pastry. It had a long hallway leading to a very modern sitting room decorated in chrome and black. The art, unfortunately for Annalisse, was modern, consisting mostly of red blotches. There was a small kitchenette with a hot plate and then a tiny bedroom with a double bed covered in a Chinese jade–printed duvet. Her closet was merely a rod separated from the rest of the room by a curtain that matched the duvet. The bathroom was like a little box, so she was very glad she didn't suffer claustrophobia.

"My flat is much nicer," Jules told her. His eyes twinkled in an expression she had never seen. Jules was happy in Vienna. The Vienna Philharmonic was pleased with him. His new music master was pushing for a spring debut when Jules would play the Tchaikovsky as featured soloist—the springboard for his future career.

Jules accompanied her on her first visit to Herr Hochmann, her piano instructor. The man looked like a cartoon from the *New Yorker*. Dressed as a gentleman from the early twentieth century, he had a full head of white hair that was unrestrained, as though he constantly yanked at it. He looked a little mad, and his expression was dour. His studio was all glass, a hothouse with every kind of tropical plant from palms to orchids.

Sizing Annalisse up and down, he sighed. "You don't look like a pianist," he said in clipped English with a British accent. "You're far too robust and well-fed. If it weren't for Grieg and Sibelius, I wouldn't give you a chance." He moved forward, peering into her face. She tried not to wince. "Scandinavia has produced very few musicians. There's too little romance in your blood."

Jules bristled. "Just listen to her," he snapped. "Her gift is far more priceless than that emerald you're wearing. Play your Rachmaninoff, Annalisse."

She was so shy about her music that the master's assessment threw her into self-doubt. What in the world was she doing here? Jules gave her a little push in the small of her back towards the Steinway grand piano.

After the first measure, she decided, "What the heck? If he decides I'm not made of the right stuff, I don't need to go through with this. Better to find out now." Relaxing inside, she gave herself over to the thundering clouds in Rachmaninoff's skies.

When Dennis arrived at the office Monday morning, his first order of business was to put a call through to the Department of Natural Resources.

"Sid? Dennis Childs. Any word on when you're going to be coming down this way?"

There was a moment's silence on the other end of the line.

"Dennis . . . I guess I should have called. We've run into a little snag at this end."

Dennis knew then that his worst fears were about to be confirmed. "What sort of snag?"

"We're tied up on another site, and we're not going to be able to get a crew down there as soon as we thought."

"Are you aware that we just had one of the heaviest rainstorms in decades and that the dioxin, wherever it is, is continuing to leak, probably making its way into our water table as we speak?"

"Well, for one thing, we don't even know for certain that the substance is dioxin . . ."

"What?"

"Well, the soil hasn't yet been tested . . ."

"And isn't likely to be unless you haul yourselves on down here and do your job!"

"Now wait just a minute. All you've got is the unsupported opinion of one country doctor that this man was exposed to dioxin . . ."

"Sid, let me ask you something. What's made you change your tune all of a sudden? Last week, as I recall, you couldn't wait to move on this thing."

"I told you, as I recall, that there would have to be certain preliminaries . . ."

"Like notifying Amalgamated and giving them a chance to cover their backside?"

"What gives you that idea?"

"Threats."

"What do you mean, threats?"

"My family. We've received a threat to leave this alone. And the only people who knew about this action, other than you, are the doctor and the patient. The patient doesn't know what hit him, and the doctor would never breathe a word. That leaves the DNR."

"You think someone here leaked the information to Amalgamated?"

"And told you to give me the runaround. Look, my client is in the hospital dying. That makes me angry. I'm not above threats myself. I think the press would love to get hold of this story."

"Hold on, Dennis. I can see why you're angry. Give me a week. I'll see what I can do. Don't call in the press just yet. Believe me, it could do you a lot more harm than good."

"What do you mean by that?"

"Like it or not, Amalgamated is probably the most powerful company downstate."

"And?"

"They've got a lot of friends. That's all I'm going to say."

To his amazement, Dennis found he was holding a dead phone to his ear. Another threat? It sure sounded like it.

Dennis slammed down the telephone and crossed to the window. What was the matter with these people? Could they not understand the danger posed by such a powerful poison as dioxin? What could be any more important than the safety of the drinking water of thousands of people? Especially to the DNR?

He watched through the glass as Little Dan Perkins entered Calhoun's Video World and Appliance Repair, no doubt to join a poker game. Whatever had given him the idea that just because these people lived simply that was a cardinal virtue? It could be and probably was just plain ignorance. In a world where environmental issues were hot topics in just about any civilized society, he had picked the one little spot in America where no one seemed to care. Well, he'd make them care. Otherwise, like Lonnie, they were going to go meekly to the slaughterhouse. That thought reminded him of his promise to Lonnie. Picking up the telephone, he called Gregg.

After a few minutes, Angela put him through to the doctor.

"Hey, Gregg. Any objection to Lonnie dying in his own bed?"

"Hospice is pretty thin in this county," the doctor said. "He needs daily care."

Once Dennis would have volunteered Annalisse without a second thought. Now he said, "What about Ada Lou?"

"She's not strong enough to bathe him and change his bed while he's in it. But I agree with you. The least we can do is get Lonnie into familiar surroundings. I'll see if someone from Lawrence County Hospice could look in on him every day. As I recall, his little piece of ground straddles the county line."

"That would be great, Gregg. Just let me know when, and I'll get Ada to help me move him home."

"I thought you'd be calling about Annalisse," Gregg said. "She was in this morning."

Dennis's heart sank like a lead weight. Since their tender interlude the night before, he had actually talked himself into believing that everything was fine. At least for the moment.

"I can't reveal our conversation, Dennis. But as your friend, I'm concerned. She really needs you to be especially understanding right now. Let her know she's safe with you. That you're not going to abandon her."

"Abandon her?" What was this? "Geez, where'd she get a dumb idea like that?"

"I'm not sure. I've probably told you more than I should. Just take care of her."

Dennis hung up the phone, completely at sea. He was utterly stumped. Then, staring at his framed photograph of the weeping willow that graced his Walden Pond, he was ambushed by memory.

It had been weeks since the Rodney incident, and Dennis had

steadfastly kept away from Jill. Bitterly, he had reflected that she probably hadn't even noticed. One Saturday night, however, as he lay listening to blues guitar and staring at his anthro textbook, his phone rang.

"Dennis?" To his surprise it was Jill, sounding somehow broken.

"What's wrong?" he asked, feeling a surge of hope in spite of himself.

"I haven't seen you in a while. That thing with Rodney . . . Well, you've got to believe me, Dennis. It was the grass. He brought it. Nothing would have happened if it hadn't been for the grass. I know you don't believe me, but I love you, Dennis."

Jill? Was this really Jill? The tough woman who had faced down the cop with her bravura? He felt the world was standing upside down. Never in his wildest dreams had he imagined that Jill-with-the-agenda loved him. And, to his surprise, he didn't know how he felt about it. "Where are you?" he asked warily.

"At a party. They've got grass. I'm feeling a little sick. A little weird. Can you come get me? I'm at Keith's."

Jill was a mess when he arrived in the ancient Chevy he had bought for forty dollars at the police auction. Her beautiful hair was tangled, and she had indeed been sick. All over herself.

He took her to her apartment and stuck her in a cold shower, clothes and all, and then brewed some strong coffee. When he went into the bathroom, she was crooning off-key, "Baa baa, black sheep, have you any wool?"'

Wrapping her in one of her giant pink bath sheets, he carried her into the bedroom and made her sip the coffee. Slowly, the blank look disappeared from her eyes, and she began to tear at her wet clothes, shivering. Dennis handed her a thick terrycloth robe and left the room.

She probably hadn't eaten in forever, if he knew Jill. Finding nonfat yogurt in her refrigerator, he poured it into a bowl and sliced an ancient banana on top of it. Peering through the door, he saw that she was now modestly attired in her bathrobe, sitting on the edge of the bed, teeth chattering.

Suddenly, he was angry. More angry than he'd ever been. Jill was fragile, despite her tough act. She was a very fine actress and had a great future ahead of her. What was she doing messing with grass?

"Jill," he said in a stern voice as he entered the room, "you've got to stop fooling around with drugs. You'll ruin your career before it even gets started."

"I wouldn't have done it, Dennis, if you hadn't abandoned me," she said, her eyes large and pitiful.

Something warned him that he shouldn't, but he let her back into his heart at that moment because he believed her.

Chapter Twelve

Weberville, the site of the postprimary campaign kickoff rally, was not even a dot on the map. Its name was written in small blue letters at the junction of double Z and H highways in the southern part of Cherokee County.

For the occasion, the volunteer fire department had driven its fire engines onto the grass, decorated them in red, white, and blue, and donated the interior of its metal garage for the festivities. A makeshift bandstand accommodated local gospel singers, and the half-dozen tables lent by the Baptist church supported the pies, cakes, cookies, jams, and jellies being sold to raise money for the cause.

Dennis smiled at it all, trying to force some enthusiasm. Grassroots politics—had it survived so thoroughly elsewhere? The only problem he could see was that there were no other Republican candidates for his prospective job, and Cherokee County seemed to have no Democratic party.

"Evenin', Mr. Chiles," Ada Lou greeted him. She had discarded her iron gray wig for a platinum blonde one tonight, and the contrast was startling.

Cheered by the sight nonetheless, he said, "Why, hello, Ada Lou. What's that you're carrying, one of your blackberry pies?"

"Land yes. I don't believe we'll ever see th' end o' blackberries this year, what with all the rain. Least I could do, bake a few pies. All in a good cause." She winked at him and passed on.

"You do have a way with the ladies, Dennis," Annalisse remarked with a grin.

"I specialize in widows," he said wryly. "Where's Jordan?"

"Right behind you, handing out your campaign cards. He's in his element. A natural campaigner."

He patted his pockets. "Didn't think there'd be so many people here."

"Give me half of what you've got left, and I'll hand some out. You go woo your widows."

For a moment he watched her departing back. She seemed more in charity with him tonight than she had been. But he had given up trying to figure out her moods. Taking himself in hand, he began to circulate. "Hi, I'm Dennis Childs, running for prosecuting attorney. I sure would appreciate your vote."

For the next forty-five minutes, he campaigned dutifully, flashing his smile at the widows, shaking hands firmly with farmers in overalls and feed caps. The pall cast by the morning's call to the DNR lifted, and he enjoyed the rally far more than he had expected to. He remembered why he'd brought his family to Cherokee County. These people were ignorant of many of the ways of the world, it was true. But they were basically good.

When the time came, Senator Cavanaugh introduced him, along with the candidates for other positions, and he was asked to make a short speech. He had thought about it carefully and decided to leave

the environmental issue out of it. It would probably, as Sid Meier
had warned him, do more harm than good in the circumstances.
The main thing to do now was to get elected.

His speech teacher and advisor, Miss Lee, would have been
proud of him. Pulling out all the stops, he made reference to
Lincoln, his mother, the Baptist church, and Ada Lou's blackberry
pies. The audience greeted his words with a foot-stomping applause.
He hadn't addressed a single issue.

Jesse Cavanaugh approached Annalisse during the gospel hoe-
down that followed the speeches. "That's a real fine husband you got
there. You'd think he'd been makin' political speeches all his life."

She forbore stating that her husband had made a few in his time
but that none of them would have been at all welcomed by the GOP.

"He's in his element. But neither of us expected so many people
to be here."

The senator chuckled. "It's a kind of a tradition to get things
kicked off in Weberville. People come from all over. For Ada Lou's
pies and homemade ice cream, mostly, I think."

"I don't suppose there's a Democrat in the whole town?"

Fixing her with twinkling eyes, the senator answered, "Matter o'
fact, there was a Democrat family moved t' Weberville, back in the
thirties. I was just a tot, so I don't know for sure, but I can tell you
how the story goes." Confident of her attention, he began his tale.
"This fam'ly, by the name of Moberly, they lived in a shanty down
by Walt Peel's place, if you know where that is."

Annalisse shook her head.

"Nearby th' old covered bridge. Humble little home, 'parently,
but they had their picture of FDR, and the daddy used to draw his

welfare check reg'lar." The senator paused for a measured sip of the coffee he was holding. "Well, someone in town offered him a job haulin' hay. He shook his head real slow an' sad-like and said, 'Nope.' Someone else offered him a job down t' the slaughterhouse. 'No, sir,' he said again. Flat out this time. Finally, some men on the fire brigade vis'ted with him. 'John Moberly,' they told 'im, 'you live in this town, you gotta take your turn at the firehouse.' 'What'll y'pay me?' he asked. 'Nothin.' But if this shanty o' yours catches fire, we'll come 'n put it out.' Well, John Moberly thought about it for awhile, but he didn't tell 'em yea or nay. That night he burned the place down 'imself, and in the mornin' he and the fam'ly were gone."

Annalisse laughed, as she was meant to do. "And the moral of the story is—"

The senator scratched his head. "Well, that's purdy clear . . . never sell fire insurance to a Democrat."

Annalisse allowed herself a grin. The man sure had a way about him, as Papa used to say about the Irish used-car salesman.

"Matter o' fact, Miz Childs, I was hopin' you and me could have a little chat."

Annalisse hauled out her armor with an effort. "If it's anything to do with the Latinos, senator, I've tried to apologize to your wife, but other than that, I've really said all I have to say on that subject."

"No, no. Not about that ol' business." He fixed her with an interested gaze. "I jes' wanted t' tell you how much I think o' yer husband. It's been a while since we had a young man o' his caliber around here."

What could she say to that? Why was the senator buttering her up?

He was chuckling. "Y' know what I like best about 'im? He's not afraid to speak 'is mind. Fer instance, when we had that little discussion about you and Miz Cavanaugh the other day, you know what nine men outta ten woulda done?"

She shook her head.

"Well, let's put it this way. Most young fellas today haven't got a lot o' gumption. But Dennis, now. He stood behind you from start t' finish. Made me see it was none of my business."

Was that true? From her husband's reaction to the incident, she could hardly believe it.

"I'm glad to hear that," she told him.

"Now, Miz Childs, I've thought about that, an' I realize yer husband was right. It's no business o' mine or Mae's how you feel about those people. Thing is, and this is what was in my mind at the time, the two o' you are new in Cherokee County. You've seen a lot more of the world than these people here. You an' I both know that nothin's as simple as it looks to them—they still see things in black and white. Fact is, they don't like gray much. It's too confusin'."

"So what you're telling me is to keep my opinions to myself?"

"You c'n put it like that if you want to." He leaned toward her and dropped his voice. "But what I'm really askin' you t' do is to try t' understand these people. Try t' love 'em. Learn what they worry about and what makes 'em happy. If you and yer husband c'n do that, ya'll be the best thing that ever happened t' this county."

The man was simply overpowering. "Thank you, senator. I'm sure we'll try," was the only reply she could make.

Dennis came over to them then and put an arm around her shoulders. Was it possible he was being protective?

"I was jes' tellin' your wife what a fine speech that was, Dennis. Fine, jes' fine."

Beaming, the man moved off.

"I feel completely snowed," Annalisse told her husband.

"He's really something, isn't he?" Dennis chuckled.

Their amusement held until they went out to the car. Jordan was the first to notice.

"Dad! Wook! What's wong with ow wheels?"

Upon examination, it appeared they had all been slashed to ribbons.

‿

"Do y' have any enemies that y' know of, son?" the senator asked later as he and Mae drove the Childs family home in his Lincoln. The police report had been filled out and the car left to be towed to a Blue Creek garage in the morning.

Instinct rather than reason bade Dennis to be cautious. "No one I can think of. But there might have been someone there that was on the wrong side of me in court. You never know about things like that, I guess. I remember one of the other lawyers in town telling me I needed to keep a loaded pistol in my desk. I thought that was a little paranoid. Was I wrong?"

The senator just shook his head. "We do have a little problem from time t' time when someone gets lickered up. But this was different somehow."

"It was downright vicious," Mae said emphatically. "I can't help but feel that someone means you real harm, Dennis."

"I think it's time I wrote an editorial to the *Sentinel*," the senator stated flatly. "I know a few things about the good ol' boys around here. They need some kind o' warning that I'm behind you all."

Dennis was stymied. He was almost certain the tire slashing was part of the Amalgamated mess, but what if it wasn't?

"It was wicked!" Mae declared. "It ought to be punished! I'm sure the Latinos are behind it, Jesse."

"Don't worry, Mrs. Cavanaugh," Dennis reassured her. "I'm

going to find out who's done this. No one's going to mess with my family."

"Just let me know if you need a hand, son," Jesse Cavanaugh invited. "I don't like to see things like this goin' on in my county."

"Why didn't you tell the senator about the threat?" Annalisse asked him once they were home.

"It may be related to that. I'm practically certain it is. But I'm playing this pretty close to the chest. I don't want even the most well-meaning of people to know about that until I figure out where this leak is coming from."

Annalisse walked over to where he was standing by the bedroom window and put a hand on his shoulder. "You know, I was pleasantly surprised by the senator tonight. I really think he was ready to do battle for us."

"It seemed that way," Dennis said, but she could tell he was a million miles away. This was another assault on his Eden.

Sighing, Annalisse returned to her rocker and picked up her crocheting from the basket next to it. She was attempting a pink blanket for Bronwyn. "I suppose that makes sense. I just hope the guy doesn't get any closer to us than our tires."

"Maybe it would be safer for you and Jordan to go to your parents' for a while."

Annalisse looked up at him, stricken. Did he want to get rid of her and her "moods"?

"But I don't want to leave you now, Dennis! Not while all this is going on."

"I'd feel much better if I knew whoever it is couldn't get to you and Jordan."

"Do you really think it's that serious?"

"Yes. I do. When I saw those tires, I felt physically ill. Violated. Then, angry. And then, afraid."

Annalisse sat silently, crocheting.

"You always said we'd be outsiders here. Has anyone ever made any cracks to you?" he asked.

She shrugged. "Oh, you know. They never come out and say it. It all goes on behind my back."

"Gregg told me the other day that Cindy had tried to get you into the local clubs. She failed. Did you know about that?"

"Cindy told me. She didn't want me to think she hadn't tried. As a matter of fact, she resigned from all of them in protest. She's as much an outsider as I am, now. I feel bad about it."

"Good for Cindy. Why don't you take her to Springfield for lunch? On me."

"Maybe I will," she promised vaguely. Right now she didn't trust herself. What if she had a flashback in front of Cindy? To distract Dennis from the idea she said, "I think they have a white supremacist group around here called Sonny's Boys. Someone I didn't know mentioned setting them on the Latinos. That's what really ticked me off at the luncheon."

"Sonny's Boys? The senator's never mentioned them."

"Oh, he knows all about them. Mae shut that woman up pretty quickly. I hadn't thought of it before, but they could be behind the tire slashing." The idea made her shiver. "It's like some kind of scary movie, Dennis."

Her husband shook his head. "Unbelievable. You know, I was thinking today that I might have made a real mistake in judgment bringing us here, but then at the rally I started feeling better about things. Now, I feel worse again. These people are about a hundred and fifty years behind the times."

Annalisse rocked gently in her chair, measuring her reply. "I know it's hard for you to understand, because you just naturally like everyone, whatever their color or creed. But these people are afraid of anything from outside that might change the status quo." She looked up at her husband, who had finally been jolted out of his "Green Dream" into listening to her.

"That's why they won't tolerate unions," she told him. "That's what enabled the Latinos to come in and take their jobs away at a lower wage. You must have realized by now they don't like anyone who's different. They have a very narrow definition of what it means to be an American."

He sighed, leaning against the window frame. "I can see their racial prejudice. I'm not as blind as that. But their laxity about the environment is incredible to me. They live in this gorgeous place, and they don't seem to care about preserving it. There's no zoning, no regulation of local industry . . ."

"They think nothing can ever happen to them if they keep the rest of the world out," she told him. "It's a kind of localized xenophobia. I think they'd actually secede from the Union if they could. I'm sorry to break it to you, but that's how it is."

Annalisse could tell by the way Dennis was shaking his head that he was incredulous. He began to pace the room. "You must think I'm a real idiot with all my stupid dreams of paradise."

"No, Dennis," she said firmly. "I don't. It's why I married you. You want to make the world better."

For a few moments, he didn't answer. Then he looked at her, his face a blank. "I thought you married me because you loved me."

She felt her own face burn. Determined to be as honest as she could, she said, "You overwhelmed me with your goodness and ideals. You were like sunshine to me. The only bright thing." She realized instantly that she had echoed Jules's phrase.

123

Dennis's laugh was harsh, his face suddenly bitter. "Another misconception on my part. And yours. It's just that I seem never to have grown up. I still think that truth, justice, and the American way should prevail. I have this personality disorder. At times I confuse myself with Superman."

He ran a hand over the back of his neck in a gesture that made her heart ache. She honestly could not bear to see him disillusioned. "Dennis, what you have is hope. It's a precious commodity. Don't give up on this. You'll find a way to save this town from itself."

"You're wrong, Annalisse. You see, you've always been my bright thing, too. I've always drawn my strength from you. And I've made you terribly unhappy by bringing you here."

The words fell between them and echoed. Dennis left the room.

Annalisse rocked in silence. Dismay pulsed through her. What had she done? What was happening to her marriage?

She'd made another horrible mistake in judgment. For some reason, she'd always thought Dennis's strength came from inside. She'd thought she could lean on him while she healed. *Dennis has always been my Jack Ryan. I've read way too much Tom Clancy.*

He wasn't the only one who had confused him with a superhero. She'd known for a long time that she'd never felt the emotional intimacy with him that one should with one's husband, and now she wondered if she ever would. She had always blamed herself, because she kept herself and her past hidden from him, but now it seemed as though he had done the same with her. Annalisse threw her crocheting into the basket. *Why is it that I am always expected to be the strong one?*

Drawing a deep breath that hurt, she began to cry. Angry with her weakness, she covered her face. But the tears wouldn't stop.

Herr Hochmann surprised her completely when he told her after her first two months of intense study that she was to make her debut. By his expression—intense beady eyes and a frown between his brows—she had supposed that she had miles more to go and couldn't imagine how she could work any harder or perform any better.

"*Fraulein*, your Jules was right. God has granted you a special gift. You have penetrated the soul of Chopin." He pounded his narrow chest with a fist. "I told you that Chopin felt that each finger produced a different color. Each one has its own job to do. Never have I had a student that has understood that as you do."

Annalisse was staggered at the compliment. "My fingers have a life of their own when I play Chopin," she replied, simply. "But do you think I am really ready for a public performance?"

"We will start slowly. One of my students lives in Paris now. She was to have performed at the opening of a new art gallery there. Unfortunately for her, she has contracted pneumonia. She asked me if I had another pianist available. You will do very well."

Jules was not at all surprised when she told him of the invitation. She had her lesson and practiced for four hours every morning, so she could be available to accompany Jules's practice sessions in the afternoon.

"Yes, Lisse, it's time you were put before your public. What are you going to play?"

"Three of the Chopin Études. I think my arms and shoulders are made of iron, I've been practicing so hard. Herr Hochmann says it's a blessing I have such long fingers."

"This calls for a celebration!" His eyes lit with his pride in her.

"We'll go to the Hotel Sacher for dinner before the Philharmonic tonight. You're going to love the piece we're playing."

"Mahler's First?"

"Yes. It's magnificent and a little bit tongue-in-cheek. There's this insane cuckoo in it that keeps sounding off. And a cheerful funeral dirge!"

The Sacher was a perfect place to celebrate. Annalisse felt like a woman of the world, dressed in her black cocktail dress that clung to her curves and then flared at the knees. Jules had accompanied her to a seamstress and given the woman the design he had sketched. This was the first time she'd worn it. Her hair was French braided like a crown all around her head.

Intimate and candlelit with stiff white linen table cloths and hothouse hyacinths on each table, the restaurant was the furthest thing from her hometown that she could imagine. Was this a sample of what her life was to become?

For dinner they had Wiener Schnitzel with tiny potatoes and hothouse asparagus. Annalisse knew she should pass up the Sachertorte, but in a reckless mood, she ordered it with extra cream.

"Jules, I don't think I've ever been so happy in my entire life," she said, sipping her coffee while listening to the gypsy violinist who was strolling throughout the restaurant. "Just think. Me. Performing in Paris!"

He didn't say anything for a moment, regarding her with a soft look she had never seen. "I didn't know it was possible to be this happy. I love you, Annalisse. I always will. My life is yours."

⌒ꝭ

Dennis clattered down the stairs, bursting through the kitchen door out onto his land and down the slope to the moonlit pond.

Looking around him, he tried to feel the boost his farm always gave him. Instead, he felt hollowness yawn. Were his marriage and his life's meaning about to crumble because of flawed foundations?

Annalisse didn't love him. Never had. He guessed he was some kind of Band-Aid she had married on the rebound from her true love. The one she was grieving for. Who was he? Where was he? Had he, like some vampire, sucked all the life and love out of her? Why had he never suspected she wasn't all his? Had his own scarred psyche prevented too deep a probe?

Of less importance, but a great irony all the same, his family was far from safe, his habitat far from "Green." There was corruption spreading through his life.

Before, he'd always run when the corruption became so evident he knew he couldn't fix it. So his wife wasn't what he'd thought her. What was he going to do? Leave her? Leave perfectly innocent children and a wife who was unaccountably fragile? Perhaps she didn't love him, but she had put herself in his keeping. She had trusted him. Or at least he had thought so. Now, according to Gregg, she was afraid he would abandon her. Thank heaven for the doctor's warning. Otherwise, what he was reading from Annalisse would lead him to believe he had failed her completely. That his leaving her would free her.

But why wouldn't she confide in him? Had he failed so completely as a husband?

Apparently he had. Annalisse's interior life was a vast unknown. *Terra incognita.*

He had seen her calm as contentment, her passivity as compliance. Now he wondered if they were merely weapons to keep him out of her inner world. *What was she hiding in there? Who was Annalisse?* His unbounded narcissism had led him to think that she was his partner, supporting him in his struggles to bring order out of chaos. It had never occurred to him to wonder, for instance, if she minded leaving LA. It had seemed to him that she was as sick of the rat race as he was.

But had it all been his fault? She was definitely in hiding. She had been, he saw now, since the day he had met her on the boat. Could it all have to do somehow with Tchaikovsky and the Latinos? He fought a sensation of drowning and realized that it was self-pity.

Dennis kicked a divot in the grass and came to a decision. He would kill two birds with one stone. He would drive the family to Burnett, Annalisse's hometown, thus getting them out of harm's way, and he would stay long enough to grill Anna Louisa and Sven about their daughter's college years and after. He had to know what had happened to her and if there was someone else. He had to begin to discover the person his wife really was. While he waited for the DNR to begin their investigation, he would start one of his own.

Chapter Thirteen

Annalisse panicked. The very last thing she wanted was to be around her father when she was so swamped by her past. He would, in his unerring way, go straight to the problem. And he would, of course, be appalled that she had never taken Dennis into her confidence. He would insist that she do so.

"How about if you take Jordan, Dennis?" she suggested. "The peaches are just ripe for canning."

"Do you think I care about peaches when my family is being threatened by some lunatic? Jerome's going to milk Henrietta for me and keep an eye on the place. I'll tell Grandma Betsy she can have the peaches."

"I really think you're overreacting, Dennis."

"Well, I don't. Besides, we need a vacation. I'm giving the DNR a week to come to their senses before I go public, so this is the right time to take one."

Jordan was excited at the prospect—he loved his grandparents—so Annalisse tried to put a good face on things. She was simply going to have to pull out of it, that was all. Pull herself up by the bootstraps. Stiff upper lip.

Unable to face the job of packing, however, she found herself wandering down to the pond the next day while Dennis went in to wrap things up at the office and oversee the move of his client from the hospital back into his trailer. Sitting on the log, she stared across the blue-green stillness, watching their goose Priscilla lead her little line of goslings across the water.

Should she just tell Dennis about Jules and get it over with? No. He would never understand why she had kept such a thing from him. It might have been possible once, in the very beginning, but now it would wound him to think she had been hiding such a huge part of herself. As she had told Gregg, she wasn't really part of the scenario of Dennis's life. And he was already hurt enough by her careless statement of why she'd married him.

She realized that for the duration of their relationship, she had let Dennis hope for both of them. It was hard to believe she had been his "bright thing." Last night she had lain awake wondering what doubts Dennis was trying to escape.

She heard running footsteps. Looking up, she saw Jordan running down the hill towards her. He was crying. Annalisse pulled herself together as best she could.

"What's the matter, honey?"

Jordan threw himself into Annalisse's arms, sobbing. "Daisy died!"

Sighing, Annalisse held the hot, hiccupping little body to her. "D' you mean Nancy's dog?" Her son nodded vigorously. "I'm sorry, Jordan, honey. How did it happen?"

"She was having babies. Nancy said one of them got stuck . . ."

"Oh, poor little thing." Annalisse soothed her son for what she thought was an adequate interval and then tried distraction. "You know what? Daddy's going to be ready to load the car as soon as he comes home. And you're not packed!"

"I don't want you to die, Mommy!" Jordan wailed, burrowing his head next to her abdomen where his sister was. "What if your baby gets stuck? Pwomise me you won't ever die, Mommy, pwomise me!"

Annalisse stroked Jordan's hair with sudden ferocity. "Honey, I don't want you to worry about this! I am going to be just fine."

Jordan sniffed. "How do you know?"

"Because I'm strong and healthy and Dr. Gregory is a very good doctor."

Annalisse felt her son's rigidity gradually slacken. His fists opened, and he settled his head against her.

In moments like this, moments when she realized the true vulnerability of her child to the hurts of the world, she felt her own inadequacy keenly. Words would fail eventually. Someday her reassurances would prove false.

Watching while Priscilla, followed by a neat line of seven goslings, glided smoothly across the pond into the wind, she thought of her own mother who radiated the same serenity and firmness. She had handled things like this so beautifully.

Annalisse remembered when she was ten and Suzy Pierson, a girl in her Sunday School class, had faded away, paler and paler until she actually looked transparent. They said it was leukemia. Annalisse had been enraged and threatened at the same time. How could this mysterious killer come out of the blue and do this to Suzy, who had beaten her every year in swimming and riding, who had never hurt anyone?

On the morning Suzy died, Mother had taken her to the Piersons' empty home. They had taken armfuls of Mother's prize roses, cleaned and scrubbed every corner of the white clapboard house, and put the roses in every room. Annalisse had never worked so hard.

Then, when they were finished, Mother had taken her home but instead of having Annalisse help with supper, she had stationed her on the west porch with a Bible. "Read St. John," she had instructed. "And watch the sun."

It was summer, and the sun had lingered above the horizon until nearly eight-thirty. Annalisse had eaten her supper on the porch, still watching the sun, still reading St. John. When the last traces of hot red had gone from the horizon, her mother had joined her.

"Now, Annalisse, has the sun gone?"

"Yes."

"No, it's still there. It's the earth that's turned." She had paused, wiping hands wet from dishwashing on her apron. "Suzy's still there, too, just like the sun. But, the earth has turned away from her. She's no longer with us in mortality—she's gone beyond that, to another place, just as the sun does each night."

For a long time, whenever Annalisse thought of death, she didn't think of darkness but of a hot, cloudless evening, with a languid breeze stirring the heavy air, carrying the scent of roses and mown grass. And she heard Chopin. Marta, her older sister, had been practicing Chopin's "Tristesse" that night, on the other side of the screen door. Annalisse's first glimpse beyond childhood's protective veil— that feeling that things were too big and too complicated and the suspicion that you didn't really matter at all—was entangled with the sweetest of melodies and gracefully yielding light. Until now.

Sighing, she released her son. Jordan's eyelashes starred around his blue eyes, but he was smiling. "I can't wait to go fishing with Papa."

"That will be wonderful, Jordan, honey." Annalisse smiled and hugged him again, but a weight pressed hard over her heart. Her son ran back into the house to choose his clothes.

Annalisse knew she had failed Jules. She had loved him with everything she had to give, but it hadn't been enough. How could she hope to teach her children about things that would never fail, about trust and hope and God, when her own failure had rent such an enormous fissure in her understanding of such things?

She dropped her head in her hands. The fissure was widening steadily now, and there was nothing to stop it. She shivered. The present kept blurring downwards, merging with the past like a watercolor before it was dry.

Though she loved Vienna, Paris took her breath away. It was so much more beautiful than anything she had seen in her life. Even the little cobbled streets held surprises. A snatch of *La Vie en Rose* played by an accordion somewhere, a painter set up along the curb recreating the façade of the different colored apartments with their laundry flapping on a line across the street like multicolored flags. And the yeasty smells of baking. She had never seen so many bakeries in her life. Nearly every bicycle that swerved around her had a bag of groceries in its basket, a long baguette sticking up like a fat golden stick.

She ate a real Napoleon pastry accompanied by real French espresso in a tiny bakery with a pink and white awning. "I feel my creative juices flowing, just breathing this air!" she told Jules.

He sat back in his chair and blew smoke rings. "You know, it's always puzzled me that the French don't have many great composers. And, aside from Gustav Klimt, the Germans and Austrians don't have many well-known artists. One culture breeds artists, and the other, musicians. I wonder why that is?"

"The light, the air," Annalisse said. "It's different here. Have you noticed how many gloomy days we get in Vienna?"

Towards evening, they strolled down the Champs-Élysées. Annalisse studied Napoleon's imposing Arc de Triomphe, looming ahead against the twilight. She imagined first the Germans and then the Free French marching through it. The traffic was wild and bizarre, honking and swerving around the monument. She was sure the crazed drivers were proceeding at ninety miles per hour. The wind they created blew her hair into her face, ruffling her black and white gauze skirt as well. She and Jules had just celebrated at a very expensive restaurant with candlelight and violins, ordering champagne and chateaubriand. For dessert they had had pears with Brie cheese, and Annalisse had never tasted anything so heavenly. It was better than chocolate.

Now, even as they endured the smell and noise of the traffic, the lights of the Eiffel Tower ahead lit a celebration in her soul. She had to pinch herself when they reached the top to tell herself she was really there, looking at the city of lights neatly designed by Napoleon.

She had never been fanciful, but Paris was doing strange things to her. Right now, standing by Jules, with the wind in her hair, she was Ingrid Bergman (whom she had always loved because she was Scandinavian and large-boned) and Jules was Humphrey Bogart (with more hair). As Ilsa, she was joyous and carefree, in spite of all the reasons she should be fearful. *We'll always have Paris.*

"The lights, Jules!" she said. "This city! I never imagined all the propaganda could be true. But I don't think words are enough to describe the feel of Paris. It's almost as beautiful as music."

Jules took her face in his hands and kissed her with unusual tenderness. "It reminds me of the first time I saw you in the practice rooms. Your face was so full of light. This same wonderful light. Now you know what I feel when I look at you."

The assertion struck the most tender chord in her soul. They were one, she and Jules. He completed her in a way she had never known needed completion. The trappings of her sensible childhood were falling away.

"Why would anyone live in Wisconsin when they could live here?" she asked.

Her father and mother, who were flying over to witness her debut, arrived the next morning. They had booked rooms for all of them to stay at the ritzy Hotel Georges V.

When Annalisse showed her mother her performance attire—a dramatic black velvet dress, floor length, with a mandarin collar attached to a triangular bodice that left her shoulders bare and free to move with the exertion of her playing—Anna Louisa was thrilled. "Sweetheart, you're turning into such a sophisticate. Why did we ever think you belonged in a lab?"

Annalisse laughed. Though nervous about her performance, she was experiencing an entirely new level of happiness.

"How will we keep you down on the farm now that you've seen Paree?" her father joked.

Sven and Anna Louisa Lundgren met Jules with gravity and aplomb. Fortunately, he was looking presentable in a black shirt and slacks and had thought to comb his mass of curls.

"We are anxious to hear you perform," Annalisse's father told him that afternoon as they strolled among the legendary trees of the Tuileries that had seen both balls and wars. "When do you make your debut?"

"This spring," Jules replied. "I'm to be the featured soloist with the Vienna Philharmonic. Tchaikovsky."

"How impressive," exclaimed Anna Louisa. "And Vienna in the spring! That gives us so much to look forward to!" Because her daughter's talent was real, Anna Louisa had apparently decided Jules was no manipulator.

Annalisse's heart warmed toward her parents. They had truly embraced her new persona and way of life. It amused her how they looked at her as though surprised that their ugly duckling had turned into a swan.

She had known she would have stage fright, but Jules stood beside her behind the curtain, caressing the back of her neck, causing the delicious sensations that always replaced whatever else she might be feeling. He kissed her lightly on her ear and whispered, *"Bon chance,* my love."

The gallery lobby, where the concert was to be performed, was large and very modern with stone floors and a high vaulted ceiling that provided marvelous acoustics. Peeking behind the heavy maroon curtain that backed the platform upon which she would play, Annalisse viewed her audience. No women in pants or men in blue jeans here. The Parisians knew how to dress. Their evening clothes and jewelry brought home to her that they expected something grand. Her hands grew clammy, and her throat closed up.

Taking a deep breath, she wondered why in the world she was doing this. The guests had come to hear genius. And how many times had they heard Chopin? He was practically a patron saint.

She could see that Jules, dressed in an evening jacket and white tie, had taken his seat in the front row next to her parents. She felt a moment's pride in the people who had raised her. How hard had it been for them to applaud her coming here and trying her wings? They had always thought Marta was the talented one. But now they seemed relaxed and proud. Jules leaned forward, elbows on knees, his head bent as though in prayer. This was probably harder for him than it was her, she decided.

A sudden spurt of adrenaline banished her stage fright. *I'll make every one of them proud, and I'll have this crowd on its feet!* As the emcee introduced her, she put her hand to her chignon—done by an authentic French hairdresser—to make certain it was still in place. This moment would never come again.

There was polite applause, and then she stepped out onto the platform. Standing with one hand on the Steinway she gave a brief bow and then settled herself on the bench. Closing her eyes, she visualized the portrait of the young Chopin that hung on the wall of her apartment. She thought of each of her fingers as a separate color and the keyboard her canvas. Then she put her hands on the keys and slipped by habit into the composer's tortured psyche. Soon she forgot her audience entirely.

She lived with Chopin in her soul. Always. All the time. In the "Tristesse," the Étude she began with, his sadness was so overwhelming that she felt the universe weeping. The weeping grew to sobbing, and tears actually coursed down Annalisse's cheeks. Chopin's pain engulfed her, spilling out in notes so evocative that she dwelt on each one with a tenderness, as though she were soothing Jules, as though his head was against her breast, and she was stroking his curly hair, telling him she would always love him, always be there for him.

In the Étude No. 4, her hands flew over the keys as though there were a street chase. Someone dangerous was trying to tackle him, but Chopin escaped triumphantly. She smiled at the end of this piece.

Then, the work that she knew inside her was the composer's dream. *The Revolutionary.* Every firework in his box of tricks declared Polish freedom. Annalisse fell into the difficult score and arose a warrior. Every molecule of her soul immersed itself in the composer's struggle against odds only a passionate visionary could overcome. When she had pounded out the last note, she raised her hands in a dramatic flourish, and the sudden sound of applause brought her back to earth.

This wasn't a revolution but a concert. And she was the performer. They were clapping for *her*. She didn't know if she had the strength to stand. Then she heard the bravos and finally looked to see the audience on their feet.

Not bad for a farm girl. The thought brought her back to reality, and she stood and took her bows, her face burning with exertion. Her whole body felt light as air, and she thought it possible that she might even be able to fly.

"Dear, you were magnificent!" her mother crowed when she came around behind the curtain. Enfolding her in a comforting embrace, she said, "You're trembling!"

"Am I?"

"Your body has to recover from expending all that passion," Jules said, coming up behind her and sliding his arms around her waist. "That was brilliant, love. It might have been Frederic himself." Then he whispered in her ear, "Our life is going to be miraculous."

They slid out the back entrance as another performer began playing a cello concerto. Sven had located a small bistro nearby. As they sat over their bowls of French onion soup au gratin, he congratulated his daughter warmly. "When Jules told us you were magical, I have to tell you, I thought it must be because he was biased. But he told the truth. I even forgot you were my daughter, I was so engrossed in those Études."

"Oh, Papa, wait until you hear *him* play. That's magic. Life-changing magic, I promise you. Jules is going to be the Isaac Stern of this generation."

After her parents went back to the hotel, Jules insisted they take a stroll along the Seine. Annalisse was glad of her voluminous black opera cape, for it was the end of February and chilly by the river.

For a while, they only walked in silence, their arms around each other's waists. Couples embraced against the ramparts, cooing French words of love. In the distance, Annalisse heard a barge hooting and the klaxon of a police siren amidst muted car horns. But then they walked into a mystical fog and entered their own private world—a fairy tale place behind a scrim that protected them from the sudden turns of fate that were occurring all over Paris this night. *I have never felt so much a part of Jules as I do at this moment.*

"Let's do it, Annalisse. Let's get married."

Jolted, she echoed, "Married?"

"Isn't that what you want? Permanence?"

"Of course. But do you think we can make it financially? Are you sure it's not the Chopin talking?"

"After that performance, I have no doubts about your future. Hopefully, I'll do half that well. I hate to admit it, Annalisse, but I really think your talent is greater than mine."

"Oh, Jules. You'll be miles better. You're truly a once-in-a-lifetime phenomenon."

"I want you with me all the time, Annalisse—day and night."

"I must have cast a spell over you," she said, laughing and ready for anything. "When do you want to get married?"

"Let's do it tomorrow while your parents are here." He paused, pulling her against the stone embankment, caressing her back with hungry hands, kissing her with escalating heat. Annalisse's knees buckled.

"I think that's an excellent idea," she answered, her voice hoarse, as he held on to her. "What could be more perfect than being married in Paris?"

She was watching Priscilla and her goslings through tears. It was so much easier when she had cut out of her life everything to do with Jules. Was she condemned to these tormenting memories forever? It was as though someone was digging in her chest with a sharp-edged trowel. She was surprised there was no blood.

Dennis drove up to the hospital with Ada Lou next to him.

"This sho' is good of you, Mr. Chiles. Lonnie will be so much happier at home. And Ah'll be able to look after him mahself."

"Now, Ada Lou, you're not to try to lift him. Hospice will be coming in to take care of all of that."

"I know. But Ah just want t' make his las' days as comfortable as can be. Ah've cleaned that trailer from top to bottom. It was a real mess. And Ah got him all set up with cable, so he can watch anythin' he wants to."

"You're one in a million, Ada," Dennis said, and he meant it.

Lonnie appeared dazed, as Dennis dressed him in the new Levi's and workshirt he had purchased. The nurses came in to say good-bye, and Gregg even showed up.

"I'll be out to see you every evening Lonnie," he promised. "I know you'll be much happier at home. Mr. Childs is right."

The patient turned his pale face, eyes grown larger, in Dennis's direction. "I sure do thank you, sir. I can't wait to see mah old dog."

Once Lonnie was gently loaded into Dennis's SUV, they drove to the backwoods where Lonnie's trailer stood. All Dennis could think about was that if their positions were reversed, he would be doing plenty of complaining. The poor human being before him was so inured to the injustices of life that he didn't even see them anymore.

⌒

Annalisse was staring at Dennis's shoes, kicked under the corner of the dresser. She could almost feel the roughness of Jules's incipient beard against her cheek, as he held her like a cherished find. She didn't know she was crying again until she heard Dennis on the stairs.

"Swedie? You almost packed?"

Using an old sweater from the open drawer, she hastily wiped her eyes and face. When she tried to stand, she found that her legs had gone to sleep underneath her and she couldn't move.

"I'm in here, Dennis," she managed, her voice sounding far away in her own ears. "Just looking for my bathing suit."

In a moment, she felt him standing in the doorway. Could he tell she had been crying? She kept her head bent to her task.

"You know what that crazy kid of ours is doing?" he asked. He hadn't seen her tears, then.

"What?"

"He's bringing a jar of frozen earthworms. Says it'll save time when he and your dad go fishing."

Chapter Fourteen

It was two long days later when they drove past the white granite chapel. Dennis announced with a flourish, "Burnett, Wisconsin! Founded by the infamous fur trader and scoundrel Louis Burnett but long since reclaimed by right-thinking Swedes. Most illustrious citizen: one Annalisse Childs, nee Lundgren. Most notable characteristic: its lack of Mexican restaurants." Jordan giggled.

Actually, Dennis had a sneaking regard for the dull Scandinavian-Americanness of Burnett. Unlike his wilder, more picturesque Eden, this land had been settled by those with stern resolve. Its tidy, broad streets, laid out in a grid and numbered north, south, east, and west from the chapel in the center, were lined with modest brick houses, neat green lawns, and white picket fences. All this had been balm to his rootless soul in the days when Annalisse had first brought him here (somewhat anxiously, he suspected) to meet her parents.

It had been quite a summer that year. After the Memorial

Day weekend when he'd met Annalisse in Chicago, he'd gone to California to meet his new stepfather, the Mexican-American vegetable wholesaler his mother had married while he'd been in Africa. He was greeted with the news that she, at age forty-five, was pregnant. And that wasn't all. Luis Fernandez, a dashing, virile widower of fifty, had informed Dennis with a smile and a clap on the back that his mother would be a Catholic now. Protestant marriages, Luis felt, weren't quite legitimate; they were going to renew their vows at St. Mary's as soon as she'd finished her course of instruction. Dennis was humiliated and angry.

His mother, glowing like a girl and embarrassingly fruitful, seemed oblivious that with a single stroke, Luis was neatly disposing of her prior life—the Methodist minister who was her husband, her own Welsh heritage, and her years of caring for an aged father-in-law. Dennis had tried hard not to blame her, but her remarriage had been the final wrench, the end of any remaining connection with his childhood.

Then, in July, Annalisse had brought him to this healing place, where people's love of the land spanned generations and bound them together with ties of tradition. Here in the white granite chapel he had married into that tradition, grafting himself onto the Lundgren family tree and drawing sustenance from its roots.

The farm was situated several miles out of town. On a modest rise, overlooking a field of soybeans, stood the rambling Victorian-style farmhouse that had housed four generations of Lundgrens, beginning with immigrants Sven and Sigrid.

The present Sven had been smitten by the world of ideas at an early age and had forsaken farming to pursue the study of Truth. Following the paths of his own unique logic, he had eventually strayed into the law and spent most of his career as a judge. On their last visit, he had stood on the porch with Dennis, overlooking the family acreage, which had been leased out since Annalisse's grand-father had died.

"You know, Dennis, when all's said and done, there's nothing quite as straightforward as tilling the earth," he had said and, pull-ing deliberately at an earlobe, he chuckled deeply and continued, "After twenty-five years on the bench, I'm beginning to appreciate soybeans. Do you think maybe I'm ready to claim my inheritance?"

Anna Louisa had come up behind them and remarked, "Dear, when you decide to finish life as a farmer, it won't surprise anyone but you." Then she had clucked them in to dinner.

From the very first, Annalisse's mother had struck Dennis as a wise and calm woman. There was no room in her life for pretense of any sort. Her house was generally cluttered, her clothes were worn with remarkable absence of mind, and except for her church work, she had little social life. Anna Louisa spared her devotion for grow-ing things—her flowers, her vegetables, and (since her daughters had gone) her prize Yorkshire sows and their litters. In the wintertime, this love of flora and fauna spilled over into the creation of har-monious watercolors that adorned the walls of the Lundgren home, mounted on foam board.

At the moment, Dennis was counting heavily on her nurturing instinct.

"Annalisse, dear," Anna Louisa sang out upon their arrival, dwarfing her daughter in an embrace. "You look a little tired. How's the pregnancy going?"

"Uneventfully. I'm fine."

Papa, solid and smiling, joined the party, solemnly shaking hands with his grandson, who handed him a jar.

"What's in here, big fella?"

"Wook!" Jordan answered.

Sven Lundgren obediently screwed open the jar, inspected its contents, and then glanced up at his daughter, bushy white brows raised over twinkling eyes. "Well, now," he said to Jordan. "If I didn't know better, I'd say that it was a tangle of earthworms."

"Wight. I fweezed 'em. We won't have to dig 'em up when we go fishing."

"Now, that's just the sort of thing I'd expect a grandson of mine to think of. Think the fish'll be able to tell they're not fresh?"

"I dunno." Jordan had evidently not considered this. "What d'you think, Papa?"

"I think, in the interests of science, that we ought to give it a try. Anybody hungry?"

Dennis sniffed the pork roast and hot applesauce appreciatively and felt the tautness in him relax as he entered the house. Nothing had changed here since their last visit. An ancient pinecone Christmas wreath, a gift from Annalisse's aunt in Minnesota, still decorated the front hall, amid vases of exquisite summer roses. Anna Louisa's easel, naked at this season, sat by the north window of the dining room, a row of cacti occupying the windowsill behind it. On the shelves of the heavy mahogany sideboard was the original blue and white Lundgren china, upstaged by various relics of Annalisse and her sisters—handprints cast in plaster, cornhusk dolls, and what looked like a dilapidated Indian headdress. The table in the dining room was set with the best china and a tablecloth printed in Christmas poinsettias.

As usual, Jordan seemed younger in these surroundings. He was anxious to visit the turret that was his special retreat. Anna Louisa kept it stocked with chips, soda pop, shortbread cookies, and a variety of children's picture books. Sven had introduced puzzles, play dough, and dominoes.

"Can I be 'scused now, Papa, pwease?" he entreated.

In answer, Sven took up the Lundgren family Bible that had

belonged to his grandfather, the first Sven to read English, and put on his little black-rimmed half-glasses. Looking at Jordan over the rims, he asked, "Well, what shall it be?"

"Daniel!" cried Jordan.

In resonant tones Sven read the ancient account of faith and courage to the family around the table. As the drama of the great hero unfolded, Dennis was pleased to feel a residue of Daniel's strength of purpose. A peace always settled on him in this house, a sense of basic rightness, as though everything was exactly as it should be. He didn't see how Annalisse could wish for any other life.

Noting his son's reverence toward his grandfather, he wondered whether Jordan regarded his own father as sufficiently patriarchal. Would he tolerate a nightly scripture reading by him? Probably not.

Jordan raced upstairs at the conclusion of the reading.

"How's the practice going, Dennis?" Sven asked, closing the old book.

"Frustratingly at the moment." Dennis helped himself to another piece of peach pie. "We've got a real nasty case involving toxic waste, and I can't get the State Department of Natural Resources down to look at the site."

"Toxic waste, huh? What specifically?"

Dennis outlined the situation for Sven, aware that his wife had checked out of the conversation. She was staring out over the cacti at the vegetable garden, twining a lock of hair around her finger.

"I don't like the sound of those threats, Dennis. I think you did the right thing to bring the family up here."

Anna Louisa spoke up, "It seems to me I read somewhere that the Ozarks plateau is limestone. Porous."

Dennis nodded. "Lots of underground water. That's what's worrying me. You'd think the DNR would be down on Amalgamated like lightning. Obviously, the company's got some connection with pull in that agency."

He could feel the fondness in his father-in-law's voice as he suggested, "The state of Missouri's not an entirely incorruptible body. Who funds the DNR?"

"The state legislature."

"Anyone at Amalgamated with pull in the state legislature?"

"I've thought of that, but I haven't researched it yet. I know our state senator was pretty influential in bringing the company into Cherokee County. I hate to think he'd be party to something like this, but my guess is that he might be."

"Is that Senator Cavanaugh you're talking about?" Sven asked.

"Yeah. The guy who put me up for prosecutor. Makes things kind of awkward."

Annalisse had tuned in at the mention of Cavanaugh's name. "But you don't think he's behind those threats, Dennis? I mean, he was horrified! Do you honestly think he's that good an actor?"

"At this point, I wouldn't put it past him. I don't trust anyone. We may never know who's behind the threats. But I wouldn't be at all surprised if it's Jesse Cavanaugh who's putting pressure on the DNR."

"Why didn't you mention this before?" his wife asked.

"I just kind of pieced things together on the way up here. There's got to be some DNR liaison with the senate committee that funds them. He may be in Amalgamated's pocket. May have been for some time."

"But would the senate committee tell Cavanaugh?"

"That's just it. He's chairman of the Senate Natural Resources Committee."

"I didn't know that."

"He's the one who got the Army Corps of Engineers down there to build all those dams that created the lakes on the southern end of the county. After Amalgamated, tourism is our biggest industry."

"Sounds like Cavanaugh is a pretty powerful fellow," Sven remarked. "What's the impact of this DNR investigation likely to be on Amalgamated?"

"That depends on what they've got hidden. If they've been hiding toxic waste all over the county and have to finance a cleanup, it could be pretty costly. I don't know how healthy they are financially."

"Well, I guess you don't need my advice, but I think you've probably got hold of the right end of the stick. Move carefully, though. Somebody wants to play nasty."

"It's not likely to do my career a whole lot of good if I'm right, either. Amalgamated is the biggest employer downstate. Plus, I can kiss the county prosecutor's job good-bye."

Sven grinned at him. "I've never known you to run from a challenge, Dennis. You'll land on your feet. You always do."

Dennis felt heartened by the confidence his father-in-law had in him. Worry had gnawed at him during the trip, making him wonder which way to turn. Was his first duty to Lonnie and the citizens of the county, or was it to his family and his paycheck? It wasn't as clear-cut a situation as he'd at first perceived.

Sven turned to his daughter and asked, "Annalisse, do you remember Pete Thorsen?"

"Chris's dad?" She turned away from the window. "The one who had the trucking company?"

"Right. They moved to Madison last year. There was a big to-do with the State Department of Transportation. Payoffs, the whole bit. Your friend Paul Piersen uncovered it—he works for a TV station in Madison now. Maybe your mother wrote you about it."

"No, she didn't." He had her attention now. "What happened?"

Grinning at his daughter, he pushed himself away from the table. "It's quite a story. How about going out on the porch for a bit? It'll be a little cooler, now that the sun's going down."

So the party wandered obediently out to the vast Victorian porch, and Annalisse sat next to her father on the white-painted swing to hear his tale. Dennis settled himself on the first step with his back against the porch rail and talked sows with his mother-in-law, who sat opposite him in a lawn chair.

It was a pleasant evening, a cooling, quiet breeze barely stirring the lilac and forsythia bushes that lined the porch rail. There was the distant sound of mowing, and nearby, a quarrelsome pair of blue jays. The sun was setting behind a glorious wash of orange and indigo that painted the sky over the green field.

"Sven," Anna Louisa said in the tone of voice that registers sudden remembrance. "Did you remember to tell Davey Long about the fence?"

Dennis changed positions, turning so he could see his wife and father-in-law. Apparently, the story of the scandal had wound down, for Annalisse had slipped back into her abstraction. Her face looked gentle, wistful, as she stared out at the horizon, blocking out the talk around her as though she were a girl again, wrapped up in secret dreams.

Fingering a branch of forsythia, he listened with half an ear to the fence discussion and watched Annalisse out of the corner of his eye. He wondered what visions she was conjuring up. Her posture was slumped, her expression contorted in what looked like worry.

Annalisse's face was only partially familiar tonight. He knew the skin, the bone, and the color of her eyes, but the essence of Annalisse remained separate, still hidden from him, shrouded by the scrim of her unknown past. It came to him that he had filled in the details of her life from his own imagination.

Annalisse had never been fully his. Something quiet and patient in her had stayed untouched, unopened, as though she were waiting. Waiting for the prince with the sun in his hands?

Turning away, he too watched the sunset and felt the peace of the evening drain away. His problems descended upon him with their full weight.

Chapter Fifteen

Annalisse left Dennis to help her mother with the dishes and walked down to her old fort. She was so carried away by memories that it was almost impossible to remain in the present. All she could feel was a compulsion to get away from everyone, especially her father, before they read what must be going through her mind.

Though nothing more than a hollow tree crawling with vines and weeds, her fort had once been a sanctuary to her, and she was still fond of coming here. There was a fallen log to sit on and the sun's last trails of glory to contemplate.

When Jules initiated her into the intimacies of marriage, that first night in the Hotel Georges V in Paris, Annalisse realized that she had been right. The heat and urgency of their lovemaking seared them together with magical alchemy, as though sealing them against the universe. She never could have survived losing this through a casual affair. They even slept bound together in the deepest of embraces, and she sensed that he was as completed as she was. The yin and the yang. Inseparable for the eternities.

When they went home to Vienna, they often put off dinner until midnight, as they returned from the day apart newly hungry for each other rather than for food. Annalisse had never known this depth of feeling. When she had to be parted from him because of performances in Venice, Copenhagen, and London, the telephone just hadn't been enough. Body and soul she had ached with the deprivation. As well as their lovemaking, she missed accompanying him during his preparations for his debut. She wondered if anyone in the history of time had ever loved each other as much as she and Jules.

―⁓―

Dennis gave a heavy sigh and went in to his mother-in-law, who was clearing the table. She had exchanged her shoes for rubber flip-flops and was heaping dishes onto an aluminum cart while she hummed a cheerful snatch of "Clair de Lune." He had no idea how to begin his questions.

"Let me get that," he offered as she started to stoop to retrieve Jordan's fork underneath the table. Getting down on his knees, he discovered half a roll and some errant peas. "How do you think Annalisse looks?" he ventured from under the table.

Anna Louisa waited until he reemerged. "Is something wrong?"

Dennis shrugged. "I don't really know. She's been crying a lot lately, but she won't tell me why."

His mother-in-law looked down at her dish cart and wheeled it into the kitchen. Dennis followed.

"She's a little pale," Anna Louisa acknowledged. "I've never known Annalisse to be weepy. And she didn't eat much. Perhaps it's just hormones."

Dennis considered this. The suggestion of hormones seemed to keep coming up. But no, there was all her weird behavior to account for. She was not at all as she had been during her pregnancy with Jordan. "No, that may be making things worse, but I have the definite sense that she's grieving. But she won't speak of it. And she suddenly hates where we live. Talks about Vienna and the opera. Latinos and Tchaikovsky. I mean, I never knew she had any interest in such things."

Filling the sink with hot, sudsy water, Anna Louisa began scraping the dishes from the cart into the kitchen garbage, which would eventually go into the compost heap.

"Annalisse was a celebrated concert pianist at one time, but you must have known that."

Dennis registered this information in silence. How could he not know such a thing? The implications rocked his world. Her talent must be an enormous part of who she really was. But what in the world had caused her to keep it hidden from him? "I had no idea," he said finally. "I've never even heard her play the piano."

She looked up at him quickly, scanning his face. Apparently registering its total lack of comprehension, she said, "Annalisse was very good. She performed all over Europe."

Now Dennis was completely winded. Europe? Annalisse? The piece he was missing was assuming huge proportions. He didn't know his wife at all. "Why doesn't she play anymore?"

Plunging the dishes into the soapy water, Anna Louisa answered, "Maybe you ought to ask her."

"She's stonewalling me. That's what's so frustrating. I keep catching her crying . . . in the laundry room in the middle of the night, in the closet, in the basement. But she won't ever explain herself. She just pushes me away."

His mother-in-law washed the dishes with careful deliberation. Finally, she paused to look at him, worry between her brows. "She's never told you," she stated flatly.

"What?"

"It's not my place to tell you anything if she hasn't. But you're going to have to get her to tell you about Jules."

His pulse exploded into a wild hammering. Pulling a chair around from the kitchen table, he straddled it blindly. The name was like a blow to the solar plexus. He had been right. There was someone. "What happened to him?"

"I can't tell you any more, Dennis. It's Annalisse's life. She needs to be the one to tell you from her own perspective, in her own way. But she needs to tell you. I'll speak to Sven."

"How will that help?"

"He's always had a special bond with Annalisse. He knows how to bring her around. She's like a skittish filly."

"Annalisse?" It was out before he could stop himself. He was fearful now. How much more was there he didn't know about his wife? What had happened to Jules? To her career? No wonder she had been pining away in Blue Creek. His hands began to shake.

Turning to him, Anna Louisa wiped her hands on her apron. "Dennis, you and Annalisse have been married more than four years. You are expecting your second child. This much I will tell you. What's past is past. Annalisse needs *you* now. You're her knight in shining armor. I have known that from the first time I saw you together."

"She's going through a crisis, Anna Louisa. And she doesn't want to share it with me."

"She will. You may be the only one who can help her through it."

Standing, he clenched his fists at his side. "Why all this secrecy? Why will no one tell me what's going on?"

"It's not my secret to tell, Dennis. This all has to be handled very delicately. She's your wife, but she's my daughter. I owe her discretion, but I think she also owes you an explanation. Like I said, I'll speak to Sven."

"Can you tell me his last name, at least?"

"Kramar. Jules Kramar."

Dennis stared at the old green linoleum floor, his eye tracing a pattern of cracks resembling a spider's web. What had been only supposition before was now confirmed. The ghost had a name. And he was powerful enough that Anna Louisa wanted to be circumspect about him. What if he was still alive? What if all this time there had been another man in Annalisse's life? The idea was so startling it was like trying to change the order of the seasons or the pattern of the stars.

Without any idea at all of what he was doing, he stood up and began to dry the dishes.

Annalisse had to wait a long time for the spell of Paris and Vienna to die. Slowly, it receded, leaving spiritual homesickness in its wake. On the way back to the house, she was still sniffing and wiping her eyes. She couldn't allow Dennis to see that anything was wrong, for she knew she could tell him no lies in this house.

She thought about the girl she had been growing up in this place she had so longed to get away from. Her magic carpet had been the piano. She had sat wrestling with Beethoven, for a while unaware that there was anything else in the world. She had desperate need of that ability to escape now.

When she sat down at the scarred ebony upright, a gift from the original Sven to his wife, she realized just how long ago her girl-hood had been. Her hands on the keys now looked more like her mother's hands with the tendons like sharp cords radiating from the wrist.

But an old book of hers—Chopin, as it happened—was waiting, open across the front of the piano, as though she had only been out of the room or away at school. Fortunately, No. 6 was one of his more manageable Études, and so she began to play it, slowly, tentatively, amazed at how much she remembered. Its nocturnal mood was familiar, but there were nuances in it now that she didn't recall. What could the girl she had been have known of this particular kind of sadness?

The world around her dropped away before she had played it through twice. Here was an old friend who had become wise over the years. Not just wise—knowing, compassionate. Vaguely aware that Dennis had entered the room, she didn't stop. She played the Étude again and then again, delving a little deeper each time.

Chapter Sixteen

Dennis watched the back of his wife's neck as she played, dipping to the keyboard and then leaning back in some kind of musical trance. The blonde hair had parted, leaving her neck bare and sweet. In the past, he might have gone up and kissed her there, casually, taking it for granted that her neck was his to kiss, that she existed in the world, there on that piano bench, solely for him to love. But Annalisse's neck and everything about her was now strange to him. She was playing the piano with a skill completely foreign to the woman he thought he knew. Why had he never wondered why they had hauled her piano with them every time they had moved? On top of that, the piece she was playing was deeply disturbing. The melody was a sad one, made more so by the incessant, running accompaniment of the right hand. He received the impression of someone trying to escape an overwhelming haunting. The sadness deepened, overtaking the runner until he resigned himself, slowing his steps and finally giving up altogether.

Jules Kramar. Where was he now? What had he done to

Annalisse? And what were you supposed to do when you found out your wife was hung up on someone from her past?

Annalisse's music flowed through the semidarkness of the well-loved room, lit only by a single standard lamp that threw long, eerie shadows onto the walls. Anna's paintings hung in the shadows, their brightness muted. Even the fiery hue of her roses on the piano was reduced to putty.

Dennis closed his eyes, blocking out the room. Whoever had written that music knew about anguish, all right. But the composer's anguish was spelled out as a kind of spiritual claustrophobia; Dennis's was just the opposite. In matters of the heart, his seemed to be the fear of opening doors, of finding a nasty surprise lurking beyond his illusions. Here he was, venturing into the unknown, treacherous territory. He didn't know if he had the courage to go further, to keep going until he had found all of the truth. But one thing was sure—there was no going back to his illusory Eden. His Eve had a past, and she'd brought it with her into the garden. Between this and the dioxin, he'd bitten hard into the apple.

Dennis smelled the burnt grease and onions of The Grill, noisy with students taking refuge from the blizzard outside. Jill's large gray eyes were fiery with an almost imbalanced excitement.

"This is really going to be big, Dennis. The biggest yet." In her outsized pea coat, she resembled a waif. "We're going to Indiana to picket Midland Steel. It still dumps into the lake. The CEO lives on the North Shore. We're going to picket his house, too."

"It's private property, Jill. The police will haul you off."

"We're going to tip off the media. There'll be television cameras there. We've seen a lot of Green sympathy on the North Shore, Dennis, you know that. We're going to make his life a misery."

"I can't see the execs and matrons of Winnetka and Lake Forest turning on one of their own. They're much more likely to turn on the movement. They don't like their privileged lives threatened."

"What's made you so patronizing?"

Dennis had been leaning back in his chair, but now he brought it down on all four legs and, putting his elbows on the table, asked, "I suppose Schwartz thought of this." Schwartz was the movement's liaison from University of Chicago and the bane of his existence.

"No." She didn't look like an orphan anymore. Her features had assumed a marble coldness. "I did. I suppose you've got a better idea."

Ignoring her sarcasm, he reached across the table for her hand. She closed it in a fist and withdrew it from him.

"Look, it's nothing personal," he said. "But don't you think we've gotten away from our objective? It's Green*peace*. Schwartz is on some kind of a power trip. All he wants is blood—anyone's blood. How is that going to positively affect the movement?"

"It has a way of making people listen to what you have to say," she observed coolly. "Since we've gotten together with Schwartz, we've had a lot of news coverage."

"Let's back up a minute, okay?" Dennis leaned toward her. "What are we trying to sell, anyway, Barry Schwartz or a Green planet?"

She grinned suddenly. "You're jealous of him, aren't you?"

Paying no outward attention to this, he continued, "We need to appeal to people's consciences, not alienate them. Do you seriously think we're going to convert people to a Green lifestyle by acting like a bunch of hippies from the sixties?"

"I'm angry, Dennis! Angry about what we're doing to this planet. It's not a legacy I want to leave to my children!"

"But what good is anger if we let it off all over the place like a loose cannon? We need a strategy."

Jill leaned back and crossed her arms over her chest. "I'm listening."

"I think we ought to get into fundraising. We need to look into the projects that people who think the way we do are financing. Alternative energy seems the most pressing need to me."

Jill rolled her eyes. "As if a few college students could raise any money."

"Hold on! We could start a nationwide campaign of college students using the Internet. Form a charity. We could raise serious money that way and call attention to worthy projects. It would be a more responsible action. What's wrong with that, besides the fact that Schwartz didn't think of it?"

"You really hate him, don't you?" Jill said, grinning.

"Are you sleeping with him?"

"Maybe." Her gaze challenged him. "That's what all this is about, isn't it? You think you have some kind of claim on me."

Dennis looked at her in pained wonder. "Evidently, I don't."

"You're such an innocent, Dennis. So pathetically naïve." She got up and left him sitting alone at the table.

❧

There really wasn't any difference between the Dennis then and the Dennis now. He was still pathetically naïve. Annalisse, his compass, was no longer pointing north. She was the opposite of everything he'd thought her. She was passionate, secretive, unhappy. The map of his future looked as undecipherable as a backwards image in the mirror. In a word, he was lost.

Chapter Seventeen

Annalisse, how about taking a walk with me down to the fort?" her father invited the following morning after a breakfast of whole wheat pancakes and bacon.

Great. Here it comes. Annalisse's breakfast turned into an uncomfortable weight in her stomach.

As they approached the hollow tree, he chuckled. "I remember all those hot summer evenings I used to find you here, curled up with a book. Who was that author you used to be so fond of?"

"There were several," she replied, inspecting the decaying elm. In spite of her trepidation, her father's words and the sharp, earthy smell of the old bark revived long-forgotten adventures—heart-stopping chases across the moors, East Indian intrigue, and Grecian idylls interrupted by terror and suspense. "Daphne DuMaurier, Mary Stewart, Victoria Holt . . . I haven't read them in years."

"Ah, yes. You were the one who was big on adventures in exotic places. Louisa liked animal stories, and I remember catching Marta with D. H. Lawrence. What do you read these days?"

"Biographies," Annalisse answered, sitting down on the fallen log. "George Sand, at the moment."

"Ah, yes. Chopin's mistress." He sat down next to her on a semi-solid bit of log, and she could feel him studying her profile. "I'll never forget our trip to Paris to hear you play Chopin. It's one of the high points of my life." He reached over and tousled her hair as he used to when she was a child. The action helped her to relax. This was only Papa, after all, who had always loved her unconditionally. "I heard you playing last night. Do you do it much anymore?"

"Was I that bad?"

"No. Not bad at all. I just wondered, with Jordan and the farm and everything, if you'd been able to keep up."

How did he do it? If ever he thought something was bothering her, he had the unerring instinct of a carpenter with an ear to the wall, tap, tap, tapping until he found the hollow spot: the problem.

"I don't play often," she told him. "It takes too much intensity."

Sven stretched his legs out in front of him and folded his arms across his chest. "In Paris I kept trying to remind myself that this was the same determined little girl who sat at the piano with long blonde braids down her back, struggling with Beethoven long after her bedtime."

Annalisse gave a half-hearted grin. "It wasn't Beethoven I was struggling with, it was Marta. And myself. I was determined I was going to catch up with her and pass her. It wasn't fair. She hardly ever practiced."

"Well, you did pass her in the end. And then some."

"Only because she quit."

"No, I'd say you really hit your stride once you went to college and met Jules."

Annalisse felt herself grow hot.

Her father evidently decided to switch tactics. "Are you going to teach your children an instrument?"

"I haven't decided," Annalisse replied. She went back and forth in her mind about this very thing every time she passed her piano. It had become almost a reproach to her. Did she really want to inflict a child of hers with an obsession with music and all that it entailed?

Sven nodded and appeared engrossed in the toes of his cowboy boots. He was silent too long. Looking up at him, she felt goaded into irritation. "Why do you always circle around things like a vulture? Why don't you just ask me straight out about Jules?"

"You need to tell Dennis about him, Annalisse."

Her heart sank sickeningly into her middle. "How do you know I haven't?"

"He was asking your mother questions last night. It seems he's worried about you. From what he said, it was pretty clear to your mother that you've been obsessing about Jules. She was shocked to realize that you had never told him anything." He looked at her full in the face, his bushy white eyebrows drawn together. "He didn't even know you were a pianist! How could you keep such an enormous part of yourself from your husband?"

She picked up a handful of earth and clutched it tightly in her hand. "What did she tell him?"

"Only his name. She said the rest had to come from you."

With some bitterness, she replied, "You should have made me stick to reading *National Geographic*." Dropping the dirt, she dusted her hands. "I think a lot of harm comes from reading romances. They don't go deep enough, or broad enough, or high enough. They end before real life begins. In real life, people hide things. They hide themselves. I didn't really know Jules. And Dennis doesn't know me at all."

Smiling at her gently, he asked, "Whose fault is that? Why

shouldn't a vibrant marriage be an endless process of discovery and redefinition? Do you really think God intended that we should stay stranded in our twenties in mind and body? It's not even logical!"

"But what will Dennis think when he knows?"

"Do you love him?"

"I wouldn't have married him if I didn't love him. But it's different from the way I loved Jules."

"No, your music was a special bond between you and Jules. I understand that. But Dennis is a different kettle of fish. More staying power. I know he loves you. And he would never do what Jules did." He leaned over and whispered in her ear, "Trust him a little more."

"Trust doesn't come easily to me, Papa."

"That's understandable. But this is your husband of four years we're talking about. I think he's mentally sound and committed. Are you?"

She squirmed under his words. "Maybe I never should have married him. Maybe it was too soon."

"Why do you think that? Is there anything else wrong?"

She hesitated, trying to put her experience into words. "I'm having flashbacks," she admitted, tears starting in her eyes. "Papa, it's terrible. I cut off my feelings and my music back then. I didn't want to feel. It was like everything happened in another life. It *was* another life! So hellish, so hard to believe."

Closing her eyes, she saw the torment in her first husband's eyes. The tears rolled down her cheeks.

"Obviously, I've never come to terms with my feelings, Papa. I feel the tragedy as though it's happening today. At the time, I remember I was numb. I think I've stayed numb until now."

Her father put his hand on her shoulder and searched her eyes. "It was the only way you could handle it and stay sane. But I worried when you came down with that double pneumonia that you might actually die of a broken heart. I guess I thought you'd processed things during your illness."

She shook her head and kneaded her hands together. "I just couldn't. I couldn't dwell on the pain. I kept escaping into my work at Scripps. But I worked too hard, not sleeping or eating, which led to the pneumonia. And then I kept escaping into sleep. But now, I can't escape. The flashbacks just keep coming. Even in my sleep. Dr. Gregory diagnosed it as post-traumatic stress disorder."

Her father thought this over. "That makes sense. Your nervous system can't subvert these emotions any longer, Annalisse. I think you got to a place where you were safe, and then all this grief sneaked up on you while your guard was down."

"The doctor told me that the only way out was through. He said I needed to talk about it, to get it out, but it would hurt Dennis tremendously, Papa. He's already carrying a load of disillusionment. I can't add to it, believe me. It's killing his idealism that someone's poisoned his Garden of Eden." She paused. "I married him for that idealism. He's always been so full of hope. So dynamic and positive."

He took one of her hands in his large one and squeezed it. "I love you, honey, and I wish you could stay here in Burnett and talk it out with me, but I think you owe it to Dennis to let him help you. I've a notion that he's stronger than you think."

Even the thought of opening up to Dennis made her panic. Her father regarded her solemnly. "The dead opposite of Jules, in fact. And, much as I like him, he's got some growing up to do as well. This earth ceased to be Eden long ago."

"But don't you see? Everything's coming apart for him all at once!"

"It's not fair for you to lean on another person for hope, Annalisse. It's not fair to Dennis, and it wasn't fair of Jules." He put an arm around her and pulled her against his chest. "You were taught a long time ago there's only one true source for hope, Annalisse. Marrying Dennis wasn't a mistake, even if your motive was a little skewed. He's a fine man, Annalisse. You need to give him a chance. You need to give the two of you a chance. And the first step is getting this business with Jules cleared up."

He stood and looked down at her with his wise smile. "Your marriage to Jules wasn't healthy, Annalisse. You're right. You *didn't* know him, as it turned out. Don't let those circumstances cripple what has all the makings of a lifelong relationship. Not just for your sake but for Jordan's, the baby's, and Dennis's."

He made it sound so simple. But it came to her then that she didn't really know Dennis, either. She couldn't bear to disillusion him further about who he thought she was. How did she even know he would stay with her when he found out the truth? His life was being harrowed up completely. Would he run from her and Blue Creek with the same cynicism he had left Africa?

Helpless tears streamed down her face.

"Annalisse," her father said. "Listen, honey, I know this is hard. But you've got to buck up. You can't help what's happening to you, but you can find your way out of it. You look like Camille in the last stages of consumption, for crying out loud. You're the woman who conquered Chopin! You're the woman who was hired by the world-famous Scripps Institute! You were accepted at Stanford from a little tiny burg in Wisconsin! Where's my fighter?"

"I'll find her again, Papa," she said. "There's more at stake here than you realize. It's complicated." She straightened her back, trying to be the person she was raised to be. "Jules and my music changed me forever. I can't go back to who I was before, and I'm just now realizing it." She looked up at her father, a giant against the sky, and became a little shy. "You have to understand. My past is trapping me like the mud in the fields after a two-day storm. But Dr. Gregory said there's no way out but through. According to him, I've *got* to feel these feelings that have been trapped inside so long. Think of it as my personal Gethsemane."

"The Savior went through His alone, Annalisse. But you don't have to. You have Him. I think you've forgotten your Twenty-third Psalm."

She had. Her relationship with Jules had never had a spiritual dimension. So it wasn't there for her in her memories.

"I'll leave you now," her father said. "Please think about what I've said."

She watched him walk away, sternly reasoning with herself. Then, when she least expected it, memory descended on her like darkness.

It was a week before Jules's scheduled debut, when Annalisse burst through the door of their flat, anxious to tell him about the first bit of praise Herr Hochmann had given her: "You should have been born an Austrian. Maybe it's there in your blood somewhere. I can't account for your extraordinary talent any other way."

She was disappointed to find the flat was empty. Walking from the sitting room/kitchen into the small bedroom, she removed her coat and threw it on the bed. She rubbed her hands together for warmth. It was really bitter outside. Hard to believe it was almost spring. Where in the world could Jules be?

When he finally stumbled in, staggeringly drunk for the first time since she'd known him, he threw himself on the couch and put his head in his hands.

"Jules! What in the world is wrong with you?"

"I thought I could run away," he mumbled. "But they've caught up with me. It's the publicity for the Tchaikovsky. Somehow word made its way to LA."

Alarm jangled through her like a fire bell. "Who? Who's caught up with you?"

"Come here, Lisse." He looked up, and she saw a face so ravaged she almost didn't recognize it. *He'd crashed.*

Going over to the couch, she drew him instinctively into her arms. Before she knew it they were making love. But there was no joy in it. Only desperation.

Later, when they were lying in each other's arms, he said, "I can't go. All hell would break loose, and it would be the end of everything. But if I don't go, he'll die."

"Who will die?"

Jules shook his head and sat abruptly. "No. I'm not going to discuss it. There's still a chance everything will be all right. I just have to believe it, that's all." He turned to her. "You do believe music is the most important thing in the world, don't you, Lisse?"

"No." She shook her head. "Love is. Music is an expression of love. It even mimics it."

Jules thought. "I suppose you are right." He hung his head again.

At that moment, Annalisse's cell phone rang. Resolved to let it ring, she stayed beside Jules.

"Get that," he said. "It must be your parents. They're the only ones who ever call."

It was her father, more agitated than she'd ever heard him. "Annalisse. Oh, thank the Lord I got you. You must fly home immediately. Use the American Express I gave you for emergencies."

Still winded from the blow Jules had dealt her, she sank to the floor. "What's wrong, Papa? You haven't told me what's wrong!"

"It's your mother. She's had a bad heart attack and might not make it. If she does, they're going to have to do surgery, even though it's a risk. If you want to see her alive, you've got to come immediately."

Sven had taken Dennis to the county seat with him that morning to sit in on a case he was trying and then out to lunch. Dennis tried his questions on his father-in-law over a good steak and baked potato.

"Will you tell me anything about this Jules Kramar?" he asked.

"Just that you need to discuss him with Annalisse."

"How do you propose that I bring it up without sounding like an insensitive clod?"

"I think maybe she'll bring it up, Dennis. I had a talk with her. Have a little more patience. She's really going through a crisis, and she may need your help coming out of it."

"Do you really think so?"

"I do. It's not her fault. She isn't doing this to hurt you. In fact, the reason she has kept her feelings from you is actually to protect you, believe it or not."

This intelligence confused him completely. But Sven was firm, and Dennis had to be content with the little he'd said. But that evening after dinner when Jordan had gone up to his turret, Annalisse showed no disposition to talk to him or anyone else. Instead, she made her way to the piano again, playing the same piece, which he now saw was Chopin. He waited in the parlor for her to finish playing. It seemed hours. He tried reading American Bar Association magazines, but he was so unsettled by the music that he couldn't concentrate.

Finally, getting up from the piano, she walked from the room like a sleepwalker, leaving him sitting on the couch. She hadn't even realized he was in the room. He heard her ascend the staircase.

For a while, he just sat there, wondering if he should go confront her, his jealousy about his rival building. There were so many things he didn't understand. Finally, going into the kitchen, he banged out of the house onto the porch and down the path. After stumbling about, he found an old hollow, vine-covered tree with a convenient log for sitting. It was dark now. Almost as dark as his thoughts. He probed his pain with questions.

This place felt like some sort of refuge. Had Annalisse come here as a child and looked at this same summer sky? What had she dreamed of? Adventure? Excitement?

In light of what he now knew, he thought perhaps she had. She must have had visions of getting away from the farm, away from all this solid security with its vast, uncluttered horizons and perfect rhythm of seasons. She'd gone away to Stanford, hadn't she? And traveled Europe as a concert pianist. Why in the world had she chosen to marry him? They'd planned to live in San Diego. Would she, after all, have been happier there? Had he ever really asked her? Or had he just assumed that she would want what he wanted? Why had this woman who seemed to be two people given up her career when it obviously meant so much to her?

Just how many things had he assumed along the way these past four years? Certainly that he, Dennis Childs, was the great love in her life. Why had he been so sure there was no one else? Had she actually led him to believe that, or was it only his own fantastic ego?

He was beginning to realize that he couldn't trust his memory. What he'd experienced and what had actually happened appeared to be two entirely different things. Where had Jules been on their wedding day? Had he known of it? Had he cared?

And Annalisse? What had she been thinking? He stood and

began to walk. The night air was cool and caressing. Their September wedding night had been much like this one. Only there had been a moon. A great, magical, silver moon.

Now there was only this mocking, dim sliver of light.

"I'm wallowing," he said to the soybeans. "Wallowing, for crying out loud."

Annalisse felt oddly fragmented here in this house, unable to bridge the gap between the child-Annalisse, Jules's Annalisse, and Dennis's Annalisse. There was no continuum inside of her; she felt jerked from one role to another.

It had always seemed faintly absurd to have separate beds. But this was the room she had shared with Marta growing up, and their single beds remained just as they had been, covered with duvets dusted with spring flowers. The first time they'd visited here after their marriage, she'd been embarrassed. "I'm sorry, but I guess this is where we have to sleep. Do you mind?"

Dennis had laughed and said, "Not at all. But would you feel terribly wicked if we slept in one bed?"

Annalisse was sharply reminded of the distance between them right now and didn't suppose they'd sleep in one bed on this trip, even if it hadn't been for the baby. She didn't know whether to be sorry or not. Her emotions were so bound up in Jules, she felt she had been unfaithful to Dennis.

Sitting on the edge of her bed holding her nightgown in her lap, she stared at the bookcase full of riding and piano trophies without seeing them. Perhaps, after all, she was neither wife nor child at the moment. The truth was that she was stranded somewhere in between, still coping with the emotions of a twenty-year-old, still trying to make sense out of a world gone wrong. She wasn't Sven's daughter, Dennis's wife, or Jordan's mother. She was alone, simply Annalisse, drifting through an unknown vastness.

But her father had reminded her that she was not alone. It had been years since she'd prayed. Opening her childhood Bible that sat by her bed where she'd left it before going away to college, she read the twenty-third Psalm. She hadn't completely forgotten it. In the last year, she'd begun teaching it to Jordan when he had his nightmares, just as Papa had done for her and her sisters. Her mind caught on the third verse: *He restoreth my soul. . . .*

How she needed that restoration! But her soul was so enmeshed with Jules's that she didn't have the first idea how to untangle it. Lying on the bed, she curled around her and Dennis's child, the fruit of their love, and prayed silently for help.

Must she give up all these memories, painful though they were? As long as Jules was still alive in her, how could she kill him? He was part of who she was, and besides, she was the only vessel left for his remembrance. What exactly did she want to be restored *to*?

❦

The next morning, Dennis decided that he had to break through the impasse. Leaving Jordan with Anna Louisa, he drove with Annalisse in the ancient Lundgren pickup to a nearby lake. The inflated orange kayak was in the back of the pickup, and their lunch was between them in an Igloo lunch bucket.

The lake was crowded on the August afternoon, fringed with pickups, heat shimmering off the water. The colorful crowd dispersed in powerboats, sailboats, canoes, and kayaks.

Releasing the tailgate of the truck, Dennis eased their own kayak onto the grass and pulled it down to the shore. Annalisse followed with their lunch, and moments later they had launched themselves onto the blue lake.

They commenced rowing at a leisurely pace. "Did you come here much?" he asked his wife.

"At least once a week in the summer. It wasn't so crowded then. Marta and I used to ride up here on horseback."

"This okay?" he asked after another bout of rowing which took them into a semiprotected lagoon.

"Perfect. This is where we always ate our lunch. Lucky Lagoon, we called it."

"Annalisse . . ."

"Yes?" Handing him the sunblock, she turned her back to him.

Dennis squirted the lotion absently into his hand and began applying it to his wife's soft white skin. Her back was studded with familiar moles—small white ones, middle-sized brown ones, and the large black flat one that he watched for her in case it should turn cancerous. A breeze ruffled her hair, and he heard the distant shouts of children echoing across the water. He'd brought her out here, away from everyone and everything specifically to make her feel something, to react, but now he couldn't do it. Everything in him shrank from it.

"Do you think we should buy a boat?" he asked, finally.

She looked at him over her shoulder. "What?"

"A boat. You know. Gregg and Cindy have one—a little Bass Tracker."

And so they talked about boats. It was an awkward, first-date sort of conversation. When they had more or less depleted the subject, Annalisse opened the lunch bucket. She handed him a deviled ham sandwich.

Biting into it, he watched his wife select a peach and pare it absently as she squinted over the water.

"Are you getting unwound?" she asked him.

"Thoroughly," he lied. Next they ate the cake Anna Louisa had packed. Or at least he did. Annalisse only pretended. "But I must admit I'll be glad when we get back to our bed."

She grinned across at him with a slight blush. Was it possible she missed him?

This knowledge pierced him pleasurably, and then the next minute, there it was: the question he had to ask, the one that would make her react.

"Annalisse. Why haven't you ever told me about Jules?"

She stared at him dumbly, her face stricken and white. Then the blood rushed into it, and she ducked her head, collecting picnic refuse with shaking hands, stowing it automatically in the Igloo. He waited, bridling with great difficulty an impulse to rush in with an apology or a "never mind."

"He isn't anything to do with us, Dennis," she said finally, her voice weary.

Dennis took a deep breath and looked at her unflinchingly. "You loved him. You still love him. He has something to do with your music and your misery in Blue Creek."

She glanced wildly at the water and then back to his face. He read her panic. This time there was nowhere to run.

"It was over before I met you, Dennis," she said tightly. "I swear."

"It's not over, Annalisse. Don't try telling me it's over. You're miserable with me."

Turning away, she began picking at the seams of the kayak. "I'm not. It's true, I've been a little emotional lately. Probably because of my crazy hormones. But believe me, it's not because I'm miserable with you."

"Then why do you cry all the time?" Dennis asked, trying to

curb his impatience. "Why do you go around like you're only half alive?"

Her eyes looked at him, wide and desperate.

"C'mon, Annalisse," he pushed. "Give me a little credit. Your piano . . . he's a musician, right? Maybe a violinist. Tchaikovsky, right? Just tell me this. Who *is* Jules? Where does he fit into your life?"

Turning away, she began fumbling with her clothes, trying to put on her t-shirt. It was inside out. "He was my first husband. We were married less than a year."

Everything inside Dennis contracted at this blow. *Her husband! She'd had another husband and never told him?* He felt sick, as though he had just been dropped from a skyscraper. A silence ensued as he hit bottom, slowly realizing that his world would never be the same.

The woman with him in the kayak was a complete stranger. This corrosive revelation was acid, destroying the image he had carried of her since that day on Sam's boat. He was physically ill at her betrayal. Looking away from her, he felt something akin to panic. *How could he ever trust her again?* She carried his child! A symbol of sacred joining. And now, he wasn't even sure he wanted to know her.

"I'm sorry, Dennis. I should have told you right away. But I was in denial when I met you. Trying to forget everything about my former life."

"That's no excuse, Annalisse," he said wearily. Then he looked at her, his eyes narrowed in anger. "Do you realize how this feels? For five years you've been betraying me, every day of our marriage! You've been playing a part. You're not the Annalisse that you pretended to be." In disgust, he closed his eyes, unable to bear the sight of her stricken face. Still not opening them, he said, his voice stiff with anger, "If you had really loved me, you would have told me about Jules. And your career—do you realize I had to find out about that from your mother? Two huge, defining parts of who you are, and I never knew. How long had things been over when I met you?"

"A year."

A year. A measly year. He opened his eyes slowly and watched her trying to avoid looking at him. "So, when you married me, you were hoping I'd provide a little diversion? Dennis, the clown. Dennis, the chaser of rainbows. Clearly, it hasn't worked."

"I think I've only just started grieving, Dennis . . ."

Before she could finish, he rushed in with the question that consumed him. "How in the world can I ever trust you again?"

Annalisse was silent, looking out over the water. She might have been cast in marble. Finally, she responded, her voice lifeless. "I don't know, Dennis. Perhaps you shouldn't. I'm damaged goods, and I've hurt you terribly. I know how you feel about imperfection. You'll be wanting a divorce."

With this declaration, his head reeled and his nausea increased. Divorce? Did he want a divorce? All he knew was that now he wanted as much distance as possible from this woman. To take it all in. To figure it out.

She wasn't made of marble. Tears had started down her cheeks, and she dabbed at them futilely. "Since you insist on thinking this is all about you, let me ask you something," she said. "Were you over Jill when you married me?"

"Jill?" He was incredulous. "For crying out loud, what does Jill have to do with this?"

"Why did you marry me, Dennis?"

"What? What are you talking about?"

She was quite calm now. "I've always wondered. I've seen Jill on TV, remember. She's gorgeous, petite, glamorous. Everything I'm not. Why did you marry me?"

"How can you even ask that?"

"Isn't that what you're asking me?"

"But how can you even think . . . I mean, it's completely beyond me how you can begin to imagine that Jill had anything at all to do with it . . ."

"Is it? Maybe you'd been so burned you wanted someone the dead opposite of her. Someone dull and wholesome . . ."

Did she really think that? "Annalisse, stop this! You know that's not true!"

"You're wrong. I don't know anything about it, except that Jill cheated on you. That's it, isn't it? I'm supposed to be Simple Annalisse, who spent her whole life in a milk barn somewhere until you showed up. Your ego can't handle the fact that I might have loved someone, too."

This was so close to the truth that he could only stare. Hadn't a great part of Annalisse's appeal for him been her wholesomeness, her complete and utter difference from all the narcissistic would-be actresses he had known at Northwestern? And yes, Jill, especially.

As though he had tasted a rotten fruit, the irony struck him. It now appeared he'd married someone who'd outperformed them all. A musical genius, and judging by what he'd heard her play, more tempestuous and certainly more deceitful than anyone he had known.

Reaching for the paddles, he began to row with great energy. "I should have known better than to have brought this up in the middle of a lake."

He rowed without stopping until they reached the shore. After formally helping the stranger who was his wife out of the boat, he dragged it to the pickup and hoisted it into the back. When he pulled himself up into the cab, Annalisse was already there, her face averted.

He started the truck, and they drove back to the farm in silence.

Anna Louisa, who had apparently been listening for their return, ran out to meet them. "Dennis! You've got to get home! Your neighbor Jerome just called! Someone burnt down your barn!"

Chapter Eighteen

Dennis caught the next flight home out of Madison, leaving Annalisse with Jordan, the car, and the fear that she had just destroyed her marriage.

Lying curled in a ball on her childhood bed, Annalisse felt Dennis's words stab her repeatedly, while the hard, bitter look in his eyes suffused her tenderest parts like a toxin. *Dennis will never recover from this. There's nothing I can do to repair our marriage.*

It was as though she had been wandering in the dark, alone and afraid, but still with the hope that light did exist, if she could just find her way back to it. But now that light was gone. Until now, until these last few weeks when she had been trapped in the past, she had never comprehended how much Dennis and his hope for a better world had meant to her. She *did* love him. He was *her* hope. The only chance she had had to step out of the blackness Jules had left her in. And now what? Would she stay there forever? And what about Dennis? Had she destroyed him in the process? What was to become of Jordan? And the baby? These questions dropped her to the bottom of her personal hell.

She stared blindly at her room with its spring-flowered wallpaper and matching duvets. Finally, her eyes focused on her the well-worn childhood Bible from which she had been taught.

She still had her parents. The part of her that had grown up in this house with the values of her beloved mother and father bred into her bones *knew* that despite all the damage she had caused, she must *try* to repair it somehow. She recalled her father teaching her about the apostle Paul, who had written his most stirring letters from the bottom of a black hole of a prison. Absently reaching for the book, she flipped aimlessly through the New Testament, her eyes blurred with tears. Perhaps the answers were here. Was there anything that could rescue her from this desolate wasteland of pain?

I can do all things through Christ which strengtheneth me. The passage of scripture was underlined in red. She knew that since Jules had entered her life, she had become increasingly estranged from Christ. Perhaps that relationship needed to be mended. What would it take to put Jules firmly in the past, to accept her new life in Blue Creek? She was terribly afraid of the next flashback that would assail her. She didn't think she could feel it and stay in one piece. Sliding off her bed, she knelt beside it in prayer.

God, help! I know I haven't asked you for anything in a long time. Forgive me, please. Help me through your grace. Please help me.

A spark of light darted into her breast. Could she fan it into a blaze that would burn away her pain? She would try. Maybe God would meet her best efforts, as he had met Paul's.

"Mother, do you know anything about PTSD?" she asked her mother as they folded Jordan's laundry. "How do you get over it?"

"Your father said you were experiencing it. I'm so sorry, honey. I wish I could help. But it sounds like something that was inevitable."

"But I'm positively hateful. I don't even recognize myself. And I may have ruined my marriage."

"Annalisse, I can't bring myself to believe that. Maybe you just have to ride this like a wave, hanging on to the raft of your good sense. A lot of it could be hormones, too, you know."

"I'm afraid I've let good sense go by the wayside. Like I said, I don't recognize myself. I hurt Dennis this morning. Terribly. I'm afraid he'll never forgive me."

Her mother paused in the act of folding Jordan's jeans. "I wish I could help, honey. I assume you told him about Jules?"

"Yes." Annalisse pulled Jordan's t-shirt right side out. "He took it hard. He says he'll never be able to trust me again. You should have seen the look in his eyes."

Her mother touched her shoulder and turned her so she could look into her eyes, "Poor man. I can imagine. He's always had you on a pedestal."

"Not *me*. The person he thought I was. I don't think he wants me anymore. In fact, I think he loathes me."

"Did you marry Dennis as a reaction to your relationship with Jules, Annalisse? I've always wondered."

"I don't know. I don't even know myself anymore. What if the real me is Jules's wife?"

"He was the stuff great obsessions are made of. A Cathy-and-Heathcliff sort of thing. And of course, it was all connected to your marvelous talent. I don't know if geniuses are ever entirely balanced."

At her mother's sigh of regret, Annalisse felt the familiar tears sliding down her cheeks.

"I suppose you've been feeling guilty because you don't have the same feelings for Dennis that you did for Jules, but I think that would be impossible. Jules will be there forever. While he was with you, there wasn't room for anyone else, not even God, was there?"

Annalisse felt the hit squarely. "No. I've only just realized that. I think I must have worshipped Jules instead."

"There should always be room for God in a relationship. Otherwise one or the other of you puts unrealistic expectations on another human being, who can't possibly fulfill them."

Annalisse thought about this. *The only bright thing.* She, Dennis, and Jules. All three of them had used those words. All three of them were wrong. The thought was cataclysmic. What *was* love then? Would she find out in time to save her marriage?

"Now what about this barn burning?" her mother asked. "It seems like that, in spite of everything else, should be your main concern. Your family's in danger, Annalisse. I think perhaps you should stay here until the perpetrator is caught."

How practical her mother was. And how wrong. The barn was immaterial. Far more than that was burning. "No," she said. "I must go to Dennis. If I stay here, I might never go back. I've got to find some way to make peace, Mother. Pray that God will help me. I know now I can't do it alone."

~

"They didn't even bother to take the kerosene cans with them," Jerome told Dennis. "Whoever it was wanted you to know it was intentional. At least they let your cow out before they lit it."

"Poor Henrietta. Where did you find her, by the way?"

"Down along my fence. She was terrified. Tryin' to get through." The old farmer shook his grizzled head. "She's been off her feed a bit."

"I can imagine. Thanks for taking her in. I'll pay to board her with you until I get that barn back up. My insurance guy tells me it ought to be pretty smooth sailing. Know any builders?"

"Mah nephew. He an' his friends can put together a barn purdy fast. It'll be sturdy, too." Betsy's husband, Jerome, fixed him with an eye clouded by a cataract. "Now, suppose you tell me why anyone would've wanted to burn your barn down."

"It's them anti-Californians," Grandma Betsy declared, bringing an enormous pitcher of lemonade out to the porch where they were sitting. Dennis always marveled at her physical strength. At age seventy-something, Grandma Betsy could still toss a hay bale into the bed of the pickup. "The preacher down t' the fundamentalist church was real inflammatory last Sunday, I heard."

Dennis scratched his head. This was a unique perspective. "What do you think of outsiders, Betsy?"

"I reckon you're fine people. You've been my neighbors for three months, and I ain't never seen no evidence of carryin' on!"

"Carrying on?"

"Oh, these fundamentals, they want us to b'lieve you've brought some kind of Hollywood poison with you. The curse of Satan. Nonsense, o'course."

"I'm glad you think so."

"You think I don't have the brains God gave me? But they do get some folks stirred up. Maybe you'd better think twice about your p'litical career if you don't want to have your house burnt, too."

Jerome was shaking his head. "They're cowards. They knew you wasn't here. They'd never burn your house with you in it."

"I sure hope not. Annalisse and Jordan will be back day after tomorrow." At least, he thought they would. Maybe Annalisse would stay in Burnett with Jordan. He didn't know if he wanted that or not. As hard as he was trying to distance himself from the revelations in the kayak, it wasn't working, even with the immediate problem.

Sometimes he'd stop in the middle of what he was doing, and his thoughts would drift off into his wife's betrayal. When he realized it, he often forgot where he had been going or what he had been trying to do.

"They can stay with us," Grandma Betsy offered, pushing her steel-rimmed spectacles up her short nose.

"I don't want to land you with my family. But thanks."

"Then you've got to take Rufus."

"Your dog? Won't he just run home?"

"Not if I tell him not to," Jerome said. "He's a first-class watch dog."

"Well, thanks," Dennis said, getting out of the porch chair. "I'm sure that'll help a lot. I know I'll sleep better, anyway." As if he could sleep at all.

Dennis was just staring out the window, trying to eat a piece of toast, when Jesse Cavanaugh called that evening. "Son, I think we should have a little talk. It looks like you've got yourself some real trouble here."

"I've got to tell you, it's got me pretty angry."

"I don't blame you one little bit. Barn burnin' is pretty nasty. Any of your livestock get injured?"

"No. Fortunately, they let the cow out first. Their problem is with me, not my cow, thank goodness."

"Your wife and son still in Wisconsin?"

"They'll be starting home tomorrow. We've got Jerome's dog, Rufus, to watch over us."

"Why don't you let them stay put until things blow over here? Don't you think that would be wise?"

"I don't look for this to be over any time soon." Dennis said shortly. How did he even know Cavanaugh wasn't behind this?

"Sheriff Webster have anything to go on?"

"Just a bunch of empty kerosene cans."

"And you're sure you don't know who's doing this?"

"Just speculation. But I'm doing plenty of that."

"Anything I can do?"

"Let's put it this way, senator. If you have any idea who's behind this, use your almighty influence to get him or them locked up." Dennis ended the call.

"Did we hear from the DNR, Leila?" he asked next day. After a sleepless night, towards morning, it had occurred to him for the first time to wonder what had happened to Jules. *Was he somewhere in Europe? Was that why Annalisse longed to be back there?*

The doughnut he had munched was heavy in his stomach as he flipped through the accumulation of phone messages.

"Not a peep," Leila answered, enjoying a doughnut of her own. "What do you think they're up to?"

"I think it's time we found out. Arlene Jacques is the one we want. She's at the Department of Corporations now—Jeff City. Think you could dig up a phone number for her?"

With a speculative glance, his secretary wheeled herself over to the Rolodex. He took another pastry and walked back to his office. It smelled musty and close, like the carpet was rotting. It probably was . . . this climate was as humid as the Amazon rain forest.

He was perusing his mail when the phone buzzed.

"Arlene?"

"Hi, Dennis! Calling to check up on me?"

At the beginning of his practice in Blue Creek, he had represented Arlene in a messy custody battle. She had retained the three children, but despite the court order, her ex-husband had continued his threats to take them from her. Following Dennis's recommendation, she'd moved away.

"How're the kids?"

185

"Fine. You remember Matt, my youngest? He starts school next month."

"Now, that's hard to believe. And how about Walt? Is he leaving you alone these days?"

"For the moment. He kept callin' the kids and gettin' them all upset. Finally, I got an unlisted number."

"You're learning. Listen, Arlene, could you do me a favor? Save me a little time?"

"Sure. Anything."

"I need to find out a few things about a company down here in Cherokee County, and it occurred to me that the quickest way would just be to call you and have you look it up. Could you do that for me?"

"Sure. No problem. Things are pretty slow around here come August. What's the name of the company?"

"Amalgamated Chemical."

"Oh, yeah. Where Walt works. What d'you need?"

"The names of the major shareholders and the board of directors."

"No problem. I'll call you back."

"That's fine. Oh, and Arlene, if one of the big shareholders turns out to be another company, it might save time if you got me the same information about that company, too."

"Right. Should take me just a few minutes."

"Thanks, Arlene."

Dennis tried to return to his mail but had made no headway by the time Leila buzzed him with Arlene's call.

"What've you got?" he asked her.

"The works. D'you have a pencil?"

"Uh-huh. Shoot."

"These are the names of the directors: Chairman—Harvey Fisk.

Others—Raymond Perkins, John Milhouse, Wendel Anderson, and Spencer Dixon."

Nothing there that would tie up with the DNR. Fisk was Republican Party chairman for the seventh district but held no elected office. "What about the shareholders?"

"It's pretty closely held. Fisk, Perkins, Milhouse, and Anderson own 10 percent each. The rest is held by Dixon Mining, Inc., out of Rolla."

Not promising. "What did you find out about them?"

"Thirty percent of the company is owned by Dixon, and the rest by a consortium called Heartland Resources. I couldn't find out anything about it, because it's chartered in Illinois. But I did find one interesting tidbit that might give us a clue."

"Yes?"

"The directors of Dixon Mining are all Dixons, except for the chairman of the board."

"And who's that?"

"Jesse Akins Cavanaugh. Does that tell you something?"

Dennis felt immediately ill. His hunch had been right. Just how deeply was the senator involved? Maybe it wasn't inconceivable that Cavanaugh could have had his barn burnt. *Wasn't it? I was only half-serious with him this morning.* "It tells me everything. I knew there had to be a connection, but I wasn't sure what it was. You're an ace detective, Arlene. Thanks."

"You gonna tell me what this is all about?"

"You'll read about it in the papers soon enough, I'm afraid."

Hanging up the phone, Dennis sank his head in his hands. Cavanaugh had enough swat in his Senate committee to drop the DNR in its tracks. Geesh, he funded them! And of course he had contacts inside the department who had let him know what was going on.

But he still couldn't make himself believe that the senator was behind the threats, the tire slashing, and the barn burning. And Cavanaugh wasn't just protecting his investment. Dennis knew him well enough to know that he really, truly believed he was acting in the best interests of the county. Perhaps he didn't really understand the seriousness of the problem posed by the dioxin.

When all was said and done, Dennis supposed he simply did not want to part with his idea of the man. He didn't think he could take it if there was one more serpent in his Eden.

But, of course, this wasn't Eden. There was death here. A man lay dying in a trailer not two miles away because of the irresponsibility of this charming man. And, faced with the consequences, what did the charmer do? Did he admit culpability and try to remedy the situation as best he might? No. He tried to cover it up. There was going to be a fight, and this was just the beginning.

In addition to feeling sick, Dennis felt suddenly very tired. It occurred to him that originally he had been exhilarated at the prospect of tackling Amalgamated. Now he felt it would be only a futile struggle that would bring down his career and his family with it. Or did he even have a family anymore? Unable to deal with another thing, Dennis went home and fell into an uneasy sleep on the living room couch.

◠◡

Dennis's father looked down into the Grand Canyon, the majestic miracle below them. The raw beauty was astounding, even to a ten-year-old.

"Makes you feel small, doesn't it?" he said to his son.

"Yeah," Dennis agreed. "I'd hate to fall down there."

"You won't. I've got you. I won't let you fall. That's what dads are for."

Dennis latched on to his father's belt for extra security.

"You know," his father mused, "as spectacular as that canyon is, we need to realize it was only made for man. God gave us this earth and all its magnificence as a gift. We're custodians of it. But remember, even if this canyon makes you feel small, there's no limit to what man can accomplish with God's help."

⸻

Dennis woke in confusion after his dream. It had been some time since he'd had a "visit" from his father. At the moment, it seemed a terrible irony. He'd always believed what his father had told him that day. But now he couldn't help wondering if the man had suffered delusions of grandeur. His own efforts to live up to his father and make a difference had proved singularly fruitless in every instance.

Chapter Nineteen

The drive through Iowa was interminable. Jordan had long since dropped off to sleep, leaving Annalisse with only her thoughts for company. She was trying to focus on the radio news program about global warming to keep Jules away, but he was perilously close. She knew her brain needed to unload the worst of it, and she was frightened. Trying instead to think of Dennis, she felt even more hopeless. *Thank goodness for Jordan.* For him, she needed to get through this, whole and strong.

Her own efforts weren't going to be enough. Silently, she prayed as she drove along the two-lane road through tiny Iowa towns. *I know I have been a stranger, Lord. I know I shouldn't have kept Dennis in the dark. Please help me now. Please help me.* Exhausted from lack of sleep, she prayed over and over again like a litany.

Could she and Dennis even live with what she had said? Or would they just drift apart as other couples did once they had lost faith in each other?

The abyss that had begun with the first haunting opened

before her, no mere crack but a merciless void, threatening to swallow the past five years of her life as though they had never been. Nevertheless, she had to take that next step into the past in order to feel it and try with everything she had to put it behind her before she got home. It was the most important step, the one she had shied away from for five years. The one that would determine everything that came afterwards. Not trusting herself to drive any farther, she pulled into a shabby hotel with a rusted sign proclaiming it to be the Economotel. Feeling as though she were racing against time, she scooped Jordan into her arms and went inside to register.

After he was settled in bed, asleep still, she couldn't even wait to carry her bags in from the car. Locking herself in the aged bathroom with its cloudy mirror, corroded fixtures, and cracked tile, she quit fighting herself and let the memory descend.

∼

After ten days, Annalisse had left her mother rallying from her successful surgery. She had been transferred out of the ICU only the day before. Jules's debut was never really out of her mind, only displaced for some days by the very real fear that she could be losing her mother.

Her flight back to Vienna was the day after Jules's performance, and she was anxious to hear how it had gone. She was, therefore, more alarmed than disappointed that he didn't meet her at the airport. Surely, if it had gone well, he would be there to tell her every detail. She didn't speak German, so it was useless to buy a paper for the reviews. With some difficulty, she managed to make her way home by bus. Walking through the peaceful Viennese evening toward their flat, she noticed with growing curiosity that the lights were out. Was he sleeping? No one responded to the doorbell.

Luckily, she had taken her key with her. Unlocking the door, she entered and gratefully let her luggage down in the middle of the sitting room. Where could he be? Turning on lamps, she searched through the apartment until only the bathroom was left.

"Jules?" she knocked on the door, hesitant to disturb him. "I'm home! How did everything go last night?"

No reply. She opened the door. The first thing she saw was the red. Red, red water spilling over the edge of the tub onto the white tiled floor. Then there was Jules, lying in the tub, fully clothed in his white tie and tails. Her mind refused to make sense of the scene. For a moment she was very, very still. Then she saw the butcher knife on the floor.

Instinctively, Annalisse backed out of the bathroom, closed the door, and leaned her forehead against it. She began to whimper. Sagging to the floor, she stared ahead at the bedroom, and when she could take it in, noticed the violin smashed in pieces. She began to scream.

***

As she relived every moment of that agony, Annalisse could feel her heart expand with a grief it had kept inside for too many years. The tears came up out of some well inside and flowed unstoppably down her face. If Jordan hadn't been with her, she might have given in to the temptation to go to the car and drive into a sturdy tree to end the pain that she could feel over her entire body. Swallowing sobs, Annalisse embraced herself, doubled over her abdomen. Eventually, she was unable to prevent the sobs from escaping. She raked her arms with her fingernails, trying to transfer the hurt to the outside of her body, but it was in vain.

After time she could not measure, the memory of Jordan asleep in the bedroom somehow made it to the surface of her mind. This dirty little cubicle was hell. Fortunately, this was more than five years later, and she had another life waiting. She could escape. Turning the cold tap on full, she splashed her face, anxious suddenly for Dennis and whatever awaited her. Surely, it would be better than this. When she thought her exterior was sufficiently under control, she went back into the bedroom and knelt next to her son's bed. He had saved her life tonight. *Thank you, God.*

She marveled that someone could escape hell as easily as walking out of a ghastly room into a place where innocence and trust reigned. *Jordan is my answer to prayer.* She heard the thought as clearly as if someone had whispered it. The product of the love she and Dennis shared, her son was a talisman against further pain from the past. Then Bronwyn kicked her, and she knew that God would continue to help her. He wanted these innocents kept safe from the tragedy that Jules had known. Love she had previously been unable to feel rose up inside her, filling the heart that had been bound so tightly against feeling. The incident in the grimy bathroom had been her Gethsemane and her Calvary. The real Annalisse was resurrected at last.

Chapter Twenty

Dennis woke to the sounds of loud barking and then a sudden gunshot. Half asleep, he pulled on his Levis and rummaged in his closet for his .22 rifle. He unlocked the trigger guard. Fortunately, he kept the gun loaded. Stealing down the stairs in his bare feet, he heard the splintering sound of his back door being jimmied. Before he reached the bottom stair, he could hear someone in his kitchen.

With his heart pounding adrenaline through him, he prayed that whoever it was hadn't killed Rufus. But he must have. The dog was silent.

The intruder was in the living room now. Dennis could hear his tread on the old floorboards of the farmhouse. Poking his head out of the cover of the stairwell, he could see a stocking-masked figure coming toward him. Dennis raised his weapon, wondering if he could possibly bring himself to shoot.

Instead, he called out a warning, "Put your hands in the air!"

The figure let off a shot at Dennis from the pistol he was

carrying. The bullet went wide. Aiming for the man's legs, Dennis shot back and then leapt into the room after him. His shot, too, went wide.

The burglar was now through the front door with Dennis not far behind. This time, the motion-sensing porch light flashed on and aided his aim. Dennis hit the intruder in the shoulder, causing him to pitch and stagger for a second. But before Dennis could reach him, he'd made it to his truck. There was some sort of logo on the side, but Dennis couldn't read it. It was beyond the range of his porch light. The dirty, light-colored truck was off down his driveway, swerving as the driver steered with one arm. It was impossible to read the muddy license plate in the dark.

Dennis was trembling from head to foot. He had just shot a man, a man who had broken into his house armed with a gun. Circling around to the back, he felt his whole frame shudder as the adrenaline in him abated. What had happened to Rufus?

He found the German shepherd by the back door, shot through the chest. Anger surged up inside him, shaking him with its intensity. Poor, loyal Rufus. If it hadn't been for him, what might have happened? What was the man after? Had he intended to shoot Dennis, too?

Walking back into the house, he instantly smelled what he'd missed before. Kerosene. An empty can sat in the middle of his living room. He could have been burned to a crisp in his bed or died of smoke inhalation. So much for Jerome's theory about cowards. This had gone far enough. He grabbed for the phone and dialed 911.

"This is Dennis Childs at Peach Tree Farm on Route H. My barn was burned a couple of days ago. I just caught a guy spilling kerosene in my living room." Dennis described the scuffle.

"Did you get a license number, Mr. Childs?"

"No, it was too dark. But I shot him and he's hit in the shoulder, so he may try the emergency room. It was a light-colored pickup with a logo on the side."

"We'll send the sheriff and firemen out there. Anything else we should know?"

"Yeah, he shot my neighbor's German shepherd. If it hadn't been for Rufus, I'd be a cinder."

Dennis didn't sleep after the sheriff left. It was nearing dawn. His life was really in chaos now. Appalled, he tried to fathom that he had actually shot another human being. That human being had tried to kill him. And what about Rufus? What could he tell Jerome?

The firemen neutralized the kerosene, and Tom Webster and his deputies looked fruitlessly for fingerprints. They made plaster casts of the footprints outside the door. No reports came in about anyone showing up in the emergency room. An APB was put out to all the surrounding hospitals.

There was only one left thing to do. He was going to have to confront Cavanaugh and level with him. It was time he got serious about looking for this perpetrator. He had to know who was in the senator's confidence about the Amalgamated investigation.

"Senator? Sorry to call so early, but I need to talk with you. Someone tried to burn down my house last night."

"This is getting way too serious for my liking, son. I agree we should have a talk. How about if we meet over t' the Roundtable Club for breakfast?"

"I think we need a little more privacy. Could you possibly come to my office sometime this morning?"

"Fine. I'll be there right about nine o'clock."

Dennis had done some thinking about his approach. He decided to begin at the beginning. As soon as the senator was seated, he said, "My client Lonnie Warner is going to die, senator."

Cavanaugh lifted his chin and looked across the desk at his protégé. "What does that have to do with your barn burner?"

"When I took Lonnie's case and found out why he was going to
die, I called the DNR. I'm sure you know this part. What I hope you
don't know is that after that call I got a threat. Then the tire slashing,
the barn burning, and last night's incident. The threat was over my
investigation of Amalgamated."

The senator wrinkled his brow. "Why didn't you tell me this earlier?"

"I didn't really figure out for sure that you were behind the DNR
shutdown until I was driving up to Wisconsin."

"What do you mean, 'shutdown'?"

"Come on, senator. Don't mess with me. I know that someone
at the DNR leaked it to you that I was calling for an investigation of
Amalgamated, and I know that you got them to back off."

"That's a pretty serious allegation."

Dennis came around his desk and sat on the edge, towering over
his former mentor. His life was going south, but he was so angry
now he was past caring. "It's true, isn't it?"

"What's being done for that boy? Is he getting the best medical
attention?"

"There's not a whole lot you can do for dioxin poisoning, senator.
Gregg Gregory's treated it before, if that's what you mean." Dennis
stood and began to pace in front of Cavanaugh. "But Lonnie's just
the tip of the iceberg. If that dioxin's in the water supply, people and
cattle are going to be dying all the way from here to Arkansas."

"That's a big if, though isn't it? Scare the heck outta people, even
if it's not true. Who says it's in the water?"

"Those drums were leaking, senator. They were buried by a creek
that floods every spring. Then Lonnie moved them. But they're not
where he buried them. We need to know where they are now. That's

why I want the DNR down here doing core samples and getting the location of every drum of dioxin that Amalgamated has ever buried during the last thirty years."

"Now, son, if what you say is true—and I'm not saying it is, 'cause contrary to your beliefs, I don't know one way or the other—if the DNR gets in here, we'll have everyone in a tizzy. Probably get the media in here with 'em. Don't you think we could settle this thing privately, take care of the problem, if there is one, our own way?"

Dennis stopped pacing and let his anger spill out. He'd had enough. "There is definitely a problem, senator. You can't wish it away. You know it, and I know it. And we don't have the resources to deal with it. The DNR *has* to be called in to deal with the pollution. It's their business. I want to make sure it's cleaned up right, and I want to make sure it never happens again."

Cavanaugh uncrossed his legs and leaned forward, fixing Dennis with his eyes. "D'you know what this'll do to Amalgamated? More than likely it'll put 'em under. I know Jeff City bureaucracy. The DNR'll go in there lookin' for a way to justify their existence. They'll bring the EPA in . . . they don't give a hoot for private enterprise. They'll throw their weight around an' turn everything upside down 'til they find a list of things long as your arm that needs doin'. An' who d'you think has to pay for it all?"

Dennis stood towering over the older man. "You relieve my mind. I had the feeling the DNR was completely under your thumb."

To his surprise, Cavanaugh met his outrage with a raised eyebrow and a grin. "Not completely, son, not completely. Once you set 'em in motion, there's not a hope in heck of controllin' 'em. That's why we gotta settle this our own way. That company means too much to this county. How many of your clients collect an Amalgamated paycheck every Friday? What happens to their families when those paychecks stop?"

"Believe it or not, I have thought of that."

The senator went on as though he hadn't spoken. "Now, you weren't here in the days before Amalgamated, so I guess I can't blame you for not understandin' what we're talkin' about here. You didn't see the smartest half of Blue Creek Senior High grads leave for Kansas City and St. Louis come June every year. You know what choice these people used t' have in the way o' work?" He held up his hand and enumerated the job opportunities with his fingers. "They could pull guts outta chickens at the poultry plant for minimum wage, or if the shoe fact'ry weren't shut down, they could maybe get on there for a coupla months. Elsewise all they could do was try t' make a livin' outta these ol' red rocks with a dairy or a cow-calf operation. That takes land, and you know as well as I do, nobody can pay the bank when ag prices are down. No sir." He paused for breath. "I might as well tell you that when I brought Amalgamated in here, I was thinkin' of my own son. But the city got him. He lives in New York City, of all places. Can you imagine that?

"Put yourself in my place. You moved out here from California to raise your family. What's going to happen to them when they're grown? That boy of yours isn't going to want to work in the chicken fact'ry. No sir. He'll be off to Kansas City, like as not." The man shifted in his chair, as though settling in for the long haul. "Now can't we just talk this out like reasonable folk instead of callin' out the cavalry?"

The man still didn't see! Was he blind? "There are people here who may be taking poison with their drinking water each and every day, senator. Lonnie got a concentrated dose, so his death is evident and comparatively fast. It's a warning. What's going to happen when young kids all over the county start developing leukemia, senator?

If you care about this county, really care about it, you'll get the DNR in here and get it cleaned up. You'll do everything you can to make sure the water's not poisoned."

"I think you're overreacting, son."

"Someone else thinks so, too," Dennis commented, bringing the conversation around to his original point. "Have you got any idea who is behind these attacks on me? I'm about to go public with this, I'm warning you."

Cavanaugh narrowed his eyes. "You'd better think what you're doin', son. You turn the media loose and who knows what this character might do."

"Who is he?"

"I've no idea."

"You swear?"

"I do."

Dennis was momentarily stunned. In spite of everything, the senator wasn't going to give him the answers he needed. Who else was involved? Coming to a decision, he slapped his desk with both palms. "Well, I guess that gives me no alternative. If I can't settle this privately, I'm going to have to give this fellow a public warning. I'm going to have to spill the whole story while I'm at it. The DNR's not going to appreciate looking like they're intimidated by anyone, so I expect they'll be down here sometime soon."

Drawing himself up wearily, the senator dropped all his affectations. "I promise you that if you forgo calling in the Department of Natural Resources and going to the media, I personally will see that Amalgamated cleans up every last drum of dioxin."

"But do you even know where it's buried? And how will we know without environmental testing what damage has already been done?"

"I give you my word. If there's poison anywhere, we'll find it," the senator promised earnestly.

"I believe you, senator. But the fact is, you just don't have the expertise to carry out your promise. We need the professionals."

Cavanaugh's jaw hardened, and the conciliatory manner followed his good ol' boy dialect. "I can see that further discussion would be futile at this point."

"Sorry, senator. I don't see that I have much choice. We're talking about life and death here. Not just for a few but for the whole county."

The man stood. "I don't know who's threatening your family, and I'm sorry about it, but I'm going to fight you on this, Dennis. I won't see my county taken back to the dark ages."

The man moved to the door swiftly and was out before Dennis could say another word. Suddenly exhausted, he drew a deep sigh. *Well, I've really stuck my neck out this time. I've got a madman trying to kill me, and the most powerful man downstate is now my enemy. Aside from anything else, how in the world am I going to keep my practice going and feed my family? No one's going to thank me for this. And I can certainly say farewell to the prosecutor's job.*

When his family pulled into the driveway the following evening, Dennis's feelings were mixed. He wished they had stayed in Wisconsin. He couldn't deal with Annalisse's roller-coaster personality at the moment, and anxiety for the safety of his small family outweighed even the problems in his marriage. Worst of all, he didn't wish to alarm them. But he had finally fallen in with Grandma Betsy's plan to have them stay with her.

"Hi, guys!" he greeted them with pseudo cheer.

"Hi, Dad!" Jordan said, running up to him for a bear hug. Annalisse slid from behind the wheel as though she ached everywhere.

He put his head to one side. What was she thinking? "Long drive?"

"Interminable. There ought to be a law against Iowa. I wonder how many people fall asleep at the wheel out of sheer boredom?"

"Did they get the bad guy?" Jordan asked.

"Why doesn't everyone come into the house? I got some micro-wave lasagna."

"Let's unload the car first," Annalisse suggested. "When I sit down, I don't plan on getting up again."

Over dinner, Dennis related the events of the previous night in as unremarkable a fashion as he could manage. He left out the part about Rufus and the gunshots, merely stating that he had caught someone in the house.

"Grandma Betsy and I think it would be best for you all to stay with her until we catch this guy. I'll take you over in a bit."

"Wheo will you sleep?" Jordan wanted to know.

"Somebody's got to stay here to catch him. Sheriff Webster's going to have a couple of deputies watching the house from now on."

Annalisse seemed to sense that there was more to the story, but she remained silent, studying him with a frown.

"I don't wanna go to Gwamma Betsy's. I wanna stay with you."

Annalisse smiled wanly, and Dennis patted his stubborn son on the shoulder. "I've got enough worries without worrying about you, too."

In the end, after dinner, Jordan finally agreed to go to Grandma Betsy's when Dennis told him she had baked a peach cobbler just for him.

As he ran upstairs to gather his quilt and stuffed animals again, Annalisse began clearing the table. "So what really happened, Dennis?"

"Rufus was killed. Jerome's dog. That's what woke me. The guy was pouring kerosene in the living room. I shot him, Annalisse. In the shoulder."

"Oh, Dennis!" Setting the dishes on the counter, she ran into his arms and hugged him tightly. He had never thought to feel her arms around him again. "Thank God you're okay. You could so easily have suffered a terrible death! You need to be at Betsy's, too."

"I need to catch this guy, Annalisse."

"But not at the risk of your own life! Besides, you're plainly exhausted. Can't you leave it to the sheriff?"

"I want to nail him myself. He tried to kill me, Annalisse. And what if the whole family had been here?"

"Dennis, you won't get a wink of sleep."

"I won't anyway." Briefly, he told her about his confrontation with Cavanaugh. "I don't know what we're going to do, Annalisse. This could be the end of my practice."

"We'll make it," she told him, an odd pleading look in her eyes. "We always do, Dennis."

He looked at her drawn face and was stabbed by his doubts about her. "We've always pulled together, Annalisse."

"And we will this time, too. I'm going to stay here with you."

"No. You're not. I can't be worried about what might happen to you. You're going to Betsy's."

Her features hardened. "You would have let me stay before."

"Before what?"

"Before Jules."

Turning away, he strode to the back door and looked through the screen. "Don't we have enough going on without bringing him into it?"

Coming up behind him she said softly, "I'm sorry."

He turned and looked into her face. She looked so repentant, so humble that he couldn't hang on to his anger. How deep did things go with her? Did she realize how really wrong everything was?

"I'm sorry I've let you down," she murmured.

Ashamed, he realized that he did feel let down. Not only let down but shaken and more lost than ever. He wondered again who this woman was that he had married.

Going to the sink, she began washing the dishes. He moved to help her, and they worked in silence, tension building between them. She was right. Before the thing with Jules he would have taken her on as an equal partner. They would have seen this through together. But now he was alone. They had cut themselves off from the comfort of each other.

Annalisse finished and wiped her hands carefully on a towel. Her eyes brimmed with tears. "I'm sorry I'm not who you thought I was, Dennis. I don't think I ever will be." Jerkily, she walked out of the kitchen, and he listened as she made her way heavily up the stairs.

Alarm flashed through him like a current, temporarily dazing him. Did she want a divorce? Was that what she was saying? Was she as disappointed in him as he was in her?

He couldn't ask, couldn't follow her. He didn't want to know any more. Hanging up his towel, he walked out the back door. There must be some place he could escape all this anguish.

But his paradise mocked him now. The air was cooler tonight with a hint of fall, the sunset lending everything a golden glow. The frogs had chosen that moment to break into their evening chorus. It was all heartbreakingly idyllic.

Walking down the hill, he crossed the creek on the stepping-stones of Jordan's bridge and went to the southern edge of his property. He could see Amalgamated's water tower sticking up through the trees.

From his seat on a stump, Dennis stared off through the forest, feeling dwarfed and impotent as the sum of the day's events settled on him. Annalisse's words beat through his mind like a leitmotif. Where did he get off thinking he had any right to perfection? Life demanded a coexistence with imperfection. There was no real Eden. Just a deep void—and a longing that had been part of him since his father's death. He thought Annalisse had filled it. But it had all been an illusion.

Looking at the tower through the trees, he extended his thesis bitterly. Why had he ever had the hubris to think he could change things? Someone far more powerful than he was had tried to stop greed and corruption and had been crucified for his pains.

But what of his marriage? Wasn't it in actuality the core around which his entire life was built? Had it been a hollow thing from the beginning? Was it now going to collapse from nothing greater than the weight of his own expectations?

Dennis, you idiot! You are such a narcissist! Why on earth should Annalisse function only as an extension of you and your dreams? Why should you project all your wishes and desires on to her? She is more than a character in the play of your life. She has her own life! Her own script!

The pain in Annalisse's eyes revisited him, and his own rose up to meet it. She was suffering, too. The blurry wonder of the other night now came to him like a shot to the midsection. He didn't even know what had happened with Jules. Why had their marriage ended? He assumed it was a divorce. What kind of hell had she been through that would change her whole personality? What would cause her to give up her career? Shouldn't he know these things? How absolutely rotten of him not to have shown some compassion for her pain! Tonight he had banged out of the house, concerned only with his own feelings when she clearly was suffering.

Dennis picked up a twig and began viciously to strip its bark. In spite of everything, he and Annalisse had two children to think of. They had created a family. He must think this through. Everything depended on it.

There had been so many disillusionments, but in spite of them all, hadn't he always been convinced that the promised land still awaited him somewhere? In a world with so much darkness, there had to be some light. Oh, he'd always enjoyed a fight, but whenever his chosen cause had revealed a taint of corruption, he'd deserted it and looked somewhere else. He was a husband and a father now. He could leave the Ozarks, but he was bound to Annalisse by vows and to Jordan and Bronwyn by love and responsibility. He was certainly not going to turn his back on them. For once in his life, he had to work things through, even though they weren't turning out as he'd planned.

"Dad! Dad!" Jordan came running down the hill, calling into the twilight. "Gwamma Betsy cawed! Henwietta's out! She's down on the woad! Dad! Wheo aw you?"

Dennis got to his feet. Why did he keep a cow, anyway? They were stupid, lumpish things with no imagination. What did she want to go down the road for?

Treading the stepping-stones across the creek, he gave a grim laugh. Well, what did he expect? Cows were only cows. They had no magical properties.

There was nowhere left to run now. He was standing on the edge of the world, and he must fight or fall off.

Chapter Twenty-One

Annalisse walked to the bedroom window when she heard Dennis bang the screen door and go out the back. She watched numbly as he strode down to the creek.

You've got to take your life in both hands and get control again. You've got to leave Jules in his grave.

In the back of her college journal, she had kept the only letter she had ever received from Jules. Perhaps she'd kept it for a day such as this. She hadn't looked at it for five years. The journal was hidden in her underwear drawer. Going to it, she pulled out the light blue letter written in Jules's crabbed script, and with a painfully accelerated heartbeat, she unfolded it. The last time she had read this letter she had been by Jules's graveside, three weeks after she had found him dead.

The small cemetery lay hushed and sullen between a soot-blackened Catholic church and a bustling street of small businesses all crowned with dirty brick flats in the working-class part of Vienna. Behind a black iron fence that reached her shoulders, tall headstones stood uneasily in their surroundings, solemn gray sentinels on a green spring lawn.

Annalisse opened the wrought iron gate with the key the priest had given her and entered. Her palms began to sweat as the gate clanked behind her. Why had she come to this horrible place again? Jules wasn't here.

An angry taxi bleeped, and a bus whooshed by, its wake stirring her skirt and filling the air with the heavy odor of diesel fuel. This familiar, temporal smell steadied her, and she began to move among the stones, forcing herself to decipher their inscriptions. The tall ones were old, many of them dated a century before and even earlier. For some reason the idea of old, respectable people buried under heavy stone monuments was reassuring.

She had had to convince the church of Jules's unsound mental condition in order to get him buried in hallowed ground. The grave was back along the fence, near the aged elm.

Yes, here it was—a rectangular slab of cold gray granite, embedded in the ground. She had been avoiding it since the burial, but coming here was to be her last act before leaving Vienna and returning to her old, pre-Jules life. It felt like the end of the world. Perhaps it was, for her.

Dear Annalisse,

Don't blame yourself for my death. I have ruined my own life by my selfishness. Because of me, my "adopted" brother Rafael was executed tonight.

What I never told you was that my father was killed while I was at school by enemies from Mexico—a drug cartel he was trying to bring down. Afraid for my life (I was only ten), I appealed to my neighbor, who responded by dumping me on the streets of East LA (the barrio).

I grew to adolescence there, part of the whole gang scene. Abuelita Emma Garcia adopted me and raised me with her grandson, Rafael, on the wages she made as a cleaning woman. When I was old enough to figure out how to do it, I contacted my mentor in the Philharmonic whom my father had hired to teach me when he was alive. He was appalled, of course, and wanted me to come live with him. But I wouldn't leave the gang, and I couldn't leave the drugs. However, I did resume my lessons with him.

Then, one day when I was sixteen, there was a fight. The only thing that made this one different was that there were guns instead of knives. A rival gang member shot at Rafael and missed. Rafael shot and killed him. I was the only witness that his action was self-defense, but frightened for my life, I called my teacher, and he came and took me away, changed my name, and coached me. I went through withdrawal from cocaine that was doubly difficult because, as they diagnosed at this time, I was bipolar.

Rafael's execution was delayed for years by appeals, but word reached me that the prosecution knew where I was when I was studying with you at Stanford. The rival gang wanted to kill me to keep me from testifying. Abuelita wanted me to accept witness protection and then testify to save Rafael. By now, there were additional charges. Every drug dealer in East LA had heaped his guilt on Rafael. In addition to murder, they were trying him as a major drug dealer. I could have cleared him but, selfish as I was, I refused to risk it.

Instead, I ran off to Vienna and experienced heaven with you, whom I love with everything good that is in me. The day you left *for home, I received another plea. Abuelita, aided by the defense, had traced me through my mentor. Rafael had been granted a last-minute stay of execution so they could hear my testimony. He was scheduled for execution the day of my concert. I know you won't understand my decision, but I was like a robot with no feelings. I had prepared myself for this performance almost all my life since I was six years old.*

You read the reviews I left with this note. I failed. I deserved to fail, because that day I got a telephone call by way of the Philharmonic ticket office. They had given a sobbing Abuelita my telephone number. She called to tell me that Rafael was dead and that I could have saved him.

I have ruined my life. Remorse over my heinous decision has overtaken me, supplanting even the fact that you don't get two chances in the music world. All I can think of is what you would have done if you had had the same choices to make. I virtually murdered Rafael. I broke the heart of the woman who raised me. I know you believe love comes before music. My self-hate tells me you are right, and I know you can never love me again. The prospect of facing you, losing you because of my selfishness, is too painful for me to endure.

Please go on without me. Your steadiness will make you the better musician. Do it as a gift of love to me, though I don't deserve it. You will always make the right choices. I have atoned for my failures with my life.

Julio del Gallego

Dropping to her knees, Annalisse felt the short turf, rough and prickly through her stockings, and wondered that this should be a place of any significance. She felt nothing. There was no music here. Her small bunch of violets looked frivolous and vulnerable beside the dark, polished stone. If her mother had not undergone the risky surgery that saved her life, Annalisse would have been here. She would go to her own grave wondering if that would have made a difference.

But she could not do as he asked. The music was dead. It had died when she found Jules in the bathtub. After screaming down the building, she had vomited, and there on the cold floor, she had rejected reality. *It simply couldn't be. She must be in the middle of a nightmare.*

She had failed him. If she had loved him enough, had made him feel that love enough, even in her absence, maybe this whole terrible tragedy never would have happened. He would have made the right choices. With her by his side, he would never have rejected life.

Without him, she was only a hollow shell who couldn't even cry.

⌒₰

Annalisse remained dry-eyed through what she thought would be the most painful of her memories. Was she still numb to them? No. The tragedy tore at her. She was no longer hollow but full of feelings that had been rising since this haunting had begun. She had never known that heartbreak could really feel like just that— physical pain that tore through her breast. Jules had been ill. He had been alone. He had thought his circumstances hopeless.

But now, as she finally felt and experienced all the emotions that she had forced down, six years of perspective were rising up and teaching her from the depths of that sorrow. She could see what she had never seen all those years ago.

Jules *had* made the wrong choice. He had sent his brother to execution. He had ignored the pleas of the poverty-stricken woman who had raised him out of the goodness of her heart. There would have been other concerts. Postponing at the last minute to save a life was something the orchestra would have understood. Jules had been a complete narcissist in the most dangerous sense.

He was right. In spite of all the joys of their life together, she wouldn't have understood his choice. It would have repulsed her. Would he have chosen music over Annalisse, if there had been another choice to make? Certainly. No matter how hard she tried, things never would have been the same. It all came down to that. All the passion she had been reliving ended because of Jules's death, it was true. But it would never have survived his decision to put music before his brother's life. At the time, she hadn't understood that. Her grief was too profound. But after almost five years of living with Dennis, she did understand. Dennis would never have made the choice Jules had.

Through her preoccupation, she heard Jordan urgently calling his father outside. What was going on? Still halfway immersed in the past, she descended the stairs and went to the bay window in the front of the house. Suddenly her husband came into view, bounding down the hill, Jordan running behind him. Going out onto the front porch, she strained to see where they had gone. Against the last shards of sunset she distinguished her husband and son silhouetted alongside a dark, obstinate shape that could only be Henrietta.

Jules had had his violin, and Dennis had Henrietta—the representative of his bucolic life choice. She wanted to laugh at the juxtaposition, but her eyes filled with the tears that wouldn't come earlier. An overwhelming tenderness for Dennis caught at her throat. In some way, that tenderness was inextricably connected with Jules, and in other ways, completely and totally separate.

She remembered with startling clarity the day she had met Dennis. It was after the three months of pneumonia, her struggle to finish college, and a few months working at Scripps. How bright everything had seemed after the grimness of her life since Jules! She had resented everything that day—the light, the long elegant sailboat, Sam's *bonhomie*, and her cousin Karin's brittle laughter. Then she had seen Dennis.

He had been incredibly handsome—bronzed and muscular—but it wasn't that. No, it was the way he had looked at her. Like she was some kind of answer. Jules had looked at her like that, and she missed the feeling it gave her.

But later, after they'd talked, she'd known Dennis wasn't a bit like Jules. Her mind still held a sharp, vivid picture of Dennis's face jutting into the wind, long blond hair blowing like a Viking's. Jason in search of the Golden Fleece. Jules had never looked like that.

A tiny crevice of light had pierced her personal darkness at that meeting. She had thought maybe someday she would be able to feel again.

The tears stung her eyes as she wrapped her arms around the porch pillar, watching Dennis and Jordan pull the stubborn beast up the incline. She hadn't known it would take five years. And now, her husband had found out she wasn't his answer after all. She wasn't the person he'd thought her.

But even with his flaws, wasn't Jules knit forever into her being? With him she had discovered the color, the taste, the substance of life. The view she'd seen through his eyes had changed her forever. Yet the happy memories had only proved to be a wedge. They'd opened her to the pain she'd never had the courage to face. She had to face it now.

Her husband knew nothing of the Annalisse who had loved Jules. She couldn't blame him if he had seen only the country-bred girl, the daughter of Sven and Anna Louisa. It wasn't his fault. There were two Annalisses, and they existed in separate compartments.

But she was neither one nor the other; she was both. For five years, she had been trying to deny half of herself. It couldn't be done.

It was time to force a truce. Wiping away her tears with the back of her hand, she wondered just how this was to be accomplished.

When her husband and Jordan arrived back at the house, she had unearthed ice cream from the deep freeze and was scooping it into bowls.

"Henrietta got into the road again?"

Nodding, Dennis sat at the table and pulled his dish toward him. "I've decided to sell her."

Annalisse looked up from the ice cream. "Why?"

"What do I want with a cow? It was a dumb idea."

"I wove Henwietta, Daddy! Don't seo huh!" Jordan pleaded. "She was naughty, but don't seo huh!"

"I love Henrietta too," Annalisse added. "At least I like having our own milk. What made you come to that conclusion all of a sudden?"

Dennis looked at her in disbelief. "I seem to recall you warning me once upon a time that dairy cows were a lot of work. You were right. All things considered, it's a lot cheaper to buy milk."

His answer disturbed her. Was he in the process of dismantling his dream? Was this the outcome of their horrible discussion on the lake? "You knew that all along," she said. "But you thought it would be a good experience for Jordan when he grew up. You've always said milking helps you unwind . . ."

"For Pete's sake, what difference does it make now?" he demanded.

Jordan ducked his head at this rare display of temper from his father. Annalisse thought she had never seen her husband look so thoroughly quenched. Angry, yes, but never quenched. Guilt smote her for the part she had played.

"Jordan," she said, "better finish up. It's time to get you over to Grandma Betsy's."

"You come too?"

"Not tonight, sweetie."

"If Papa was heo, he'd wead the Bible to make us feel bwave."

"Yes," agreed Dennis, "he probably would."

"Can you do it, Daddy?"

"Sure." In spite of his obvious weariness, he agreed to his son's request. "What do you want me to read?"

"Why don't you choose?" Annalisse intervened. She had to give the poor man some stake in this.

"My father always read me the twenty-third Psalm. Do we have a Bible around somewhere?" he asked, looking around vaguely.

Annalisse went to the bookcase in the living room and pulled out the Bible her parents had given her when she and Dennis were married. Her husband settled himself in the rocking chair. Annalisse and Jordan seated themselves on the sofa.

She watched as her husband carefully opened the scriptures and then, finding his place, began to read aloud: "The Lord is my shepherd; I shall not want . . ."

He read magnificently, of course. Legacy of a Northwestern degree in oral interpretation of literature. But how much of what he read had he really felt? When he finished, they were all silent.

Chapter Twenty-Two

Dennis lay tense and restless next to Annalisse's sleeping form. He was glad she had elected to stay, though still somewhat puzzled as to why, considering his earlier rudeness. Was she offering him some kind of hope for reconciliation?

Getting up, he walked over to the window to see if the deputy's car was still staking out the driveway. It was. Right next to the place where the barn used to be.

Perhaps, as long as he was awake, he'd take a walk around the back of the house to see if the other deputy was at his post.

As he pulled on his Levi's, Annalisse stirred. "Where are you going, Dennis?"

"I can't sleep. I'm too strung out. I want to make sure that deputy in the back is still awake."

She swung her feet over the side of the bed. "Maybe I should send them out some food. I've got chocolate chip cookies somewhere in the freezer."

"Sounds like an idea. I wouldn't mind some myself," he told her.

Together they went downstairs, Annalisse tying the belt of her terry cloth bathrobe. In the mudroom, his wife switched on the light and began rummaging in the deep freeze, finally emerging with a tin canister in her hands.

"Would you feel more comfortable if we kept watch ourselves?" she asked. "Since we can't sleep, we might as well sit in the living room."

An expression of deep concern was etched on her tired face. He remembered the long drive she had just made. Reaching for her, he smoothed a lock of hair behind her ear. "You go back to bed, Swedie. I'll take these cookies out to the guys. I really don't think this joker's going to try anything tonight. Remember, he's wounded."

"Then why are you so tense?"

"I'm trying to figure out who he is, for one thing. It's driving me crazy."

Hoisting herself up so she was sitting on the chest freezer, Annalisse faced him at eye level. "He's not working for Cavanaugh?"

"No. I had a long talk with the senator. He's opposed to my investigation and intends to fight me, but he seemed genuinely horrified at what had happened."

"And you believe him?"

"I do. He's honorable according to his own world view. He may be against the investigation, but he's doing the wrong thing for the right reasons, if you know what I mean. He sincerely believes the poison isn't as much of a threat as the DNR is."

His wife shook her head. They were silent for a moment. "Could it be someone Lonnie told?"

"Lonnie says he didn't tell anyone but Ada Lou. And she didn't know who he was hauling the stuff for."

"What do you mean?"

"I mean it was a contracted job. The outfit Lonnie worked for

217

had a contract with Amalgamated. She knew the haulers but nothing about Amalgamated."

His wife looked at him, puzzled. "But Dennis, wasn't it illegal for those guys, I mean Lonnie's company, to be burying toxic waste on public land?"

"Maybe they didn't know it was toxic waste."

"I'll bet they guessed it. What else would Amalgamated be trying to get rid of? And I bet they were paid plenty to keep their mouths shut. They're liable to be closed down if this gets out."

He slapped his hand on the freezer as the revelation hit him. "That must be it! Why didn't I think of it? Ada Lou would certainly know who Lonnie's boss was. And she probably threatened the guy before she brought Lonnie to me. She thinks they're the bad guys. She doesn't know about Amalgamated. As far as she's concerned, it's just a worker's comp case, like all the others she's brought me."

"She could be in danger, too."

"You're right, Annalisse. I've got Lonnie's file down at my office. It has the name of the trucking company in it. I can't remember it off the top of my head. But I don't feel right leaving you here alone. Could you come with me? I don't want to wait until morning. I want to know *now*. If they can get this guy tonight, I'll feel a whole lot better."

"I'll come."

The first indication that something was wrong was that the flimsy lock on his office door had been forced open. It didn't register that he'd actually had an intruder until he looked inside and found his office in chaos. It appeared that every single one of Leila's green Pendaflex files had been pulled out and its contents strewn wildly across the floor. For a moment, that's all he could take in. Then he saw the bare desk where Leila's computer usually sat. Leaping across the papers on the floor, he went into his own office to find his desk equally bereft. Both computers were gone. Worse still, a hasty search confirmed that every backup device had been taken.

He felt as though he'd been slugged.

"Oh, Dennis! What a mess!"

Collapsing in Leila's chair, Dennis could only stare. "That isn't what matters, Annalisse." It was so unthinkable, he almost couldn't put it into words. But she had to know. "I'll never recover from the loss of my data files. I had much more on that computer than in the file cabinets."

Kneeling on the floor, his wife was making a vain attempt to begin straightening up. "Leave it," he said. "The sheriff will want everything just as it was." He pinched the bridge of his nose, squeezing his eyes shut. "It's a good thing I got that malpractice insurance. I'm going to be sued for sure."

"What do you mean?"

"A whole lot of my practice went out of the door with that computer, Annalisse. I have a million deadlines in my cases, and they were all on my electronic calendar. All the law office finances plus our own are on those computers. I don't even know how much money I have in the bank right now. It will take a titanic effort to reconstruct even a portion of what's missing. I have clients who are going to be harmed by this. Not to mention all the business records I need for the IRS." Picking up the telephone, Dennis dialed 911.

When they returned home, finally, it was nearly dawn, and Dennis sent a white-faced Annalisse to bed. He had told Tom Webster about Annalisse's idea about the identity of their terrorist, and the sheriff had promised to get in touch with Lonnie Warner right away.

Dennis felt angry and frustrated that he couldn't take immediate action. What was left of the practice he had tried so hard to build? Would this madman get to his family before they could stop him? Everything was up for grabs; nothing was certain. Leaving his fate in the hands of others was not a feeling he was familiar with. Anxiety gnawed at him as the adrenaline ebbed and flowed through his body.

What could he do? Pacing the living room, he reviewed various strategies in his mind. Even if Tom Webster caught the malefactor, he was willing to bet the computer and backups had been destroyed. Selling his practice and leaving Blue Creek was now out of the question. He had nothing to sell. He could never salvage the information that was lost, and he knew the senator would use all his influence to turn potential clients against him. Should he obey his conscience, his basic sense of rightness, and go ahead with his plans to expose Amalgamated to the media? Cavanaugh had vowed to fight him. There would be no county prosecutor's job. Could he really, in good conscience, expose his family to the risk of bankruptcy? But if he didn't act, who would? Lonnie would be only the first victim. Countless more might die, or be sick already without knowing they were poisoned. How long would it take before Cavanaugh finally realized that the danger was real?

The weight of decision only added to his anxiety. Sitting down on the couch, he reached idly for the first thing that came to hand. After a few moments, he realized he was paging through the Bible.

Jordan's scripture study. It had been oddly comforting at the time. He had almost been able to feel that all would be well.

Trying to still the turmoil in his mind, he turned back to the Twenty-third Psalm. "He maketh me to lie down in green pastures: he leadeth me beside the still waters . . ." Dennis thought he had found green pastures and still waters in this place. Hadn't he been looking for them all his life? What a laugh!

He nearly closed the book but decided, more for the sake of argument than anything else, to continue. Who was this shepherd, anyway? According to the Psalm, someone who had a transcending love of sheep. Did Dennis believe in that love?

He'd believed in it certainly when he'd met Annalisse, when he'd been taken in and nurtured by the pure goodness of her family. But what about now? What was the promise of the Psalm?

"He restoreth my soul: he leadeth me in the paths of righteousness for his name's sake . . ."

"He leadeth me . . . The words struck him hard. When had Dennis Childs ever allowed himself to be led? What kind of claim did he have on this Shepherd and his green pastures, after all?

Surely, not much of one. Like a recalcitrant sheep, he had always been so sure he knew a better way. He had always known there must be a perfect place. A place where little boys' fathers wouldn't die, a place where life was safe and serene. But what did the Psalm say? "Yea, though I walk through the valley of the shadow of death, I will fear no evil: for thou art with me . . ."

Perhaps he had missed the significance of the Shepherd entirely. Life wasn't about avoiding death, avoiding pain. It never had been. That was why the Shepherd was necessary. That was why whatever he, Dennis Childs, did, in the cosmic sense would never be enough. As Annalisse had so aptly warned him, even he couldn't keep Lonnie from dying. He had been trying to take on the Messiah's job. What hubris!

The weight subtly shifted from his shoulders until he could almost see it on the page before him. If anyone in the world needed the grace of God at that moment, surely it was he.

Maybe, just for once, especially since his back was against the wall, he ought to trust in some force outside of himself. It couldn't hurt to give it a try. He certainly didn't have any other ideas. Closing his eyes, he pictured himself as a lost sheep, draped over the shoulders of the Shepherd.

The sheriff called just when Dennis had dozed off in his living room. "We've picked up John MacCavity at his house. He runs Lonnie's outfit. There's about eight cans of kerosene in his shed, and he has a dirty white pickup with a logo for MacCavity Hauling."

"Has he got a wounded right shoulder?"

"That's the bad part. He's healthy. Right now we're charging him with conspiracy to commit arson. The kerosene cans are identical to those left by your barn and in your living room. It's pretty thin, but we're hoping you can identify the truck."

"Maybe someone saw a truck down by my office last night. That could give you probable cause for the warrant to search the house. I'm right across from Calhoun's, you know. Did they have a poker game last night?"

"We've got a deputy checking. Let's just say those boys in Calhoun's are generally a little shy about helping the law. We were lucky with the shed. It was missing a wall, and the kerosene cans were in plain view."

"So what's our next step? Do you want me to see what Lonnie knows about other members of the company?"

"That makes sense."

Showering and dressing, Dennis left the sleeping Annalisse a note telling her he was going to visit Lonnie. The deputies had changed shifts, but the law was still protecting his home.

Lonnie was just finishing his breakfast. Ada Lou had made him pancakes and sausages before leaving to feed her chickens.

Dennis's client's face looked more drawn and his eyes hollow with melancholy. Sitting on the arm of Lonnie's recliner, Dennis tried to explain the situation.

"Someone's burned down my barn, Lonnie, and tried to burn my house. We think it's probably someone who works for MacCavity. Can you give me any idea who the other employees are?"

"Well," Lonnie scratched his head. "There weren't a lot of what y'd call permanent employees. He'd just call us if he needed help."

"How many trucks did the company have?"

"Two 'r three. But only the MacCavitys got to drive the trucks. Most of us just did the diggin' and the loadin'."

"So what other MacCavitys are there besides John?"

"Well, there's John's wife, Tina. She'd drive once in a while. Then there's his brother, Terry, what lives out t' Eagle Point."

"Where in Eagle Point? Have you been there?"

"Jes' once. It's out at th' end of a road overlookin' Beaver Lake."

"We'll find it. Thanks a lot, Lonnie."

The man returned to picking at his pancakes. "Sure am sorry about yore barn. Looks like I jes' brought you bad luck."

Dennis patted his shoulder. "I don't want you to worry about this now. We're going to get it taken care of."

Back in the car, Dennis used his cell phone to call Webster. "Terry MacCavity drove trucks for the company. He lives in Eagle Point on a road that dead ends into Beaver Lake. Any idea where that is?"

"I know the area like the back of my hand."

"Any luck with the fellows at Calhoun's?"

"Yes, as a matter of fact. You've got a fan there in Chester Calhoun. Seems you did a little service for him after that flood."

"Just shoveled some mud."

"Well, he's grateful. He said he'd call up the boys and see if any of them saw anything. Tell 'em it was okay to speak up. If they did see anything, I think we'll find out about it."

"Good. I'm going into the office. You can catch me there if you need me. I'd appreciate a report on Terry MacCavity."

"You'll get it. We're keeping a deputy out at your place, by the way."

"Thanks, Sheriff."

Leila was kneeling among the files in a state of shock when he arrived at the office.

"Who did this?"

"We're trying to find out. I'm hoping the sheriff will be able to get my computer back, but it's probably been junked by now."

"I don't even know where to start to clean up this mess!"

"Well, we've got nothing else to do. As of right now, I haven't got much of a practice. I want you to make a list of every judge you can remember that I have a case pending before so I can call them. Then I'd like you to call the clerk's office down at the courthouse and let them know what happened. Let's get started."

At noon, they were joined by Annalisse, who arrived bearing submarine sandwiches and lemonade. Dennis told her what the sheriff had told him. Not long afterward, they received a call from him.

"Bad news, Dennis. Terry MacCavity's healthy, too. No shoulder wound. Any other ideas?"

They had the call on the speaker phone, so everyone could hear the conversation.

Annalisse interjected, "Did you see Tina MacCavity when you arrested her husband?"

"No. As a matter of fact, she didn't seem to be there. I'd have expected her to come out and say something when they made the arrest. She hasn't been down to the jail either."

"She drove the trucks, too, Lonnie said," Dennis replied. "I'll bet you anything she was our intruder the other night."

"A woman?"

"Women can do lots of things these days, Sheriff," Annalisse said grimly.

"Any luck with Chester Calhoun's boys?" Dennis asked.

"Yes. That's the good news. Seems you've got another fan. Jake McClellan. He saw one of MacCavity's trucks parked across the square outside your office when he came out of the poker game last night. He said he'll swear on a stack o' Bibles."

"Well, there's your probable cause. You can get your warrant and search the MacCavity house. You'll probably find Tina there and hopefully my computer, too."

"We'll need you to come along to identify it. I don't suppose you have the serial number?"

"Hold on. Let me see if they left my desk drawer intact."

Dennis returned in a moment with the receipts for both computers. "Had to save them for the warranty. Yeah, I've got both serial numbers."

They arrived at the MacCavity house an hour and a half later in the sheriff's car with their search warrant. To Dennis's surprise, the home was a tasteful neo-Victorian, painted slate blue with white trim and geraniums in the window boxes. Pretty upscale for Blue Creek.

Sheriff Webster rapped on the door with the brass knocker.

No answer. The door was locked.

They went around to the back of the house. Again no answer. Again the door was locked.

"Well," the sheriff said. "Looks like we're going to have to do a little breakin' and enterin'."

Using the butt of his gun, the sheriff broke a pane of glass on the back door and then, hand wrapped in a bandanna handkerchief, reached through and unlocked it from the inside. Holding his revolver ready, he entered, motioning Dennis to stay behind him.

"Mrs. MacCavity?" Sheriff Webster called. "I've got a warrant here to search your house. I suggest you come out."

No answer. They entered the surprisingly lovely home. It looked like it belonged in a decorating magazine. Dennis had never seen anything like it in Blue Creek. But a search of the house revealed no one. Neither did it reveal any computers.

"They must be at Terry MacCavity's or else in a dumpster somewhere," he said.

"How about in the dumpster here? There's a big one out back. I saw it from the second floor window. Looks like they just finished doing some remodeling or something. It's full of old carpet," the sheriff said.

Dennis carefully lowered himself inside the dumpster and began pulling apart the layers of dirty mauve carpet. Then he saw them. Both computer towers were lying askew several layers down. Treading as carefully as possible, he went through every layer of trash, recovering the backup devices as well.

"D'you get everything?" Sheriff Webster asked.

"I've no idea. But I'm pretty sure I got everything that's here. I just hope the computer memory hasn't been wiped out."

"Any ideas where this Mrs. MacCavity could've got to? She must've been the one you shot at, if she's the only other one who drove the trucks."

Dennis was busy transferring his cherished computers to the back of the sheriff's car, but he paused to think. "Well, she might have relatives in the area. Ada Lou would know."

"That woman's an encyclopedia, but y' know what just occurred t' me? When we put out that APB the other night, it was for a man.

Could be she's laid up in a hospital somewhere and they didn't report it because she was a woman."

"Could be," Dennis mused. "Good thinking."

After helping him carry the heavy computer towers into Dennis's office, Sheriff Webster left, promising to keep in touch. Annalisse and Leila stood by as Dennis tried to boot up his computers. Nothing happened. Whether a technician could retrieve the data was anyone's guess.

Leila said, "At least we have the backups, Dennis. We'll get everything restored eventually."

Annalisse and Leila were still trying to get the paper files in order. They had made some progress. About half the floor was now cleared.

"Do we have insurance on the computers?" his wife asked.

"No. Heck, I didn't dream anyone would break into my office in Blue Creek!"

"But we do have the resources to buy a new one, Dennis. This isn't the end of the world."

Dennis looked pointedly at Leila. He certainly wasn't about to discuss their financial affairs in front of his secretary.

As though reading his thoughts, Leila stood and brushed herself off. "I've got to run a little errand. I'll be back in about half an hour."

When she had gone, Annalisse turned to him, her eyes full of apology. "I'm sorry. I didn't think."

Sitting on the edge of his secretary's desk, Dennis surveyed the mess around him. "We can probably afford one new computer. That will have to do for the time being, I guess. The good thing is that we have the backups, so I shouldn't feel too sorry for myself. It could have been a whole lot worse."

His wife was scrutinizing him carefully. "We'll get through this, Dennis. You'll see."

"The MacCavitys have a nice house. They've probably got assets. I could bring a civil suit and recover damages, but it'll take a while."

"You'll get it. Everything's going to be fine."

Annalisse's anxiety for everything to be instantly better was somewhat galling. Looking at her, he was struck by her plaintive expression, as though she were begging for him to agree with her, as though she needed reassurance. It wasn't like her. She looked like a small child, eyes round, forehead puckered. She was biting her lower lip. It struck him suddenly that she was caught up in some fear that transcended what was happening to them at that moment.

"Is Jordan still at Betsy's?" he asked.

"Yes. And he has strict orders to stay there until he hears from one of us."

"That's a relief. We haven't got Tina MacCavity, yet. She could be anywhere."

Chapter Twenty-Three

They had baked beans and corn bread for supper at Jerome and Betsy's.

"Mommy says yo' computeo got took," Jordan said.

Dennis looked down the red-and-white-checked tablecloth to where his son sat at the other end of the huge kitchen table. "Taken. Yes. The computers were trashed, I'm afraid," he replied wearily. "But at least we know who we're looking for. The MacCavity clan. They must know they're in trouble for burying toxic waste on public land. They probably did it on a pretty big scale if they're scared enough to try to run me out of town. What do you know about them, Jerome?"

"They're white trash predators," the old man told him. "Charge places like Amalgamated and the other fac'tries top dollar to do their dirty work, and they keep most of the cash. Take folks like poor Lonnie Warner and pay 'em nearly nothing to work at all sorts of mucky jobs. They also own the local junkyard. Surprised you haven't come up against 'em before."

"Me, too. They're nasty all right. What's Tina MacCavity like? Would she be likely to come into my place packing a revolver?"

"That'd be Tina. She's tough as nuts. Rodeo rider, as a matter of fact."

"I wouldn't have guessed it from her house. It's so refined."

Grandma Betsy laughed. "She's tryin' to compete with Mae Cavanaugh. Jes' dyin' to get asked to join one o' Mae's clubs."

Annalisse shook her head. "Mae's not about to let any what you call white trash into her little group."

"Tina's a desperate critter," the old woman said. "Her family was dirt poor, and she can't forget it."

"Who are her family?" Dennis wanted to know.

"She's kin to Ada Lou, as a matter o' fact. Not that she has anything to do with her. I think Ada's her aunt or something. Her daddy ran off when she was a babe an' her mother's dead."

Dennis pondered this. "I wonder what Ada Lou would do if Tina showed up wounded on her doorstep?"

"Take her in," Grandma Betsy said positively. "It wouldn't matter what she'd done. Tina's the only family Ada has, except Lonnie."

"That makes it awkward," Annalisse remarked.

When they were home in their own bed, Annalisse said, "I'm surprised you didn't call Sheriff Webster. Tina's got to be at Ada's."

"I want to think for a while about how to handle this. I don't want Ada to be an accessory."

"What do you mean?"

"I'm sure as can be that Ada doesn't know what Tina's up to. I think if it were between Tina and me, she'd choose me. I intend to phone her to meet me tomorrow, and I'll tell her what's going on. She'll know that Tina's going to the pen, so I've got to convince her that it's her fault Lonnie's dying."

Annalisse twirled a lock of hair between her fingers, a thoughtful expression smoothing out the anxiety that had played across her face all day. "You're an awfully nice guy, you know that?"

"Not exactly an asset in my profession," he said ruefully. "Don't nice guys finish last?"

"Depends on where they want to go," his wife said with a touch of wistfulness. Curling around him, she put her head on his chest.

His concerns dropped away. What was this? Why in the midst of this uproar had his wife suddenly changed—again? It seemed like weeks since he'd held her like this. Looking into her face, which was tilted upwards so she could see him, he saw that her eyes were full of affection. Something had resolved itself inside her. Now that he thought about it, she had been different since last night, when she offered to stay up with him. Her physical closeness was as welcome as water in the desert his life had become. His thoughts switched from Tina McCavity and Ada to deeper concerns.

She was such a puzzle. Should he try, just once more to find the key?

"Annalisse . . ."

"Hmm?"

"Is Jules a nice guy?"

He felt her go stiff and then struggle up onto one elbow. "Not very," she answered finally. She managed to keep her self-control this time, clearly trying hard not to flinch. She looked straight into his eyes. He could only guess what it cost her. "And it's *was.* Not is. He's dead."

Instantly, shame poured over him at the remembrance of his wrath. At his narcissistic personalization of the situation. *Oh, Lord! What have I done? What unknown pain has Annalisse suffered? And I've as much as poured salt in the wound!*

Carefully, he gathered her to him. She went willingly. Stroking her hair, he said, "Forgive me, Annalisse. Please."

"If you can forgive me. I should have trusted you. Gregg says I'm going through post-traumatic stress disorder. But I think I'm finished with it. It's been like going through hell naked, Dennis. I'm sorry for the way I've acted."

"So his death was traumatic?" he asked. "Can you tell me about it?"

Her hands clenched on his chest. "It was suicide. I found him in the bathtub with his wrists slashed."

He clinched her closer to him. *How could I have been so self-centered that I didn't see the horrible pain she was in?* "Can you ever forgive me, Swedie? I should have known something truly awful was going on inside you. But I thought it was me, the farm . . ."

"You were partly right. At least, about the farm. I'm not a farm girl, Dennis. Unfortunately. I thought I could do it. For you."

"Why did you give up your music? Your mother told me you performed all over Europe."

She seemed to ponder this question before answering. "I thought I had buried it with Jules. I never wanted to play a note again after he died." She was silent for a few minutes. He waited. "Music was his god. He put it before everything. It caused him to do something really terrible. Maybe someday I can talk about it. Just know that I never wanted it to do that to me. I certainly don't want it to cost me my marriage and children."

He took a deep breath and said what he knew he must say. "It's a gift, Annalisse. A huge part of you. You can't just bury it."

"No. I know that now. Somehow I've got to make peace with it. It's like I'm two Annalisses, Dennis. They're at war."

"My Annalisse and Jules's Annalisse?"

"Yes."

"You know what I think?"

"What?"

He steeled himself to tell her what he must. "You married two selfish, self-centered men. You shouldn't be defined by who you're married to! You should be who God made you. Who is Annalisse's Annalisse?"

What if her answer took her away from him? Her revelations had changed his heart. For once in his life, he cared about someone else more than himself.

"I don't know, Dennis. I really don't know." She began weeping softly.

He had a sudden vision of a younger Annalisse trying to cut her feelings dead. Casting such a talent out of her life! Becoming a biologist, of all things. How ruthless she had been! But it hadn't worked. She'd still suffered, smothering the substance of her soul, because she thought that's what life demanded, what he demanded.

"Annalisse . . . don't," he murmured softly, pulling her hands gently away from her face. "I'm to blame for a lot of this, you know."

"You?" She shook her head in wonderment. "You have no idea what you're saying."

"I'm your husband. I've lived with you on terms of the greatest intimacy for four and a half years. Don't you think I should have realized somewhere along the line that you weren't whole? But no. All I saw is what I wanted to see . . . I've always assumed you were contented, that you wanted what I wanted, and all the time you were locking the biggest part of yourself away . . ."

She tried to interrupt, but he shushed her gently. "After all this time, do you think it might be possible for you to let another person in?"

He felt her shrink beside him, but he went on. *All at once, things were dazzlingly clear.* He saw the Shepherd carrying the wounded sheep, Annalisse this time. "I'm going to ask you a question,

233

Annalisse, and I want you to answer. Truthfully. Not the way you think I want you to answer."

Swallowing, she turned her head and eyed him warily.

"Now think about it—do you really want to forget Jules?"

She looked away, biting her lip. He took one of her hands in his. When she spoke, her voice was high-pitched and trembling. "I . . . I don't know, Dennis. I'm sorry. It doesn't mean I don't love you . . ."

His heart bumped painfully at the anguish in her face; he knew how much she wanted to answer differently. Unable to stop himself, he cupped her head with one hand and began to kiss her hairline, her ear, and finally her weeping eyes. "It's all right, Swedie," he soothed into her hair. "It's all right. I've been a real idiot about this thing, but I'm not asking you to forget him. That isn't what I meant at all."

He let her cry herself out. She didn't seem to care what it was he did mean; it didn't matter.

He felt a strange exhilaration. *Why, in spite of everything, do I feel such a delicious sense of peace?*

It came to him slowly that he was holding the real Annalisse. After all the turmoil inside her, she was finally giving her grief to him. Willingly. It was a precious gift, a gift of her truest self. He marveled, as though seeing it all on a screen in front of him—the two of them groping toward one another, merging, like amoebas. So thin was the wall between them now that he could feel her sorrow moving into his own soul, displacing all the fear and bitterness that had been there.

For a long time he didn't say anything more. He couldn't. When he did, he tried to make his voice firm and matter-of-fact, but it came out as shaky as he felt. "I love you, Annalisse. This sounds crazy, but if Jules is part of you, I don't mind anymore. I guess I'll have to take him, too. I just want you to be you. I love all of you."

She didn't speak but only clung to him. Her need for him spoke poignantly. He had never felt needed by Annalisse before.

"When everything is settled, we're going to leave this place."

"Where will we go?"

"Some place where you can study and perform again. Somewhere you can hear the symphony and sit up all night in cafes discussing the opera."

"But how will we afford it? And can you ever be happy in the city again?"

"We'll figure a way. We'll work together this time. Not New York, but maybe somewhere around Boston. There's plenty of green in Massachusetts and New Hampshire . . ."

Reaching over with one hand, he turned off the bedside lamp. Then, pulling the sheet over them both, he kissed her face with a new tenderness.

"I do love you," she whispered.

"It's all right," he told her. "Everything's going to be all right now."

For a long time he lay there, still shaken, holding his wife and feeling a lingering warmth in his breast. Somehow they had done it. He had no real idea how it had come about, but he thought perhaps he had met her at last.

It was raining the next morning. Instead of getting up when she awakened, Annalisse lay quietly beside her slumbering husband, listening to the clamor on the roof. This morning, she could lie there and savor the security of her cozy bed and dry house. She could lie there next to Dennis without guilt, without being in a hurry to do anything or go anywhere. She could enjoy the rhythm of the rain.

No longer compartmentalized, the loves of her life were spilling together, spanning the schism inside her. Gazing at her husband's sleeping face, she wondered if he even knew what he'd done. How gentle he had been, dismantling that last wall but leaving everything intact. Somehow he had rescued them all. Now her choosing to remember Jules, to grieve over him, and to take up her music again no longer meant rejecting Dennis. In some way he had shouldered part of the burden, taken part of it upon himself.

There was a sense of completeness now. A circle had closed.

Standing on the very edge of Point Loma, Annalisse could see the San Diego Harbor stretching out below them. They watched together as a Navy frigate slipped her moorings and made her way out to sea. Small white sailboats flitted back and forth in her wake, the Coronado Bridge framing the entire scene gracefully from behind. When the frigate reached the harbor's mouth, the white wake sprang larger off her bow, and she began to disappear in the sea haze of a color that rendered her invisible. It was all very fitting to the occasion.

"Annalisse?"

Anticipating the question he would ask, she turned away. "Is there any place around here that isn't covered with ice plant? It looks okay, but it won't be very comfortable to sit on . . ."

"There are some benches somewhere."

"Great. Motorcycling always makes me feel I'm starving."

"Probably the sea air," he mumbled, locking the Triumph and taking her hand. His palms were sweating.

On the bench beside the asphalt path, Annalisse opened the backpack. Hovering over her, Dennis refused to sit. "I hope you like pita bread," she remarked. "I tried it for the first time the other day . . ."

"For crying out loud, Annalisse, put that stuff down!"

"Don't you want to eat?"

"In a minute. There's something I want to say first."

Laughing at his cross expression, she put everything down beside her on the bench. Hands in her lap, she smiled primly at him. "Shoot."

He only looked at her, his annoyance evaporating. He wore his Jason the Argonaut look today—intense, hopeful, determined. After a moment, she lowered her eyes.

"I'm not really a bum, Annalisse," he told her. "I mean, I don't intend to spend the rest of my life cruising around on Hannibal."

Smiling, she looked up again. His nervousness had returned, and he was running a hand over his head.

"I've been trying to decide what it is I really want to do." He paused. "How would you feel about law school?"

"I'd make a terrible lawyer."

"Annalisse, be serious, for crying out loud."

"Okay, but why do you need my opinion?" There was temporary safety in obtuseness. "I mean, if you want to go to law school, go to law school. It doesn't make any difference what I think."

"It makes a lot of difference. I've actually been accepted, as a matter of fact." His voice was almost grim, and she repented of her levity.

"Oh."

Placing a foot on the bench beside her, he leaned forward on his knee. "I've spent the week rereading Thoreau. I still think he could save the world, but philosophers don't seem to carry much weight these days. You know who does? Lawyers. Everywhere you look, every step you take, there has to be a lawyer. There's a lot of action in environmental law."

"My father's a lawyer," she murmured, struck by the idea that perhaps Sven had followed a similar line of reasoning in his long-ago youth.

"He is? I thought he was a farmer."

"Actually, he's a judge."

Dennis appeared to contemplate this fact. "How does he feel about long hair and motorcycles?"

Laughing, she answered, "He likes Thoreau a lot."

"It's time I got my hair cut, anyway." He sat down with a sigh. "My stepfather's getting high blood pressure over it."

"Dennis, I'm awfully hungry."

He affected not to have heard her. Seating himself next to her, he folded his arms across his chest and studied the lighthouse. "So, you think law school's a good idea, then?"

Suddenly, for a reason she could never explain, everything came together in her mind—the crystal-bright sky, the gabbling seagulls, the clean, perpendicular lines of the lighthouse, even the idea that there might be a blue whale swimming in the waters below. The presence of Dennis, with his quixotic dreams and explorer's face, enhanced everything around her and temporarily banished her ghosts. She grinned hugely.

She saw the tension leave him, and he turned to her, laughing. "I want to catch that smile and bottle it. You have no idea what it does to me."

He kissed her, and she felt something. His kiss wasn't like Jules's kiss, but it was sweet and tender. "That should make things easier, but it doesn't," he remarked after a moment. "Have I been too pompous?"

Unable to speak, she shook her head.

"What good is poetry if it abandons you in a crisis?" he demanded of the heavens. "Here." Standing up, he pulled her to her feet and down along the path until they could see the harbor again.

With a sweep of his arm, he indicated the view. "There we have the romantic scenery." Taking his tiny radio from his pocket, Dennis turned the dial until he found something that sounded like "Strangers in the Night," with a lot of static.

"Perfect," he placed the radio at her feet. "Don't move now," he warned. Wading in among the ice plant, he began to pick its spiky magenta blossoms.

Tucking his offering behind her ear, he declared, "There! Now we're all set." He took her hand in his and went down on one knee. "Dearest Annalisse, all that I have, all that I am, all that I have in me to become, I lay at your feet. Hannibal, my transistor radio, and me. How can you turn that down?"

"I can't possibly," she said laughing.

He got to his feet quickly and took her in his arms. "Then you'll marry me?" he asked gently. "You'll have my children and be my love?"

"Oh, yes," she answered. Perhaps it was the comic nature of the proposal, but she felt a moment's daylight through her numbness. Something was telling her that this was the right thing to do. Marriage with Dennis would be the absolute opposite of her first marriage. An adventure, a much different kind of adventure.

"Thank God," he murmured into her hair. "Thank God."

Chapter Twenty-Four

The rain on the roof sounded like applause. Annalisse knew she must tell Dennis everything now. Last night, he'd gone the whole way alone.

When he awoke, however, it was to the ring of their bedside telephone. Annalisse answered it.

"Hello? May I speak to Mr. Childs, please?"

"Who shall I tell him is calling?"

"This is Sam Dunston from KYTV, Springfield."

Covering the receiver, she relayed the information to her husband. He took the phone from her, and she listened as he gave out a few monosyllables.

Then, "How did you find out about this?"

Squawking on the other end of the line.

"Well, as a matter of fact, I do have a story for you, but it goes far deeper than the barn burning and so on. I was going to draw up a press release this morning. We have a real problem down here in

Cherokee County. We should be making an arrest this morning, but that's just the tip of the iceberg."

More squawking.

"Sure, I'll give you an interview. How about one o'clock?" Dennis swung his legs over the side of the bed. "Yes, a cameraman would be essential. I think you'll find this is a lead story."

A short time later, her husband hung up the phone. "Some guy in the sheriff's office called KYTV. I guess he gets paid for tips. He told them about our barn burning and the office break-in and the MacCavity arrest.

"I need to call Ada Lou and meet her somewhere for breakfast before I sic the sheriff on her."

"I'm sure she has no idea that Tina got that wound shooting at you. I'll bet Tina told her some story about an accident or something," Annalisse assured him.

"I hope so. I wouldn't want to think of Ada Lou harboring a felon."

Annalisse went to sit next to her husband on the bed as he contemplated the telephone.

"I love you," she said, smoothing his hair out of his eyes. He perpetually needed a haircut. She kissed the frown lines between his eyes. "You'll do the right thing. You always do. And when it's over, we need to have a talk. I have a lot to tell you."

He kissed her on the ear and on the tip of her nose. "This is liable to be a rough ride, Swedie."

"I'll hold on tight."

She listened as her husband called Ada Lou and made arrangements to meet at the Roundtable Club. Then he called the sheriff and told him the probable whereabouts of Tina MacCavity, explaining that he would appreciate it if he picked her up while Ada Lou was eating her breakfast.

Dennis took another phone call from Gregg when he finally got to the office after advising a tearful Ada Lou of Tina's activities.

"Dennis, I just thought you ought to know that Lonnie died this morning. Hospice called me. They were there. They said it was peaceful."

A memory of his client as he had last seen him, hollow-eyed and gray, visited Dennis, and he felt deep stirrings of pity. "I'm really sorry. But I'm glad he died at home." Dennis sighed. "Well, I've got an interview with a TV reporter this afternoon as it happens. They'll probably want you to show them where that dioxin was buried. Do you mind going on record?"

"Heck, no. I'm angry, Dennis."

"Me, too. But this could put a lot of people out of work."

"Says who?"

"Cavanaugh. He thinks the cleanup will put Amalgamated under."

"I doubt it. He's just pulling his tear-jerker act. He's a wily old son of a gun."

"You've had run-ins with him?"

"Cindy's dad knows him really well. They've been pals all their lives. But even he knows when Jesse Cavanaugh's being a politician."

Before the morning was out, Tina MacCavity was arrested at Ada Lou's and charged with assault, breaking and entering, and conspiracy to commit arson and murder.

"Ada Lou was real upset this morning, Sheriff. She didn't know a thing," Dennis told Tom Webster on the phone. "I'm going to see if Annalisse will go sit with her for a while. Her nephew died this morning, too."

His wife agreed to perform this errand of mercy. Jordan loved Ada Lou because she always made homemade ginger snaps.

Annalisse told Dennis that she thought maybe their son's presence would bring Ada some comfort.

"You'd better tell Jordan the bad guys are in jail. I know how he worries," Dennis advised.

He left for his meeting with the reporter without any idea of how he was going to handle it. But he needn't have worried. After taking Sam Dunston to meet Gregg, the matter was taken out of his hands.

"This patient of yours died this morning from dioxin poisoning?"

"Yes. I can show you where the drums were buried, the ones he was digging up when he was exposed to it."

"And these MacCavitys who have been terrorizing Mr. Childs hired Lonnie Warner to bury the dioxin?"

"Yes. But Dennis can tell you about that."

On the way to the dumping site, Dennis gave an interview about the MacCavity threats and incidents and then explained the relationship between the MacCavitys and Amalgamated.

"The barrels have been moved, Sam. We have no idea where they are. And when we tried to get the DNR down here to investigate, they stonewalled us," Dennis said.

"Any idea why?" the reporter asked.

"Amalgamated is a big company. Maybe they have connections."

"Do you have any concrete reason to believe that they are intentionally delaying their investigation?" Sam queried.

"None but the fact that initially they couldn't wait to get going and then they suddenly lost interest. I'm glad you're investigating this, because since the DNR isn't doing anything, we've got to get the warning out about this. People need to be made aware of the hazards."

"And you think the danger is sufficient that people should avoid using the water from Blue Creek?"

"That's a question for the DNR, really, which is why I wish they'd get down here. All Gregg and I can tell you is what the dioxin did to Lonnie."

The cameraman followed Dennis and Gregg to the spot where Lonnie's barrels had been and videotaped the rain washing the soil into the creek. Then, taking their leave, they went off to tackle Amalgamated.

Gregg whistled. "I wonder what Amalgamated will have to say?"

"I imagine Cavanaugh's briefed them pretty well," Dennis told him. "They'll be ready."

He was home in time for the six o'clock news that night. Annalisse and Jordan were already sitting on the couch. Jordan could barely contain his excitement at the idea of his father being on TV, but Dennis felt the tension in Annalisse and knew that it mirrored his own. From this point on things were likely to happen pretty fast. Who could tell what the final outcome would be? Sitting down next to his wife, he gave her shoulders what he hoped was a heartening squeeze.

It was the lead story. First there was footage of the hospital, with Sam Dunston standing out front under an umbrella, unfolding the sad saga of Lonnie Warner. Then came snippets of the interview with Gregg, followed by an edited version of his own interview, the part about the DNR being broadcast in full. The creek was shown, and the façade of Amalgamated Chemical. Sam stood outside and told his audience that the management of Amalgamated had issued the following statement: "It is the policy of Amalgamated Chemical Company to follow a very strict procedure when dealing with toxic waste chemicals that derive from our manufacture of hexachloro-phene. We contract all disposal to 'responsible third parties,' which parties have assured us that all care has been taken to dispose of the waste in a safe and judicious manner. To our knowledge, no waste has ever been buried in the vicinity of Blue Creek."

The seedy exterior of MacCavity Hauling office was then shown, and the story was told of their persecution of the Childs family, culminating with the arrest of Tina made that morning.

"I hate to say it, but I think I sense the Cavanaugh touch," Annalisse said.

The phone began ringing almost immediately as the newspapers picked up the story. Reporters, anxious to beat deadlines, interviewed Dennis at length, promising to send down photographers in the morning.

"How was Ada Lou?" Dennis asked, as they at last, crawled into bed.

"Mortified. I think I calmed her down. But I felt really sorry for her, Dennis. She's such a loving soul and so alone."

"If we survive this, we can adopt her as another grandma," Dennis said, pulling his wife into the hollow of his arm. They slept entwined as they always had until Jules had shouldered his way into their lives. Dennis knew Jules was still there somewhere, but Annalisse was Annalisse, not the stranger she had been.

The St. Louis and Kansas City television stations picked up the story from the wire services and helicoptered their own crews in the next day. It was all just as Dennis had dreamed while milking Henrietta the day he'd first met Lonnie, but he didn't feel gratified. Instead, for a reason he couldn't name, he felt a growing unease. Something was going to go wrong. Somehow Amalgamated was going to get away with it. They had hunkered down and were refusing to make further statements.

He was not terribly impressed with any of the media's follow-through. So far no one had made the connection to

Cavanaugh. He had intentionally left the senator's name out of it, certain that someone would uncover it. The MacCavitys, at the advice of their lawyers, had declined to give any statements at all, so the public was left with the impression that they were the villains. Dennis was sure that suited Cavanaugh just fine.

The day following the appearance of the story on the Kansas City and St. Louis stations, the DNR held a news conference.

"This entire thing has been a misunderstanding," a spokesman said. "We are sorry for what Mr. Childs has had to endure in his pursuit of the truth in this matter, but there was never any intention on our part of shirking our responsibility. We have always intended to be down there by the end of this week, and we will be."

The next day, Dennis received a call from his friend Arlene Jacques in Jefferson City. "I don't care what they said in the news conference, Dennis. Sandy Templar works at the DNR, and she says heads are rolling over this. Good work!"

It was hard to believe the news media would swallow the DNR's statement, but there was no evidence they were looking beyond it. His own investigations had been so elementary, surely his own suspicions would have occurred to a seasoned reporter! However, there wasn't even a whisper about the Cavanaugh connection.

Annalisse was indignant. "I'm going to write an anonymous letter, Dennis. Why should he get away with this?" she demanded three days later.

"Hold your horses, Swedie," he told her. "This isn't over yet." For the first time he noticed the rows of jars lining the kitchen counters. Apparently, she had been canning peaches all week.

"Wouldn't you rather play the piano?" he asked.

She shrugged. "I couldn't let them rot."

His days had taken on a strobe-lit frenetic quality foreign to Blue Creek. On the one occasion Dennis saw the senator, he echoed those sentiments. "Well, now, you sure did what you set out to do, didn't you, son? Never seen so much excitement in Cherokee County."

Reporters had swarmed the town, staking out the Roundtable Club, where they interviewed a sampling of residents. Taken all together, Blue Creek's reactions didn't even come close to outrage.

"I sure don't know what all this fuss is about," Little Dan Perkins told the camera. "Lonnie Warner always has been simple. Poor boy didn't know one end of a shovel from t'other . . . he was bound t' git into trouble one day . . . it don't nec'ssrily mean nuthin'."

Ada Lou recovered from her agitation over Tina, and anxious to weigh in on the opposite side, she put on her new lavender-tinted wig and sought out reporters. "Yes, 'twas me took Lonnie in to see Mr. Chiles. He's a man who cares 'bout people, Mr. Chiles is. There warn't another lawyer in this town would o' had any use fer Lonnie."

"I've et fish outta Blue Creek for forty years, and there ain't nothin' wrong with that water," Chester Calhoun asserted. "Now I always liked Mr. Chiles. But I think he got the wrong end of the stick this time. I don't think I'd b'lieve anything that someone simple as Lonnie Warner told me."

"We're just going t' have t' wait 'n see," Sheriff Webster remarked, shifting a wad of tobacco to the other side of his mouth. "Dennis Childs was almost killed by people threatening him over this investigation. He put his life on the line by refusin' to hold back. Those MacCavitys were afraid of somethin', that's for sure. I'd hate to think Amalgamated knew what was goin' on, though."

Mitch Reeves, a reporter for the *Springfield Daily News*, summed up the situation in his Sunday editorial: "A preindustrial naïveté exists among the citizens of Blue Creek that disappeared in most places a hundred years ago. It is foreign to these people to suppose that manufacturing could be anything but an unmixed blessing. Most never seem to have heard of toxic waste. All they see is that

Amalgamated Chemical has given them jobs, the jobs have given them money, and the money has freed them from the poverty endemic to these rocky red hills."

Cavanaugh knew his constituency, all right. Dennis folded up the Sunday paper, his anxiety building into black futility. Obviously, the town perceived him as an enemy. Ever since his TV appearance, people had kept their distance. Even the barn burning didn't seem to weigh in his favor anymore. People had known the MacCavitys all their lives. Dennis was a newcomer, an interloper. His office calendar was ominously blank.

The DNR had come and gone, taking their core samples from the area where Gregg said Lonnie had buried the barrels. It was Annalisse who called him on Monday to tell him that she'd heard on the noon news that the DNR had called a press conference for two o'clock. It was to be carried live on KYTV. Had he heard anything?

No, he hadn't, and that made the whole thing a foregone conclusion. Telling Leila to go someplace where no one could find her, he locked the outer door of his office, turned on the answering machine and watched the conference alone on the little TV in his law library.

"We are happy to inform the media and the citizens of Cherokee County that we have thoroughly investigated the site alleged by Mr. Dennis Childs and his client Lonnie Warner to contain dioxin. We have made core drillings at the site. These samples have been analyzed by Simmons Laboratories, an independent concern with an outstanding professional reputation, utilizing the most comprehensive testing methods. We find no indications whatsoever that dioxin was ever present in the soil. While the department will always follow up any reports of toxic waste in any part of the state, no further investigation of the Cherokee County site is planned at this time."

Gregg had gone with the DNR to show them the place where he and Lonnie had marked the digging with the three tires. Just since the TV interview, someone had moved them. They were gone. Had someone guessed their significance? Had one of the MacCavitys seen them on TV? Without Lonnie to tell them where he had been digging, Gregg wasn't precisely sure. Clearly, the DNR hadn't conducted a very thorough sampling of the area, no matter what they claimed.

Annalisse was waiting for him at the end of the driveway, her hands in the pockets of her denim maternity jumper. Stopping the car, he let her in and saw that she was calm.

"I took Jordan to Betsy's. I thought you might want to get away."

He felt tremendously tired, as though he had just stepped out of a chamber where he had been battered ceaselessly by sound. "No."

"We can't sit here."

"I don't want to go into hiding like some kind of rat," he said with all the vehemence that was left in him and drove up the driveway.

Chapter Twenty-Five

Getting out of the car, they walked down the hill behind the house until they came to the pond and then sat down on the late summer grass. He was grateful she didn't rush in with reassurances; he couldn't have stood hearing them.

"It's not just that I blew it," he said bitterly. "It's that I took so many down with me—you, Jordan, Gregg and his family . . ."

"Dennis, think about this rationally. Even with all this rain, obviously there's got to be dioxin left in the ground. Maybe not as much as before . . ."

"No, not obviously. Nothing's obvious in the law. Now they will say that Lonnie's condition has nothing to do with any drums he may have moved . . ."

"But you can prove that Lonnie had dioxin in his body!"

"We can?"

"Didn't Gregg run any tests?"

"He never said so. He saw this stuff in Walter Reed, some kind of skin acne plus the leukemia . . . he was sure."

"But there's a test. Remember, I'm a biologist. We did those tests at Scripps. It's expensive, and maybe Gregg didn't think it was necessary. But don't you think hard evidence might help now? It's not too late."

"What good will it do if we can't prove a connection between Amalgamated and the dioxin?"

"If we can prove it was dioxin, the MacCavitys are bound to talk once their case comes to trial. They're not going to carry this alone. They would be liable for the entire cleanup!"

"I don't think you've really grasped the essential fact, Annalisse. The people in this town don't give a damn. They're all on Amalgamated's side."

"They don't understand, Dennis. They're ignorant, that's all."

"No." Her insistence made him weary. "The important thing to them is jobs. They don't care about some poor old simpleton who got poisoned. They can't see it happening to them."

"But it will." Annalisse's voice rose, and he looked at her. Surprised, Dennis saw that her hands were shaking as she pitched a rock with some violence into the pond. "How are these people going to feel when their kids start getting leukemia?"

"Are you all right?"

"No! I'm not all right." She looked at him squarely. "I don't want you to give up on this, Dennis."

Her attitude stirred him out of futility into a flash of anger. "And what do you expect me to do? Skulk around with my shovel in the middle of the night and find the dioxin myself?"

"Why not? You've done crazier things before. But do something! Do anything except turn all weary and cynical."

"What's another cynic, more or less?" Stretching out on the grass he propped himself on an elbow, exploring the turf with his fingertips. The flash of anger had died, and the apathy closed in on him again. Encountering a pebble, he flicked it lazily into the pond. "Besides, you hate this place. I'm ready to admit my experiment with rural life has failed. We can leave with a clear conscience. We've got to find you a concert grand somewhere."

"Dennis, you can't run away from this!"

She was so totally in earnest, he sat up and faced her. "Annalisse, what else can I do? We have to eat. My practice is finished . . . It was hard enough to get going the first time, but now my reputation's completely shot."

"Do you believe Amalgamated has got dioxin buried all over the county or not?"

Gritting his teeth, he looked past her into the forest. "Of course, I do. Cavanaugh as much as admitted it."

"Then there must be some way to prove it. We won't starve. I'll go to work."

He began, dimly, to see the shape of something solid and fixed behind her words and was moved in spite of himself. She really, honestly believed he could do it. She believed he ought to do it.

"Annalisse, what on earth would you find to do in Blue Creek? Sling hash?"

"I could go to work in Springfield. It's only an hour's commute . . ."

"No, Annalisse. That would make a ten-hour day. And there's your piano, not to mention the kids . . . You're about to have a baby, in case you've forgotten."

"Our baby," she corrected and then looked up at him out of eyes full of tears. "But do you know how I feel about you? How I really feel?"

Everything else dropped away before the intensity of her look. "I think so."

"You don't," she told him, bending her head and picking at the grass. "And it's not your fault. It's mine. In order to understand how I feel about you, about all of this . . ." she waved her hand vaguely in a gesture that might have meant the farm or the whole mess, "you need to understand about Jules."

"Jules," he repeated dumbly. "What does he have to do with it?"

"Just listen," she told him firmly. "I'll try to explain, but it's complicated." Looping her hair back over her ears, she continued. "First I need to tell you something I should have told you the first day I met you. Part of falling in love with you was that I wanted to put the past behind me, to make a fresh start." She smiled a brief ghost of a smile.

"Jules thought I was a genius on the piano. He pushed me into a wonderful career. And, suddenly when he died, there was this huge hole in me where he had been."

"I can understand a little, I think," Dennis said. "Your life with him must have been pretty glam. Europe and everything. And then I bring you to Blue Creek, telling you it's paradise."

"You made the mistake of visiting here first in the springtime," she said tolerantly, caressing his hair with a sudden grin.

He shrugged. What she said was true. To a weary LA lawyer, the rolling green, studded with red bud trees, lilacs, and creamy dogwood had seemed like a slice of Middle Earth. And the land had been dirt cheap. For the price of their house in LA, he could buy a house with eighty acres and still have money left to set up a law practice.

"Anyway, back to my story, Jules was an incredibly talented violinist." Here she paused, swallowing and taking a breath. "I wish you could have heard him play. All of this would make a lot more sense. It was truly life-changing to see the world he communicated through his playing. I fell in love with Jules the violinist. I'd never experienced such feelings at home in Burnett or in the bio lab."

Though privately reeling from her revelations, Dennis was grateful for this additional information so he could at last understand the puzzle that was his wife. "Did you accompany him? Were you planning some great life where you lived all over the world?"

"Yes. We studied together in Vienna. I performed solos in Paris, Copenhagen, and other places. He was about to make his debut as a soloist with the Vienna Philharmonic. Playing Tchaikovsky." She stopped speaking, picking at the grass and biting her lip.

"Annalisse, I've already accepted Jules as part of you. I've felt your pain. You don't need to tell me the rest."

"I need you to understand. So you can understand why I was drawn to you, why all these things you're fighting for mean so much to me. And I need to explain about the Latinos."

What followed was a long and heartrendingly ugly tale of murder, a lonely little boy with a huge talent, drugs, mental illness, and ghetto warfare. And to cap it all off there was a suicide. It was beyond difficult to place the Annalisse he had known in the midst of this scene. It had the scope of tragic opera. And he had thought her so calm, so uncomplicated! More likely, his wife had been battered to the core and lived in fear of any real attachment. That he had succeeded in getting her to marry him, to have children, and to affirm life, was in the nature of a miracle.

"I think it's a tremendous tribute to you and your upbringing that you were able to survive emotionally, Annalisse. But how could you love an ordinary Joe like me after Heathcliff?"

She kissed him above the eyebrow. "Well, he was dark and broody looking. But you're far from ordinary, and well you know it. You're a hunk. Do you know, you and Jules both lost your fathers when you were ten? In your own ways you were seeking to fill a tremendous void in your lives, I think."

"Ah. The Divine Void."

"What?" she asked, her voice puzzled.

"All this drama we're going through can't compare with the tragedy of Jules, but it's taught me something."

"What?"

"We all need comfort, safety, and love. We're born that way. And if we don't get it, say because our fathers die, we look for things to fill the void. Jules had his violin. I had my crusades."

"Go on."

"There's only one thing that can fill the void, Annalisse. I learned the night you told me you couldn't give up Jules."

"What is it?"

"Surely you can guess?" For some reason all tension had gone from him, and he felt as though he held the sun in his hands.

Annalisse turned thoughtful as she sat gazing at Priscilla and the goslings. Finally, she said, "Unconditional love?"

"Yes. I'm no savior, Swedie. I can't save your Latinos or find lost barrels of dioxin. I'm a frustrated dragonslayer. But I can love you and accept you with all my heart, no matter what. I'm not going to leave you."

Her face was turned away, but he heard her sniffle. She reached blindly for his hand.

"Is that why you're so determined that I not give up on this?" he asked. "Are you afraid that you're going to fail me if I give up and go off somewhere to lick my wounds?"

"I've put an unfair burden on you, Dennis. I'm sorry. You've always been such an idealist. You've been my hope. And that's not right. But it's all because of the mess with Jules. I needed to believe that the world could still be a safe place . . ."

He let silence fall between them for a moment while he decided how much to tell her. "Annalisse." He tipped her chin up with his finger. "I can't speak for Jules, but I can tell you this. You haven't failed me."

She looked into his eyes, her own sad and unbelieving.

"Not because you played the milkmaid to perfection. Forget about that. You seem to have these heroic illusions about me, but I'm really not so different from Jules. I imagine I love you for the same reasons he did." Lightly caressing her cheek with his finger, he continued, "I know I'm no great violinist, and I've never been to Vienna, but I've been to some of the places he'd been in his head." She frowned, and he cupped her chin firmly in his hand, willing her to listen.

"The day I met you, all I could see anywhere I looked was pain and no possibility of making a difference. You were the only bright thing, and you came just in time."

"I couldn't have looked very bright. Oh, Dennis." She buried her head in his shoulder and held on to him. "You were my only bright thing, too. How have we gotten this far with all these ridiculous expectations of each other?"

Remembering the Twenty-third Psalm, he was silent, stroking her hair.

"There's only one Savior," Dennis told her. "Even for Jules."

A flock of starlings took flight from the bottom land, circled, and flew over them in a chirping mass. Despite the disappointments of the day, he felt his heart lift. Here in his arms, this was what mattered. They would move away and start again, this time as whole people. Annalisse would have her career, and he would pledge to the child she carried a life of love, even though he couldn't guarantee her a carefree existence.

Annalisse sighed heavily, as though reading his thoughts. A great weight seemed to be taken from her.

Then suddenly, they were hailed stridently from somewhere in the direction of the house, "Den-nis! Dennis Childs!"

A figure appeared at the brow of the hill waving a sun hat. It was Grandma Betsy. Rising as one, they motioned for her to join them. She began her message halfway down the hill, but the wind carried her words away from them.

" . . . mad as fire . . . cows . . . right in the creek . . ."

Dennis stiffened. "What's that, Betsy?" he called, beginning to move toward her.

"You've got to come right now, Dennis! I've got George Crane over t' my place in such a state. He's been tryin' t' call you. Thought maybe I knew where you was . . ."

"What's the trouble?"

"It's that poison! It's killed ever' one of his cows. They been sickenin' for months, but now they're dead and lyin' right there in the middle o' that creek . . ."

"The creek?"

Betsy took another breath and began again. "George Crane's cows are lyin' dead in the middle o' Blue Creek. Thirty-five head . . . all dropped over sometime last night . . . Right by that place where those idiots were looking for that stuff you said was buried!"

For a moment, all Dennis could do was stare.

Annalisse's voice was triumphant. "Oh, Dennis! Don't you see? Now we can have one of the cows autopsied. We can even get someone from Scripps to do the testing. Then we'll have proof! People will have to listen!"

The remaining weight that had borne down on him lifted at once, as he looked at his wife's shining face. It had never been so bright.

"Bless you, Betsy!" he crowed, and snatching the large woman off her feet, he swung her around in the air as though she were a child.

Astonished, she batted at his arms with her hat. "What in the world? George Crane loses his cows, and you start carryin' on like you won the lottery!"

Setting her down gently, he rejoiced, "Don't you see? Those cows are going to save everyone's lives! People will have to listen now! And George can get himself the best herd in Cherokee County, courtesy of Senator Jesse Cavanaugh and Amalgamated Chemical!"

It took her a moment, but suddenly the old woman put her arms around his neck and kissed him on the cheek. "God bless you, boy!"

Seizing her about the waist, Dennis began singing "I'm a Yankee Doodle Dandy" and waltzing Grandma Betsy around the pond. Her hair tumbled down, its pins flying into the water.

Annalisse watched it all with intense satisfaction. Even Jules got a kick out of the scene. *"Lisse, I was wrong about this whole gig. He can't carry a tune in a bucket, but I like your Dennis!"*

Laughing aloud at the thought, Annalisse joined in the singing.

About the Author

G. G. Vandagriff began this novel twenty years ago when she was first experiencing the effects of PTSD, although it was years before she discovered what the disorder was. Working out her feelings through the book, she then abandoned it on her hard drive. At the urgings of her oldest son, who vowed he would publish it posthumously if he had to, she took it out again, updated it, and created *Pieces of Paris*. Through events of those past twenty years, she had learned lessons and experienced tender mercies that made the story more poignant.

The story takes place in a fictional community similar to the one where she lived in southwestern Missouri and where there was a dramatic toxic waste incident that involved dioxin.

Before her family moved to Missouri, they lived in California. G. G. studied writing at Stanford University and later received her M.A. from George Washington University. She worked as the assistant to the treasurer of Harvard University, as an assistant bond analyst at Fidelity Investments, and finally as an international banker.

She has taught part-time at three different colleges while raising her family. Despite the impressive finance resume, creative writing is her true love. G. G. received the 2010 Whitney Award for Best Historical Fiction for her novel *The Last Waltz: A Novel of Love and War.*

Now living in Provo, Utah, G. G. and her husband, David, are the parents of three children and the grandparents of two. She loves to communicate with her readers through her blog, ggvandagriffblog .com, and her various websites: ggvandagriff.com, last-waltz.com, deliverance-depression.com, and arthurianomen.com.